Salmon

To the essential ones
B and E and J

The Night Game

Frank Golden

salmonfiction

Published in 2015 by
Salmon Fiction (an imprint of Salmon Poetry Ltd.)
Cliffs of Moher, County Clare, Ireland
Website: www.salmonpoetry.com
Email: info@salmonpoetry.com

ISBN 978-1-910669-00-6

COVER ARTWORK: Cover photo © Lynn Saville
Courtesy Yancey Richardson Gallery
www.lynnsaville.com

COVER DESIGN & TYPESETTING: *Siobhán Hutson*

Printed in Ireland by Sprint Print

Salmon Poetry gratefully acknowledges the support of
The Arts Council / An Chomhairle Ealaoín

"One night she went too far. Something happened. We're not sure what."

Other People/ MARTIN AMIS

1

The motion of the world shows in a veil of weather. The vast-scaled elevations of the city disappear. Along Roosevelt Island waterway an unseen riverboat pushes wake water against slanted wooden pilings. The sloot bellow of a distant foghorn gutters in darkness. It is late February, New York, 7p.m.

The night has drawn in. Drifted river fog has eased up through the wharf sidings and low-rise streets on the margins of the Lower East Side. Crashes have been reported on the city's exit roads and highways. A soft cloud of car beams moves inexorably along Pelham Parkway. Light refracts off particles of fog.

A crosstown bus mooches along 14th street. Mary drags the outline of a face through misted glass. She can smell the stale hair of the brunette in front, and the urine-high stink of the old guy in the crumpled flat cap across the passageway. Inside the doorway of a vintage clothes shop a young woman flips a cardboard CLOSED sign and locks up. A bus passes by opposite, a child's ghost face pressed up against the glass. As she nears her stop the blue and pink neon lights on the corner of 10th flash on and off. She pulls on a pair of kid gloves before pressing the bell on the glossy yellow bar. Stepping off the bus she immediately feels the freedom in occlusion, the draped secrecy of befogged streets, the cling and obfuscation of the particle world. In that barren, beautiful moment of discrepancy between the seen and the unseen, footsteps sound and fade. Behind her rises the long echo and astringent beat of steel heels and soles.

Mary walks through a covered arcade of grossly bright

shopfronts. The arcade is empty, the individual shop units closed for business. She stops and stands before a sex shop window. There is a smell of citrus and something fetid. A sudden night alarm shreds what would otherwise be the routine hum of urban noise. She looks around then returns her gaze to the mannequin in the window and to the sex paraphernalia surrounding it. The female mannequin is on her knees, hands behind her back and yellow corded rope around her neck. Mary imitates some binding gestures, crossing her wrists in front and behind. She imagines the mannequin's pain in the abstract.

Footsteps scuff the pearl-white tiles a short distance away. Mary looks to the side, her eyes wide, instantaneously watchful, anticipating danger. She imagines she sees a host of others watching her: oddities, freaks, derelicts, perverts, lurkers, reprobates. She knows these streets, its railings and crumbled kerb margins, its basement grilles and stained stoops, its hoardings and rusted fire escapes. She moves away quickly, alert to the controlled pace of following footsteps. She hears them gather and close. She walks steadily at first, the figure behind her. She doesn't turn but her flight hairs attest to a tangible presence threatening. She doesn't attempt to rationalise the nature of the threat posed. She accepts the reality of something malevolent about to possess her. This she knows to be the first response of the aware. She runs through fogbound streets and alleyways. There is a terrible coarseness to her breathing, a kind of climactic rise and fall. As she runs her mind conjures a scarifying sequence of images: the dishevelled dresses of women, men sluicing slick tongues, a figure exhaling fire. Mary runs up the steps of an old brownstone. She fumbles for her keys then stops. The road is empty of cars with only the vague bloom of white streetlamps alleviating the opaque dark. The footsteps behind her have stopped. Has she evaded danger or imagined it? It is no longer clear that she is or ever was being followed. There is only the fog. Her eyes are drawn across the road to a brightly lit, uncurtained window. She sees the blur of her Germanic, housefrau neighbour, Hilda. Mary raises what she imagines might be a vaguely perceived hand in a kind of wave and smiles warmly, before plunging her key into the inverted slit, and double turning until the lock tumblers and bolt release. The front door is heaved open then banged shut. Silence.

Mary moves some strands of matted hair off her forehead, leans back against the door, and exhales loudly while flicking the hall switch on with her outstretched hand. She calls out, almost shouts.

– Darling, I'm home!

There is no reply.

The hallway has a decorous if old-fashioned flavour as though no substantial redecoration has occurred in a generation. The burgundy-and-gold-striped wallpaper with intermixed florets and urns capsizes what would otherwise be an elegant and welcoming entrance. She sets her keys down on the mirrored hall table and her mini backpack on one of the coiled antlers of the old wooden hallstand. She catches sight of herself; angular, cheek-boned, flushed. No distortion, just brutal, eviscerating age. She can feel herself becoming disconsolate. She hangs up her coat, loosens her hair, and turns on the first-floor landing light. Smith, a small white cat with a gimpy, aberrant black tail appears at her feet and brushes against her calf. She picks the cat up and holds him close. Walking towards the back room on the ground floor she replays in her mind her lunchtime therapy session from earlier that day.

2

Dr Orin Lavender's rooms are minimal and warm, cream walls, chocolate chairs, a burgundy carpet. It is what Mary likes, their difference compared to the spaces she engenders for herself. Orin himself is urbane, bearded, inscrutable. She finds him easy, unthreatening. She has grown to trust him and cannot imagine how she will cope if he relocates. On clear days she can see Brooklyn Bridge from the window, the high towers and cables holding it all together. He occasionally indulges in bridge language when constructing his metaphorical conceits:

– There are foundational constructs we all need, there are spanned transepts from one self to the other that we need to originate. A bridge can serve as a consciously imagined structure connecting diverse selves to the primary self.

There are no pictures of his family, extended or otherwise. Mary likes the fact that he is not distracted by normality. No cosy pictures of enfolding love, no lawns, no dogs. The sole piece of personal information she has retained about him is that he likes offal, testicles or brains forward themselves as possibilities. It had come up once though she forgets the context. She is disdainful of her memory and cannot always remember the transitions and actions she negotiates in a given day. She thinks that Dr Lavender is good at hiding the fact that he is frustrated with her. The afternoon session had gone badly.

– I feel like the only thing I can identify with is catastrophism, where the earth is heading towards collapse. Everyday it *feels* like living but not *really* living, says Mary. It's like everything is suspension, or everything is ending.

– Why should your concern over climate change, which is

entirely legitimate, lead you to that conclusion? You're not in obvious peril.

– I feel I have only so much time left. Don't other people feel that way, that things are happening, accelerating, beyond their control? You know, surreptitiously. I mean there's all that methane in the North Pole waiting to be unleashed and then what?

– You tell me.

– It makes everything else, *this*, everything, meaningless. What's the point in trying to be better if it's all inevitably going to end up badly anyway? Isn't it in the nature of things that they corrupt – whether it's me or the polar ice caps? Think of all that methane! Aren't some things best kept suppressed?

– It's not a useful linkage Mary. Whatever about our individual or collective futures we have an obligation to confirm who we are to ourselves. If we are to be of value to ourselves let alone anyone else we need to move towards the integration and resolution of self.

– Do you think it's possible?

– What?

– To resolve the self?

– Better to be in progress towards it than to be unconscious, surely!

– But all I'm really conscious of is failure, my failure to hold onto my marriage, my failure to keep time with myself, my failure to meet my basic emotional needs. What is my value? Who am I important to? Why do I feel so inadequate?

– If you concentrate on the needs you can reasonably meet you'll be okay. Don't try to envision things beyond the scope of your immediate reality.

– So what do I end up with Dr Lavender, a kind of disabled survival?

– I don't know what you end up with Mary, you decide that.

Mary's shoulders slump over.

Dr. Lavender takes Mary through a routine fractional relaxation, starting at the top of her head and getting her to relax different areas of her body. He gets her to slow her breathing and focus on a chrome disc.

– Let's try a visualisation, says Dr Lavender. Close your eyes.

Imagine you are floating high up. You are in total control of your actions. You decide to glide down through the clouds into clear air. You can see the rooftops of houses below you. Visualise your own house. Imagine floating down until you are standing in the kitchen you grew up in. Go to the window and look out.

– We've done this before!

– Just go with it. The curtains are open. Look out of the window. What time of year is it?

– Winter.

– Look around the kitchen. Do you notice anything in particular?

– There's someone there.

– Who is it?

– A man.

– Do you recognise him?

– No.

– What is he doing?

– He's asleep in an armchair by the cooker. There's a kettle boiling in the corner. Steam is beginning to fill the room.

– And?

– And what?

– What do you do?

– I make tea of course. I go over to the wall cabinet above the sink. The tea box is full of... that's strange!

– What? asks Dr Lavender.

– Sachets of dried blood. That's what it says on the box. DRIED BLOOD. Whose blood is it, I ask myself, and how will it restore me?

– Do you make the tea?

– I make the tea.

– Then what do you do?

– There's a drawer underneath the sink. I pull it out. Inside is a little ornate knife with a black and white onyx handle.

– What do you want to do with it?

– I don't know.

– Take it in your hand.

– Okay I've got it, says Mary.

– Now what do you want to do?

Mary begins to laugh.

– Go on, says Dr Lavender.

– It's sharp. It cuts the hardest things. It's such a brutal, malicious little knife. I can see him sitting there. There's a roll of fat falling over his belt. His left hand is resting on his crotch. Does that matter? No. His head's back, mouth open. I think he could be dead except for the noise. I can see the light hairs in one of his ears flecked with wax and one or two sticking out from his nose. They move with each –

Mary inhales and exhales deeply.

– I place the tip of the knife in front of his left nostril, then grab his hair roughly and push the point up as far as it will go. His eyes bulge open. I screw the knife into his brain. I can see weird things happening in his eyes like parts of his memory are being digested by the knife. He's changing before my eyes, becoming like a…cavity, a brain imploding. When I pull the knife out –

– All right, says Dr Lavender, you can stop there.

– No, don't say anything! I hate when you do that. Just let me go with it.

She closes her eyes briefly once more.

– I want to pull little bits of his brain out. I want to pick his brains. Then I'll know.

– What will you know? asks Dr Lavender.

– I'll know how it feels, says Mary.

– Is it not that *he'll* know how it feels?

– What?

– To have his memory marred or his body.

Mary looks towards him, confused.

– Is there anyone else in the room? asks Dr Lavender.

– No.

– Is there anyone upstairs?

– No.

– What about Sally?

– Sally's dead.

– Let's go back to the tea, says Dr Lavender.

– Whose blood is it anyway? asks Mary.

– Good question. Do you press him to drink the tea you have made?

– Yes.

– Do you force him?

–Yes.

–What does it do?

– It fires him up. Suddenly. SUDDENLY he bursts into blood.

Mary's eyes open. She stands up, frantically gesturing.

–Water! she says. Throw some water over him. For God's sake throw some water over him! His blood is burning! It's all my fault.

– It's not your fault. Mary, listen to me! It's time to save yourself. Leave the room. Close the door. Run out of the house. Save yourself!

Mary continues to stand in the centre of the room.

– Who hands on my blood anyway, if not me? Love is a consummation like fire. Isn't that the truth? Isn't love like fire?

She begins to cry.

Dr Lavender leads her slowly through an abdominal breathing technique, and then brings the session to a close.

Silence envelops them both.

Mary watches as the gross fog falls.

Dr Lavender levers himself up from his chocolate leather chair, walks over to Mary and helps her on with her coat. The thickening afternoon light has deepened the air of somnolence.

– Have you to go back to work? asks Dr Lavender.

–Yes.

–You wouldn't think of taking the afternoon off?

–You think I need to?

– Just to process.

– No, I'm afraid not.

– Not to worry. It was interesting what you said about memory being digested.

– How do you mean?

– Follow the metaphor. Digestion is only part of the process, memory is a kind of digestion, but you need to evacuate the negative. What you have to do Mary is confront your fears.

– I don't know what that means Dr. Lavender. You see I don't know what I'm truly afraid of.

– I can't tell you that either Mary.

– Why do I get the feeling that you know and won't tell me? Is this some kind of game?

3

Mary lets Smith out onto the tiled patio to the rear of the brownstone. She tries to avoid noticing the overstuffed green receptacle bin, which she has failed to put out for collection three weeks running. She views it as a kind of systems failure indicative of some deeper malaise. The bin will, she knows, persist as a kind of psychic nag until she does something about it. She could burn the garbage, she thinks, and perhaps she will.

She checks a tub of half-eaten paté in the fridge, winces at the whiff of fouled meat and takes it and some black-leafed lettuce and mushy cucumber to the wormery, painted blue and set against the lattice fence outside. Lifting up the active end of the wormery her fingers squelch against what she knows are the large white slugs that sometimes colonise the underside of the plywood top. She throws the lot in, plastic and all and runs back into the kitchen, then plunges her hands under cold water and averts her eyes.

She turns on the radio and gets the end of the drive time evening news round up.

...the toddler, who had walked for over a mile holding his baby blanket, was spotted by a 21 year old student returning from his night security job. The student, who wishes to remain anonymous, alerted the police and the child was reunited with his mother at 4am.

And now to the weather.

For the third day in a row a thick fog is covering the city. Humidity levels are at 100%.Visibility is down to less than ninety meters. All major airports are experiencing delays, and there are tailbacks on roads leading into and out of the city. Winds from the North East are expected to slacken later tonight. Some fog will burn off late tomorrow morning with temperatures rising to 6°C, falling back to one or two degrees above freezing tomorrow night. However, general conditions are not expected to change dramatically over the coming days.

She fills the kettle and turns off the radio. Her hands are cold. She rubs them together then joins her fingers until they whiten. Distractedly she gnaws at a hangnail. She wishes she had a larger life, a more complex life, more commitments, responsibilities, charges, dependents. She tries to think about what this would mean for her, about the loss of control it would dictate. A cordoned and contained life, that is what she has wanted to achieve these last years, to minimise the challenges to what she knows can be tolerably survived, and to shunt everything else to an apportioned place in a chambered space. That is what it always comes down to, the avoidance of distortion. Isn't that always what it comes down to? Perhaps her occasional and occasionally overwhelming desire for complication is a foolish one. She recants, telling herself she has enough to be going on with. She has herself after all, tip of the iceberg, all those parts of her self still to disclose. These are the metaphors Dr Lavender has guided her to rely on: emergence, submergence, generation, regeneration.

Smith meows to be allowed back in. Mary fills a saucer with curdled milk. She has a sudden urge to mop the tiled floor. She switches on the boiler in the utility room. There'll be warm water in an hour or so.

Maybe a bath.

Mary walks through the kitchen, along the connecting corridor lined with photographs, and up the three steps, off which lies the entrance to the dining room with louvered doors to the adjoining drawing room. She fingers the still-unopened mail from the previous few days. She tears the corner of one envelope, looks at it again then puts it aside. She opens the doors to the drawing room, turns on the main light, dims it, then clicks the tall pink-shaded standing lamp behind the TV. She notices Smith's hairs on the end cushion of the red sofa and makes a mental note to vacuum it later. She looks out onto the fogbound street, the aureoles of light, the brownstones and apartments opposite. She opens the glass-fronted cabinet set into the left corner of the room and takes out a half-empty bottle of whiskey. She fills a cut sherry glass almost to the brim and takes a sip. The blinking light on her telephone indicates at least one message. She distrusts the mild uplift that comes with knowing that someone has thought of her. She keys in her number and puts the phone on speaker. What follows is a wrong-number kind of silence and the receiver being replaced. Second message. A man's muffled voice comes on.

– It's been a long time Mary. Too long. I've come back. You always knew I would. You hurt me Mary. I have to hurt you back. You think I don't know where you are. I've always known where you are. I've always known who and what you are.

There's a pause in the message. The pause elongates, interminably. For a moment it appears that it might be finished, then the voice erupts.

– I can come whenever I like.

Then louder.

– I can come whenever I like. I'll come and get you soon. Not yet. Soon. You be ready now.

From the first word of the playback Mary has slumped down to a crouching position, her back against the wall. She looks physically diminished, the phone still in her hand.

– To delete your message press 7, to save it press 9. To listen to your message again press 3.

Mary presses 9. Another message begins.

– Mary! IT'S SHEILA! Got your call! Thanks for that. Sorry I haven't been in touch. So, any news! Got yourself a new man or anything?

Sheila laughs and continues.

– Listen, I'll be home around seven. Give me a call when you get in or sometime over the next few days and we can catch up, okay! Hope you're well. Bye!

– To delete your message press 7, to ....

Mary cancels the voice and remains slumped. Smith rubs against the side of her thigh, shedding some black-tipped white hairs which Mary brushes off immediately. Her eyes furtively scan the room then the ceiling.

What if there's someone in the house? What if they're listening for her now? What if they're waiting for her? Why does she have to cope with so much? She picks up the phone and scrolls for the man's number. The number comes up but she doesn't recognise it. She does the same for Sheila. She calls it and takes the phone with her as she walks out into the hallway and up the main stairs. At least if anything happens someone will know. She stops on the first floor return beside the stained-glass copy of one of Monet's windows and listens to make sure Sheila's number is ringing. She looks upstairs. Nothing. Automatically she counts out the final nine steps, looking for stains or debris along the red-and-black carpet runner. She stops beside the heavy mahogany chest of drawers on the first floor landing and turns on the lights to the second floor. She goes into her room and locks the door. The bed remains unmade. She sits at her cluttered vanity and brushes a clutter of lipsticks and creams to one side.

To her right there's a stand holding five or six wigs. She takes the top one of these, a short, dark, bobbed wig, and puts it on.

Sheila picks up.

– Hello!

– Hi, can you hear me?

– Mary? Just about. You sound far away.

– No, I'm right here, says Mary. In my head as usual. I rang you at work and they said you had moved. I thought of Africa for some reason. I don't know why.

– I wish. I decided to change jobs then I crashed my car. A total write-off. Other than that there's no evidence that I'm trying to sabotage my life. Hello Mary?

– I'm still here.

–You sure you're all right? You don't sound yourself.

–To be honest I feel like…a turtle, except I don't have a shell anymore.

Mary pauses and begins to comb her dark hair.

– Sheila I feel cold. God! If I could only hear myself. I must sound like I've been in therapy too long, or alive too long.

–You sound a bit low.

–You say that like you're surprised.

– I'd hoped things were better.

– For your sake or mine?

Sheila doesn't rise to the slight.

– Has anything unusual happened? asks Sheila. You're not pregnant? You weren't abducted by aliens?

– Nothing really unusual. I had another one of those calls. But I don't know if they really affect me.

– What kind of call?

– Not really obscene, more threatening. It's someone who wants to hurt me or wants me to believe they're capable of hurting me. Sounds like he knows me. In fact I think it's David. I'm almost certain.

– No, it couldn't be, says Sheila.

– What makes you so sure?

– I just know. Are you on your own? Have you reported it to the police?

– The police, says Mary. No I haven't. God, I feel so stupid and incapable.

– Ease up Mary, you've had a tough time these last few years. You've managed it well.

– I suppose. Anyway, I shouldn't be getting stressed about this. In fact I resent getting stressed about this. It's probably no big deal. Just some prick. But you know when I think about it I actually can't stand it. I thought I could but I can't. As if I didn't have enough to deal with, and now this.

– Calm down! says Sheila, I'll come over. I can always stay with you. In fact it would be great to spend a bit of time together. It'd be fun. Just like old times.

– That would be nice Sheila. You don't have to, but if you wanted to, it'd be great.

– Ok I'll pack an overnight bag. Has the fog lifted over by you?

– No. Sometimes I get the feeling it never will. Do you have a car?

– Sure do.

– Could you pick up some liver? It's for Smith. And some milk and cookies for the policemen when they come.

– No problem, I'll be over as soon as I can.

– You don't think I'm going to die, do you? asks Mary.

– No, of course not, says Sheila. No one is going to die.

4

Mary is finishing changing the linens in the spare bedroom when the front door knocker clangs twice. The sheets are pink, the first she had put her hands on. Another moment and she would have found the nice white cotton ones with the matching embroidered duvet. Her stomach rumbles. She recalls that she only had a pitta sandwich earlier in the day. These are the things she has to watch just to demonstrate to herself, if to no one else, that she's managing her life. She is halfway down the stairs when she remembers the wig. There are another couple of knocks, louder this time.

– I'll be there in a minute. Just hold on! she calls.

Just hold on, she thinks, just hold on.

She throws the wig on the vanity and quickly brushes out her blonde hair. She swivels to the side checking her profile in the mirror, smoothes her midriff with her left palm and sucks in. After all it's been over nine months since she's seen Sheila.

She almost falls down the stairs.

She opens the door.

– Sheila, sorry about that, says Mary.

– I was beginning to get worried, says Sheila

The two women embrace. The cloying scent of Angel from behind Sheila's left earlobe overwhelms Mary, while the metal of her friend's shoulder-bag-clasp digs into her arm. Odd, she thinks, that this seizing pain is the first thing I feel. Sheila steps back still holding onto Mary's shoulders. She eyeballs her.

–You okay m'dear?

– Sure. Nothing's happened. I'm okay.

– Okay then.

–You look great Sheila.

–You too. You cut your hair.

– Just shows how long it is since we've seen each other. That was months ago.

The two women go through the hall, down the steps and along the corridor to the kitchen.

Sheila unzips her tracksuit top and sits down.

–You call the police? she asks.

–Yes, I did.

– Do you mind if I put the kettle on? Here's the liver you wanted by the way.

Mary opens the plastic bag and places the meat on a wooden cutting board. Smith smells the meat and entwines himself between her legs. Mary takes out the knife with the black-and-white onyx handle. As she cuts the liver into strips she sucks each strip before putting it in the cat's bowl.

– I'd forgotten you do that. It's so weird. You should have called me before this, says Sheila. You should have called the police.

– I know. Sometime I'm so frivolous.

– Do you want a cup of tea? asks Sheila.

– Sure, says Mary. I thought it would stop. I thought.... well I didn't think really. I went shopping. Can you believe it? I thought I could shop my way to a different me. I thought I could shop my way free. Isn't that funny!

Mary stoops and offers Smith his food.

– It's just a coping mechanism, we all have them.

–You're so sane and reasonable Sheila, I envy you. I'm glad you're here. When I hadn't heard from you in so long I thought you were upset with me.

Sheila opens a fresh pack of Marlboro Lights.

–You mind? she asks.

– Just open the door.

– I wasn't upset with you Mary. It's just that I needed some time to myself. And you know what they say; the greatest cure for loneliness is solitude.

– You lonely! I can't see it. Guys love you. You sure you weren't seeing someone?

Sheila takes a long drag of the cigarette and exhales towards the partly opened door.

– No…well I was, but it was casual. Nothing came of it.

– No, of course not.

– How about you? Any action?

– Any action? No, no action. Although I did place a personal ad a few weeks back but I didn't act on any of them. I didn't *action* any of them.

Mary is drawn to Sheila's face. She wonders what kind of moisturiser she uses. She always does herself up so well, and she looks so fit and trim, even though she smokes. Some girls have all the luck. Immediately she hears the Robert Palmer melody from the eighties in her head and begins to hum it. She stops.

– Was that why you changed jobs? asks Mary. Was it someone at work?

– No actually, work was something else.

The door knocker sounds loudly, twice.

–That'll be the police.

– Are you all right?

–Would you get it? Bring them into the drawing room. I'll be in in a minute. Offer them the good chairs. Oh and stick on the heater.

– Sure thing.

Mary prepares a tray of tea and cookies. While getting the sugar bowl from the cupboard she notices Sheila's cigarette burning down in the Budweiser ashtray that's been in the house for as long as she can remember. She takes it from the ashtray and stubs it out in the centre of her palm. She exhibits no facial reaction, no sign of pain. When Sheila returns Mary presents herself as though she were a little girl, spic and span, waiting to be passed by a parent. In fact that is what she says.

– Am I presentable?

Sheila flicks a piece of fluff off Mary's shoulder and some of Smith's hairs off her bum.

–You look fine!

5

Sheila has turned on the electric fire and the radiator behind the sofa, and drawn the curtains. With the pink-shaded standing lamp and the small porcelain wall light both lit, the room, she feels, is warmly and invitingly defined. She puts the police officer, who has introduced himself as Sergeant Keaney, in the pale green rocker near the fireplace. Looking at him she figures he's in his thirties, his blond hair gelled and slicked back, his features and gestures refined. As he sits facing both women, who are seated variously in different sized armchairs, he tries to achieve a comfortable point of balance on the unstable chair. Tea and cookies rest on a small table in front of them.

– Sergeant Keaney's partner had a panic attack in the car, says Sheila.

– We can do this now or you can come down to the station later, says Sergeant Keaney.

– Now is good. I don't need two cops to tell my story to.

– You'd no trouble getting through the fog? asks Sheila.

– No. I knew where I was going.

– Some more tea, Sergeant? asks Sheila.

Mary is momentarily unnerved by Sheila's unctuous tone.

– Please, Ms Deane! says the Sergeant. I must compliment you both. That's quite a cup of tea! Just what the doctor ordered.

– Thank you, says Mary, corralling the compliment. With tea, she continues, you never let the water boil, just before boiling whip it off and then over the tea leaves. Perfect every time! When I was seventeen I worked in a wine and tea company…before I went to college. Of course, the tea leaves play a part too, and the coolies who pick them. In Ceylon, isn't it?

– Sri Lanka I think it's called now, the Sergeant corrects her. India's another place.

– I'm sure you're right, says Mary.

Sheila passes the Sergeant some more cookies.

– Thank you.

The Sergeant takes the last two chocolate cookies.

– I hope you don't mind, he says, I'm a *savage* for these ones.

– Not at all, says Sheila, go right ahead.

The chitchat evaporates.

– I should listen to the message, says the Sergeant.

– I'm sure you've heard this kind of thing a million times, says Mary.

– Even so. That's what I'm here for.

Mary plays the message.

– And again, says the Sergeant, can you play it again?

He eats his cookies as she does so.

– So, Sergeant, do you think he's dangerous?

The Sergeant tries to clear his stuffed mouth. The two women glance at each other.

– Yes…yes, it's a possibility, although it's impossible to be sure at this stage.

– Clarity is impossible is that what you're saying? asks Mary.

– I don't know, says the Sergeant.

– You know I was being followed this evening. It wasn't the first time.

– You're sure you were being followed Ms Reid?

Mary's frustration, anxiety and anger pour forth.

– I'm sure of *nothing*, Sergeant. I'm afraid. I feel vulnerable. It's not a feeling I like.

– I understand.

Sergeant Keaney eyes both women. He taps his teaspoon against the inside of his index finger.

– You phoned Ms Deane here directly after listening to the call. Have you mentioned them to anyone else?

– No, says Mary.

– Why is that?

– There's only been one other. I thought it was a once-off.

These people get off on fear don't they? I mean they have an appetite for it. I didn't want to submit to that. And I know you're not meant to talk to them. There they are...wanking. At least I suppose that's what they do.

Sheila reaches out and comfortingly pressurises Mary's forearm.

– Mary, I don't think you should...

– It's disgusting! Do you think they wear condoms when they do it? What about the ones who phone the girls who talk dirty? I mean what kind of person?

For a moment Mary feels overwhelmed by the darkness she perceives. She looks directly at the Sergeant.

–Why is the world so sick? she asks.

– I can't answer that Ms Reid but for me self-control has a big part to play. The absence of it is an ingredient in this whole ugly business. Inner discipline, that's what's missing.

Sheila nods approvingly. She is clearly at one with the Sergeant. If there were one more chocolate cookie she would offer it now.

The Sergeant continues to unfold his thinking on this matter. Both women lean forward ever so slightly.

– Believe me Ms Reid, Ms Deane, if I had my way I'd punish them severely. It's one of the things that's missing in my view – extreme measures. It's the only thing these people understand. In my experience it's the only thing that makes a difference. Now I don't mean to rush you but time is pressing on, I need some details about your personal life. Do you mind?

– No. Well that depends, says Mary.

– Let's see how we get on.

– Should I leave? asks Sheila.

–That's up to Ms Reid, says the Sergeant.

– Of course not Sheila. There's nothing I wouldn't share with you. Besides, I have no secrets and it's not as though my life is so lurid.

The Sergeant writes some details at the top of the page.

–You live alone?

– In a manner of speaking. I have Smith of course and Smith has me.

– Boyfriend?

– Oh this is so pathetic! Next question.

– Are you sexually active?

– Go to hell!

Sheila looks anxiously over to Mary. She feels an instinct to ameliorate Mary's abrasiveness.

– Mary, the Sergeant is only trying to help.

– Any casual affairs recently? asks the Sergeant.

– God, the pristine logic! Yes I screwed myself, that's what I do all the time, I screw myself up.

Sheila whispers in Mary's ear.

– If you go on like this, says Sheila, he'll leave, or he'll stop caring.

– Sorry! Sorry! I'm just a little upset. Okay!

– No affairs then, you're sure.

– N…no.

– There was a slight hesitation, remarks the Sergeant.

– There was someone I was interested in but I didn't do anything about it.

– Was he aware of this interest?

– He wasn't aware period. That was the problem. It would never have worked out.

– And you haven't noticed any of your co-workers being more attentive to you of late?

– Maybe there was some unwanted attention. It's not a perfect world.

– I understand you're upset. That's a given. But if you want me to help you…

– We're only here to help, says Sheila.

– Stop ganging up on me!

– Believe me I know how difficult this must be for you.

– How can you know?

– In your phone call to me you mentioned your ex-husband David.

– About time! says Mary, exasperated. He's got to be the prime suspect. Shaw…David Shaw.

– He threatened you?

– He violated me. I left him two years ago. This is his idea of revenge.

– You recognise the voice then?

– It's muffled of course, he's not stupid but it's him all right.

– And his motive?

– I've created a new life for myself. That's what he can't stand. He still wants a part of me, and this is his sick way of going about it.

– Was there a history of violence in the relationship?

– Not violence *per se*, more cruelty, mental cruelty.

Mary becomes aware that he has stopped taking notes.

– You don't believe me, do you?

– Ms Reid, as you probably know the majority of calls of this nature come from acquaintances, friends, even intimates, so I'm discounting nothing. If it is in fact a stalker then it's a little more worrying. Can you think of any other possibilities aside from your ex-husband?

– No, says Mary.

Sheila looks at her.

– Tell the Sergeant what you told me, about the dating site. They might be a factor.

Mary stiffens. She wishes now that Sheila had left the room.

– Don't you think I would have mentioned them if I thought they were important. Whose life is this anyway?

– I'm only trying to help, says Sheila.

– I know, I'm sorry, says Mary. To be honest I don't see it as a possibility. All the replies were to an online account and I haven't answered any as yet.

– Can I see the responses that you've had? asks the Sergeant.

– I'll have to get my laptop. It's upstairs.

Mary leaves the Sergeant and Sheila together and goes upstairs. The Sergeant adjusts himself in the chair, touching his inner thigh in a discreet effort to loosen his crotch. Sheila does not avert her gaze. Her unflinching look intrigues him.

– Do you have any other insights into this Ms Deane?

– I'm one of Mary's oldest friends Sergeant. She's certainly been through a hard time these past two years, since the break-up of her marriage.

– Yet she instigated the break?

– That's not strictly true.

– Do you think it's her ex-husband?

– No, it just doesn't fit. It's a long story but ultimately I never felt that David and Mary should ever have gotten together. They were just too different. If there was mental cruelty, then it worked both ways. As far as I know David's in a new relationship and quite happy by all accounts.

Mary returns and hears the tail-end of Sheila's chat with the Sergeant.

– Who's happy by all accounts? she asks.

Sheila doesn't betray any defensiveness.

– It's nothing I haven't said to you before Mary. I think you're wrong about David.

– Sounds like you're more concerned about David than you are about me.

– You know that's not true.

A cold silence ensues.

Mary isn't happy with the way the whole evening has turned out. She'd like to revise it.

– I have the number that came up on your phone and I'll check that out first thing and I'll take a list of these names, says the Sergeant, and run a check on them. You never know what might turn up. I must say I find it amazing that so many people use these sites.

Both women meet this observation with a stony silence.

– Of course I'll talk to your ex-husband. However, in the meantime you should think about changing your number. You can do it now if you want.

– I'd prefer not to have to do that but you're right it's probably the easiest solution. I'll do it later.

Sheila and Mary begin clearing up. Mary takes the tray full of empty cups down to the kitchen.

The Sergeant scrolls through the various respondents. He identifies one in particular.

– There's one here from an Ed Perlov. Something about the face looks distinctly familiar.

– Do you remember the context? asks Sheila.

– No, I'm afraid not. He's good looking though you've got to admit that.

The Sergeant turns the laptop towards her.

– You're better looking, says Sheila.

– That's kind of you to say.

– Is there an address with it? asks Sheila.

– No. But I'll be able to requisition it from the dating site and I'll cross reference his name against the files.

Mary on her return stands under the lintel of the doorway.

– Do you have a card we could have in case we need to get in touch? asks Sheila.

The Sergeant rummages, takes one out of his wallet, and hands it to Sheila.

– So your name's Gerard? says Sheila.

– Well, Gerry actually.

Sheila passes the card over to Mary.

– One more thing before I go, says the Sergeant, can you tell me precisely when the calls started?

– I'm almost sure it was the evening of January 10th.

– Did something happen that day?

– It's my birthday.

The Sergeant looks at Mary's online description of herself.

– So the first call was two days after you placed the ad.

– I suppose.

– You don't think that's significant?

Sheila drops a water glass, which shatters. Mary kneels and puts some broken pieces in her palm. She hides the welt that has arisen from the burn. The Sergeant makes no effort to help.

– Sorry, says Sheila, I hope it's replaceable.

– It's not.

– Both calls were recorded, says the Sergeant, so you've never actually spoken to the caller?

– You think that makes it any better?

– No, no, I'm sure it doesn't.

– You really inspire me with confidence, Sergeant. What about protection? Don't I get an officer outside the door or something?

– I'm afraid we don't have the manpower for anything like that, but the house will be under surveillance at hourly intervals. It's the best I can do.

– I hope this creep's a good time-keeper!

– I understand your anxiety but in turn you've got to understand our position. You've had two calls, you may have been followed. It's not enough to warrant…

– You think I'm being irrational. But my life is being threatened, says Mary.

– Mary, you can always stay with me or I can stay here, says Sheila.

– For how long? A month, a year? He'll find me. That's what he said. He's probably watching me now. He knows where I live. He can follow me.

Sheila goes over and gives Mary a hug.

– Take it easy. Come on Mary, you're all right. Everything will work out.

– Do you mind if I take a quick look upstairs? asks the Sergeant.

Sheila, with Mary still in her arms, nods for him to go ahead.

6

Upstairs, the Sergeant enters Mary's bedroom. Clothes and hangers lie strewn on the bed and on the floor. He goes to the window, opens it and closes it again. He touches some of the wigs on the stand beside the vanity, taking a curly red one off the holder and examining the inside. He picks up a pair of discarded knickers and smells them. He leaves the room and goes upstairs to the second floor. If the first floor has an air of unruly habitation then the second by comparison looks almost derelict. There are no floor coverings; cobwebs and dust cover the ceilings of the two rooms, one of them packed high with storage boxes, the other completely empty except for a rotten mop and bucket. Off the second floor landing four steps ascend to a reddish-brown door leading to the top-floor rooms. He turns the knob. It's locked. He tries to force it but it won't budge. He checks the overhead lintel. Nothing. He makes a cursory examination of the four steps, running his fingers along the wooden overhang. Nothing there either. He turns off the lights and returns to the first floor. He looks into the spare bedroom with the pink sheets turned down. He notes that the pillows' openings have been properly turned in towards the centre of the bed. Before returning downstairs he goes past the chest of drawers stabled by the bannister railings, stops at the windowless end of the first floor landing, unzips his trousers and urinates on the floor. A pool of deeply yellow urine spreads around his feet which he sidesteps neatly.

7

In the drawing room Mary is finishing writing something on a piece of paper. She rises and hands this to the Sergeant.

– This is David Shaw's address and telephone number. You have to go round there.

– I will, don't worry.

Sheila returns from the kitchen wiping a droplet of urine which has seeped through the loose floorboards,off her forehead.

She tastes it.

– The door to the third floor is locked, remarks the Sergeant.

– Yes.

– Can you tell me why?

– They're just junk rooms up there. I lost the key a while back and just haven't done anything about it.

– Okay I think that's it for the moment. I'll be off unless you have any questions.

Mary shakes his hand formally.

– I hope the next time you call it will be in a different capacity.

Sheila takes his elbow.

– I'll see you to the door.

Fogged streetlight enters through the elliptical fanlight window. Sheila opens the door and stands with him looking down the fogbound street towards a cluster of shops and bars at the next intersection. The city has grown quiet, unobtrusive, unpredictable. If it were not for the sordidness of the situation she wonders if the aftertaste of danger would be quite so strong.

– If you could stay Ms Deane, suggests the Sergeant.

–Yes, of course. Do you think this freak is likely to carry out his threats?

– I really don't know, says the Sergeant. If it's a stalker anything is possible. My hunch is that it's not but I've been wrong before. You have my cell number. Call me if there are any problems.

Sheila stands up straight, chest out, and appears to measure herself against the Sergeant.

–You're quite small for a cop. I thought you had to be bigger.

– Oh, I'm big enough!

– I'm sure you are, says Sheila.

– Goodnight Gerry and thank you. You've been a great help. Now I'd better close the door. We don't want to let the fog in, now do we?

The Sergeant grasps her upper arm.

– I'll be in touch, he says.

8

When Sheila returns to the drawing room, Mary is standing by the window, the curtains partly drawn, her right hand wringing her other wrist.

– He was cute! remarks Sheila.

Mary turns around.

– Thanks a lot, Sheila! I think what I need now is a little support not one of my oldest friends going behind my back and contradicting me.

– I wasn't trying to undermine you.

– All that stuff about David. Why is it that I'm the one who feels guilty? I haven't done anything wrong.

Mary feels a contraction in her stomach as though some necessary evacuation needs to take place.

Sheila licks her lips.

– You didn't spill anything upstairs did you?

Mary's whole demeanour is distracted, unsettled.

– What do you mean he's cute? Sometimes I wonder about you Sheila. How can you expect anyone else to treat you decently when you flaunt yourself like that?

– Oh for Christ's sake stop being so critical! I like men. I let them know I like them. What's wrong with that?

– It just seems so contrived, you know, false. Men deny me. How can I trust them after that?

– Trust isn't that important, says Sheila. Sex on the other hand…

Sheila laughs.

– C'mon let's have a drink, she says.

Sheila gets some proper glasses from the kitchen and pours a couple of stiff whiskeys.

The two women sit down in the armchairs in front of the glowing electric fire.

– I know you don't want to hear it but I still think you're way off-beam about David. Have you been in touch with him recently?

– Why do you ask?

– Have you?

Sheila knows that she's pushing it.

– I might have called him once about something, says Mary. I don't remember.

Sheila is surprised by this admission even though she has suspected it.

– Mary the truth of it is you can't let go. You're still obsessed with him. Admit it, he's still a part of you.

– I resent him if that's what you mean. I resent his capacity to move on, to forget me, to find someone new. Do you understand that?

– Yes. To me that's completely understandable, I know as well as anyone that there's nothing worse than rejection, there's nothing that destroys self-esteem more than a break up. But equally there's no use trying to blame this on him. You're just going to confuse things.

– God! Why do I feel so alone?

Sheila looks over at her with utter sympathy.

– You're not.

Silence. One of the three clocks on the marble mantlepiece strikes once on the half hour. Sheila looks at the framed print above them. A semi-abstract of what might be two intertwined bodies and what looks like the ghostly echo of their bodies arrayed behind them. Mary picks up Smith and begins to stroke him. Sheila lights up a cigarette.

– Not in here if you don't mind, says Mary.

– Sorry!

Sheila stubs out the cigarette, and turns the laptop around.

– Mind if I have a look at some of the guys who got in touch.

– Go ahead!

Sheila scrolls down to one. Putting on a fantasy Southern Belle accent.

– I like this one. Big and strong! He'd make you do exactly as you was told, sugar!

Mary laughs, and pulls up her chair alongside Sheila's.

– God no, not that one. There was one, though.

Mary scrolls through until she finds the contact she's looking for.

– What gave you the idea to join this site anyway?

– Just a whim.

– At least you're in control.

– Here it is!

Sheila reads it.

– You've got to be kidding!

– Why what's wrong?

– Another painter! Just like David. And his name!

– I like his name.

– Germain. That's a girl's name. C'mon Mary. You don't want a fag. Or maybe you do.

– So they're both painters. What's so unusual about that? Maybe I should have put: no artists need apply! Anyway I think I know him. There was a Germain that did a show with David a few years ago. He fits the description.

Sheila reads on.

She hollers.

– You can't be serious! Listen to this.

"I want to make it clear from the start that I suffer from a disability. I contracted polio when I was five and although the crutches don't appear in the photograph I do need them to get around."

He's a cripple!

Mary looks at her, unperturbed.

– Aren't we all, in one way or another?

9

Unable to sleep Mary rises at dawn, not that dawn light is hugely discernable in this fogbound dreamtime at the close of winter. She dresses and leaves a note on the kitchen table should Sheila rise and notice her absence. She moves through the streets in the gloopy light. She has lived here all her life. She knows it blind, and can trace this place as you would a body, its declivities and smooth expanses, its crenelated protrusions and subsidences.

She takes the subway fifteen stops to Deer Island beach. She buys the early edition of the *The New York Times* in tabloid format. There's a report of a fifteen-car pile-up on the highway the previous night. Three generations of the Ellis family wiped out, the sole survivor a four-month-old infant. Mary briefly imagines the trajectory of that future life, a narrative of loss, a life distorted by ghostly alliances. No hands to compare to, no eyes. Every serious, future relationship prefaced by this story of absence.

For the last five stops the train emerges onto an overground track. She thinks about what it would have been like to have had a child. Not that it's beyond her. She's still young enough. She touches her stomach; she pictures it bulbous, blooming, the uterine wall tick and sturdy. She always imagines a girl. Buying mobiles, dresses, swings. It's not too late, she knows that, maybe a sperm donation online, or maybe buy a baby somewhere else, somewhere exotic – Central America or Vietnam.

From the *News Around the World* column she reads about a woman who superglued her philandering partner's genitals to his stomach, and the cheeks of his ass together. The thought strikes her that people are endlessly creative in revenge. Justice is never obscene. She speculates on what the woman was thinking in acting as she did. Was she hoping to stop up his essence, his waste, to block his life? He was a shit. Even he would come to feel that in time. She wishes the woman well.

As the train pulls into Holbrook, figures and faces fugue in the fog then come into focus. It is like a world in imminence, the fog creating a liminal space between worlds, forms appearing and disappearing. The fog like memory, amorphous, depth charged, spurious. Images retrieved, held, and lost. The world suddenly capsized to small space, intimate space. As Mary looks around her references for what she believes exists remain occluded. Her memory accretes on the basis of what she locates but she finds that she has little or no memory of what actually exists here in Holbrook station, or elsewhere. She knows there are houses, hypermarkets, garages, cinemas, but it is an imagined assemblage of nominally predictable elements; she cannot locate a detail that might cohere the truth of what she believes exists, what she knows on some level to exist. She is faced with the momentary illusion of having no coherent corroboration of memory. The evidential lights seem like small annunciations in declensions of darkness. The fog creates a page onto which anything might be written, or narrative or image conjured. She imagines herself as the Ellis child thinking of her lost family, instating memories of accord and ideality.

So much of what is lost remains lost, so much of what is remembered remains unheeded. She has an instinct for the memory fudges others create in order to survive. Isn't that why she's in therapy – to regain what is lost, to encode and integrate what is remembered? One day she believes she will be full of herself and lose no more time in the present.

Unexpectedly the rhythm of the train lulls her to sleep. When a ticket inspector taps her shoulder she wakes from a small dream of hanging, her child's body lolling over the edge of a pond in an ornamental garden, giant yellow and orange goldfish opening and closing their blobby mouths below.

– We're on turnaround. Do you want to go back to the city? asks the inspector.

– Do you have the time?

– Five after seven.

She has time.

– No, I'll get out here, thanks.

Mary puts the newspaper on her seat, leaves the train and walks from the station to the boardwalk. Not a soul in sight. This was what she had imagined, a soulful, soulless place. The tide is in. She can see the low waves lap against the pebble shore. It feels elegiac, romantic. The place reflects her in this instance perfectly. She and David used to come here in the past. They had constructed a narrative of joy, had they not? He was the song of manhood, she was the animal of loving vigour. She can feel the grace memory of her hand enfolded in his, the strength and tenderness of his painter's grip. It is not the memory of that evanescent and evinced joy that saddens her, but the lost possibility of its reoccurrence.

She shifts her inner gaze, breathes deeply and is present. To be in tune with the greater world even for a moment is a solace. She believes this, but somehow she doesn't really believe that all her moments of solace ease her. Her breath still stalls, her sleep pattern remains random and shallow, there is something deeper in her mind that kills her bit by bit.

She leans out over the rusting blue balustrade. Some shore birds, loons and shearwaters, skirt along the sandbar. Routines of food, shelter, and regeneration are what possess animals. Urgent physical needs simplify existence. To be purely animal. There is a wish. To be devoid of mind, to be emotionally void.

To void, to walk into the sea, to simply desire erasure of one's nature, to feel a kind of osmotic mergence of the sea with the body, to feel integration before death. There would be a kind of bliss in that.

She understands that no one will maintain a memory of her. Her life will pass and it will be as though she had never existed, there will be none to even carry her name for a generation. Better that way, cancelled before she becomes completely ridiculous, or worse utterly resolved and nondescript.

She walks towards the curved, port-holed, concrete shelter newly painted mint green, its wooden slats carved with the names of youthful infatuates. Steps lead down from the shelter to the beach. Her feet shift stones making a kind of sheer earth music. She imagines her water-wasted body rolled by the waves, her body eroding to small parts, hands rounded, bones rounded, organs pebbled. She takes off her shoes and socks and trembles her toes in the freezing water, unperturbed that the bottoms of her jeans dampen slightly. The shore curves and she can see the dark outline of a near headland. She is unaware of her tears until the air cools them on her cheeks. It is not that she is in mourning for her life but ultimately for a death she feels she cannot accomplish. Lifting her head she sees a dog running towards her and beyond the dog a figure. She scans the concrete wall underneath the balustrade, thinking she can veer off and avoid having to nod or acknowledge another human being, but her route to avoidance is not obvious. She walks on. The dog approaches her, all legs and muscular body. For a moment she feels threatened. She stops dead. There is a scream inside her she wants to emit. Just stand, she tells herself. Let the dog pass. Let everything pass. She wishes she had not come. She had expected to be alone. She roots herself to the spot. The dog – a boxer, chestnut brown with a white diamond between its black eyes – stands with its legs slightly splayed. It moves towards her. Where is its owner? The figure seems not to have moved but to be stationary by the shore's edge, contemplative, eternal. The dog will be debased by her fear. It will maul her. No sooner has she thought this than the dog growls menacingly, lurches forward on the first bark, retreats, then surges again. She feels faint. Were she to swoon, she has no doubt its jaws would clamp on her flesh. Although derisive of her own fear, she cannot command it, or repress it.

– Help me!

It is no more than a strangled, guttural whisper. But once voiced all dignity is lost. She says it louder, the dog barking frenziedly in response until there is a kind of dialogue of terror set up between the two. The figure, alerted from his reverie, responds by calling the dog's name.

– King! King! Come here. Good boy!

The dog retreats, retrieved by the call.

Moments later, the dog approaches again, now tightly leashed and held tautly by a vigorous, striding man in a long woollen black overcoat.

– Sorry about that. Hope he didn't scare you too much. He's just a young dog, a little high-spirited.

– I just didn't expect it that's all.

– He's really quite gentle. Here do you want to pet him?

Mary bends down and somewhat obligatorily fingertips the top of his skull. She dislikes the too intimate feel of bone. She is reminded that these were her father's favourite dogs. She surprises herself by communicating this fact to the man.

– I shouldn't be so afraid.

– They really are quite gentle, says the man.

Mary bends and strokes the dog some more.

– There, friends now, says the man.

The man pulls a small velvet purse from his pocket and extracts his phone.

– I wonder if you'd mind taking a photo of me and King by the shore? It's so atmospheric. Haunting, don't you think?

Mary takes the phone. The figure and the dog loom against the fog. They look diffused by it, lessened by it. She moves them to the side of the frame so that they are almost incidental. Before she taps the screen she has an image of her father standing in the man's place, his lips thick and sensuous, his legs splayed like those of the dog. She blinks and sees her reality.

– Done! says Mary.

– I can take one of you if you'd like, and send it on to you.

– Why would I want that?

– I don't know. A memento maybe! It was only a suggestion. I'm an inveterate recorder. I expect everyone else to be the same.

Mary finds herself walking with the dog a little distance away, occupying almost the same space as the man did, and yet it has been an almost unconscious agreement to do something she has no wish to do.

She stands holding the leash slackly. She hears herself imitating the dog's owner.

– Good boy! she says. There's a good boy!

As she waits she recalls how French women used to repeat the words *petite-pomme* before the camera flashed, in order to create a simulacrum of sublime, refined bliss, their lips a fulsome bee-sting, alluring and sensual.

She imagines how she will place this photograph with all her other photographs on the cork-lined corridor from the kitchen to the hall, titling it humorously, *The King and I*. For a moment she feels entitled, dignified. Courage, she tells herself, is not, after all, so hard to secure.

10

It is after eight thirty when she gets back to the house. She is surprised to find Sheila's blue Ford still parked outside. She sees a travel guide to Sicily on the back seat amongst some tumbled garments. She recalls a journey she had made in her mid-twenties into the interior of the island to Corleone, the huge field systems with their shoulder-high cereals, the poplar-lined country roads, the rolling hills. She recalls picnicking by a lake's edge under an olive tree, the sound of harvesters in the distance.

An image comes to her of Corleone and the Mafia Museum sited in an old convent orphanage. She still has copies of the black-and-white pictures detailing the symbology of the mafia killings, and other pictures of grassed-on dons manacled to policemen: the dons' murderous arrogance, the fear in the policemen's eyes. Terror was what they were good at, casual and fickle brutality. She wonders when Sheila could have gone. She never remembers having spoken to her about it.

Mary closes the front door.

– Hi Sheila, she calls out, still here.

– In the kitchen. You need to get to a store Mary. There's nothing to eat.

Mary's eye stops on an old photograph of the two of them in Cyprus years before. Both in summer dresses, thick-haired, fleshy, sunburnt.

– Didn't you find anything?

– Some old muesli, it's no wonder you're as slim as you are.

– There are crackers somewhere if you want me to look.

– No I've got to run. What's your schedule like today?

– I've an appointment in Brooklyn at 11. I've got to show some business types around an industrial unit, so I'm going to take the car. After that I'll be in the office, but I should be back around seven or so. How about you?

– I have a presentation at twelve and just routine stuff after that. I can do dinner if you want, says Sheila.

–You're going to stay tonight?

– That's the plan. I've no problem doing this for a while Mary if it helps sort things out.

– Ok then. I'm going to have a shower. See you later.

– O I saw your note. How was the shore?

– Interesting! I couldn't sleep and I just felt like seeing the sea or not seeing the sea. The fog is as dense as ever today. Before I forget here's a spare key.

– Cheers! It feels like old times doesn't it?

–Yeah, I suppose it does.

– Ok see you later!

The bathroom is still steamed up from Sheila's earlier shower.

Mary notices Sheila's moisturiser, toothpaste and toothbrush set neatly to one side on the countertop. She opens the moisturiser and smells it. She squeezes out an iris-sized blob and smears it between her fingers. She swabs the mirror clear.

Undressed, she looks at her breasts and bottom. She thumps the cheeks of her bottom with her fists, then her ribs, then her bottom once more. She feels a mild pain, a mild relief. She takes her steel nail-scissors from her wash bag and begins to clip her pubic hair, which has bushed up. She slides the scissors between her hairs until she feels it rest against her skin. She is careful not to cut herself. She thinks about leaving a centre line of hair along her slit. The reddish-blonde hairs pile up in the sink. She cuts everything off until she looks like a girl again. Wetting a tissue, she gathers up the bulk of the hairs then turns on the warm tap to flush the loose ones down the plughole.

In the shower she soaps herself down. She imagines Sheila's body, so much fatter than her own. She presses her palms against her stomach and breathes in until it concaves against her spine. There is an emptiness that makes her feel a little safer.

She pours a palmful of Sheila's jojoba oil and rubs it over her breasts and nipples and then between her legs. She imagines it as a kind of anointing, a playful, sacramental treasuring of her body. She feels more ready for the world than she has for days.

Mary gets a call from Grace, the department secretary, at nine-ten.

– Mary, your meeting with Bob Jodorowsky and his associates has been moved back to eleven thirty.

– That's fine. I can do some work from home in the meantime. I should be back in the office by 1.

Mary makes a quick cup of coffee and slathers a staling cracker with raspberry jam. Sheila's cleaned up, she can see that. Dishes racked, table cleared, the curtains on the glass frame of the door pulled back so that a mute sun through fog brightens the kitchen. What every woman needs – a maid, or better still, a wife!

Before leaving, Mary rings the telephone network's main enquiries number and is transferred to their malicious-calls unit. The line is busy so she is forced to listen to Vivaldi.

–You are now caller 2 in line.

More Vivaldi.

She is about to hang up.

–You are now caller 1 in line.

–This is Nina. How can I help you?

– Hi Nina, this is Mary Reid. I've been receiving threatening phone calls over the last while. I contacted the police who suggested that I change my number.

– I have your current number up on screen. All you need to change are the last three digits. The new numbers must be over three one zero. When you give it to me I'll confirm it by calling you back.

Mary chooses her numbers. She likes Nina's tone.

– Hang up now and I'll call you right back, says Nina.

Mary picks at the bulb of raised skin in the centre of her palm. She wonders what caused it. The phone rings.

– That's it! Your new number is now in operation. Good morning, says Nina.

– Bye Nina, and thanks.

Mary has a look over the spec on the industrial unit in Brooklyn, which she has to show Jodorowsky and his associates round later. She makes a series of notes on its potential suitability and covers any negative points she thinks are likely to come up.

In front of the hall mirror she applies some startlingly red lipstick, grabs her car keys, her cell phone, and leaves.

Her neighbour Hilda Wobbe is wading towards her as Mary descends the stone steps from her house. Hilda is carrying a cheap blue-and-red canvas bag full of groceries.

– Isn't it vonderful, that dammed fog has cleared a bit. I bake some cinnamon cookies last night. You vant I give you some?

– You're always giving me things, Hilda. One of these days I'm going to have to do something for you.

– You don't need do nothing for me. It makes me happy. Beside, you way too skinny. Haves to fatten you up a bit. Men they like the vobbly bits.

Hilda gesticulates with her hands as though weighing and seeking an impossible balance between two heavy balls.

– Why you don't have a man?

– I'm late Hilda…

– With a man first thing in morning! Better than cinnamon buns. Much better! Much, much better!

Mary finds it hard to abide her neighbour's chuckling face.

– I have to go, really I do.

– I saw police last night. You got trouble?

Mary immediately feels violated.

– You saw the police!

She moves a step closer to Hilda.

– Isn't there such a thing as privacy around here, Hilda? I don't like people snooping on my life.

– You don't get uppity, Miss. So it's a crime now I vatch the vindow?

Hilda pauses for a moment.

– You need me, you know where I am. Hilda your friend. I vatch out. Then she says laughingly, I don't have anything else to do.

Mary begins to sidle away from her neighbour.

–You remember! says Hilda.

–What? says Mary. Remember what?

– I bring cinnamon buns round later.

Mary, completely fatigued, concedes her thanks and struggles to get the door of her car open.

11

The early morning rush hour traffic is over. Mary takes the Brooklyn Battery Tunnel. She trails a burgundy Audi and pulls up alongside it at the toll station. The balding slouch-jowled man is talking into a hands-free set and tapping his fingers on the leather-twined steering wheel. Mary's silk panties feel smooth against her body.

She says the word – cunt – aloud.

She goes through the toll-booth. The toll-booth woman's fingertips touch hers. She thinks of it as exceptional contact and allows it to register as a touch of desire. She drives onto the Keith Street exit and wends her way down along the East River Road. She puts on Bach's cello suites 1, 3 and 5, with Ralph Kirshbaum's fuliginous sound, perfectly appropriate to the vast-spaced uniformity of the fog.

Mary drives down by Sweetman's Meat Packers, and up through some low rise public housing units, some of which have been newly acquired and gentrified. Young kids are gathered in ones or twos on either side of the street.

Must be a day off, or mid-term or something. Mary slows down. She can barely see the end of the street. The car judders on the old concrete surface. Cello suite number one comes to a close. Mary feels hemmed in with cars parked to left and right making it a tight squeeze. She can't be going more than fifteen kilometres an hour. She sees a blur of pink before anything else. In the fog it looks like the shimmer of refracted neon. Only when she is on top of the little girl in her pink anorak on her low tricycle does Mary jam on the brakes. She feels the left front tyre hump over something. The car stops. For a moment she cannot breathe. The car is still running. Someone screams at her to turn off the engine. She does so mechanically, on order.

She sees people milling in front of the car. An image of swarming insects overwhelms and paralyses her. Someone knuckle-taps the driver's window. Others palm-bang the windshield. How long has she been sitting like this? She craves to be anywhere but here. She feels reduced, culpable. She presses the central unlock button on a panel beside the gearstick. A woman with wiry greying hair pulls the door open. It sounds to Mary as though she is screaming at her.

–You stupid bitch, didn't you see her?

There's an echo of this from someone else.

– She wasn't looking where she was going.

Who does this apply to? she wonders.

Voices and bits of sentences move into and out of range.

– She's ok…the bicycle…is it ruined?…let her get up herself…don't touch her…don't move her…is she damaged…take the bicycle out of there…the car needs to move back…on part of the handlebars…don't move her until the father comes…here he comes now……she looks all right does she?

Mary has got out. The little tricycle with its stabilisers lies crushed and still partly trapped by the front wheel of the car. The little girl is crying and one of her knees looks scraped. Mary wants to touch the little girl. She wants to be able to show something approaching a decent impulse. One of the older women puts a comforting arm around Mary's back.

– It wasn't your fault dear. She just rolled out between the cars.

– I was going slowly, truly I was. I only saw her at the last minute. It was just the barest nudge.

– The barest nudge, someone echoes. Look at the fucking bicycle!

– Here he is now, says the woman.

– Peter it's all right. Susan's all right.

Peter, the father, brushes past Mary, checks that his hysterical daughter is substantially uninjured then gathers her up in his arms.

– Are you all right my darling! There! There!

He holds her close and shushes her. Peter looks at one of the women.

– Evelyn, would you go into the hall and get one of Susan's beanie babies?

Evelyn runs off.

Peter looks towards the other women.

– What happened?

– It was no one's fault Peter. We had our eye on her and next minute she's pushed herself out between the cars. This lady here stopped as soon as she could. Just thank God that everyone's all right.

– Peter, bring her home and I'll come and wash the wound out. Then you should take her to the doctor, just so as he can give her the once over and make sure everything is okay.

– Thanks, Veronica.

Peter turns to his daughter.

– It's just the shock, sweetheart. That's the worst thing.

Susan continues to bawl. Peter holds her ever closer. Evelyn comes back with the soft toy, an elephant. Mary is pushed to the margins as parents and children move Susan inside one of the ground floor apartments.

Cars have begun to back up along the street.

– Better move your car, lady, so we can get the bicycle out.

Mary gets back into the car. She finds she can't turn the key. Her hand is frozen. The street appears to have narrowed to the point where she can't imagine driving to the end of it. She gets out and asks one of the young men to do it for her, and to leave it at the end of the street.

– Sure thing, lady. Nice car!

Mary stands forlornly to one side as she watches one of the men attempt to straighten out the handlebars of the tricycle. The front wheel looks partly twisted, but the bike, Mary thinks, is probably repairable. She separates off from those still standing on the pavement and walks in a kind of stupor to the end of the street. Retrieving a blank sheet of paper from her briefcase she writes out her insurance and contact details.

The woman in the corner store has turned to go inside, the drama over. Mary follows her in and scans the top shelf behind the register.

– That big box there with the pink bow, please.

– Did you see the accident? asks the shopkeeper.

– No.

– Some woman, by all accounts.

Mary takes the florid, pink-bowed box of chocolates with her details attached over to the little girl's building. The front door to the ground floor apartment is half ajar. She knocks tamely and moves inside. The place looks clean but untidy. She can hear voices coming from the back kitchen. The little girl, still cocooned in her pink jacket, is sitting on a wooden chair. There's a basin of hot water on the floor and the smell of disinfectant. Thankfully she has stopped crying. Mary looks on, peering through the group of adults standing with their backs to her. An image of Rembrandt's The Anatomy Lesson of Dr Nicolaes Tulp comes to mind.

– After the doctor we'll do something extra special, says Peter. How's that?

The little girl looks up and sees Mary standing in the doorway. For a moment Mary thinks the girl is going to start crying again but she just looks at her. Mary is afraid of what Susan might see, that she will see her completely and be repelled; just like the dog her child instinct will make her want to shun her.

– Can we get a treat? asks the little girl of her father.

– Of course we can.

One of the neighbourhood women tapes a piece of gauze and muslin gently across Susan's knee.

Peter lifts her up and enfolds her in his arms. She looks so small, so protected in his broad arms. Mary stands, infatuated at the sight of the two of them together. Peter notices her standing under the lintel of the kitchen door.

– I just wanted to leave these, and my contact details.

– There's no need, says Peter. I realise it wasn't your fault.

– If there are any problems. Something may crop up. I'd like to pay for any repairs to the bike.

– There's no need.

– Please!

– All right, I'll let you know.

She goes over towards the little girl who clings ever tighter to her father, and leaves the chocolates on the deal table. Turning to go, she touches Susan almost imperceptively on the shoulder.

– I'm sorry sweetheart, she says.

12

Mary leaves the car where the young man has parked it and calls a taxi. Something about what has happened, the little girl, the bike, the damage sustained, the response and the feelings it has promoted, remind her of an incident years earlier when she had been with Maurice – her first real boyfriend, her first real obsession.

Maurice would regard her current attitude of compassion and remorse for the child's near death as feeble-minded. Better to see it as subliminal, intentional caprice on her part, her own little play of power, her desire for autonomous cruel ecstasy.

– Admit it, he would say, some part of you wanted to kill her, some part of you wanted to witness her anguish. Remember disdain for other people's pain gifts you a sovereign strength. Accept it.

She had met Maurice when she was fifteen and working as a part-time attendant at a local gas station, to earn some money during school term. Sometimes she had responsibility for locking up. He would stop by. He was only three years older but he had a car, a red Mustang his mother had bought him. He would watch her fill the tank and chat to her. Sometimes he sat with her in the office listening to music, throwing out ideas he had culled from his reading of philosophers and ideologues.

– Conformity is passive, he would say. Religious conformity is an idiocy. God conformity is irrational.

– Physical pleasure is the only real value.

– Acceptance of the moral values of others is a denial of the rights of the individual to determine their own power.

– You can sleepwalk through your life Mary or you can honour your innate superiority and obtain as much pleasure as possible from your life.

You can be depleted by the majority or you can stand in rarefied isolation rejecting the precepts of the masses.

– There are always choices Mary, and if you are motivated by pity and compassion then you will renege on the latency of your personal power to inflict what it is your will to inflict, and if you renounce that power you will render yourself irrelevant. Are you irrelevant Mary?

This last hadn't seemed like a question she would ever have answered yes to, and she didn't.

– Are you irrelevant?

– No.

– You must be contemptuous of the moral morass others will try to draw you into. Society is corrupt and dishonest. There is no good reason to adhere to its laws. There is a will to power Mary. There are the dominant and the weak. The laws that obtain are there to contain us. There is no reason to be constrained by them. What they deem criminal, we can be contemptuous of. Ours is a plausible disdain, our acts are secure intellectually and morally, believe me.

It went on like this for weeks with Maurice outlining the moral relativism of his position. He brought her for drives at the weekend into the country. Sometimes he bought her clothes. That someone of Maurice's calibre was interested in her brought her into an awareness of her own power. She believed in him and in turn she began to believe in herself. The sham of societal morality became apparent to her as did the knowledge that she stood outside of its gravitational field. He convinced her. He could have convinced her of anything. She had a hunger for him, and for what he knew. When he named her latent power as being a mirror of his own she felt directed by a blind love. When they had sex for the first time she became aware of what she really had to offer him. He thrived on her. He exhausted her. Then he bought a time-lapse camera and began to take pictures of her. He said they constituted a record of their time together but she knew he sold them. He bought fetish clothes for her to wear. She was only fifteen.

They spent so much time together that he said their link was telepathic, transigent, ancient. He knew what she was thinking when she was thinking it. He said that he knew she wanted to have sex with another boy, to faithfully objectify the act, to fuck analytically.

He picked her up one day. She remembered it as winter but it may not have been. They drove downtown to a near empty railroad apartment, with its end window barred, facing out onto a rough car park, beyond which rose the top fifty stories of the Empire State. It was one he had used before. There was a boy there around her age with long hair and bruises on his neck and body. Mary looked at him, his dulled strength and unnatural sadness. She wanted to go home. She had never said she wanted this. She felt sick suddenly.

– I did this for you Mary. Don't pretend this isn't what you wanted. Come on, let's do it.

– What do you want me to do?

– I want you to play with him. I want you to fuck him. I'll take some photographs.

He was brusque, business-like. She could see he liked the orchestration of things. He was captivated by this semi-ritualised play.

Mary went into the narrow corridor which ran through the kitchen and took off her clothes. When she returned to the room the boy was completely naked. When she touched him he flinched. She could see the delicate curve of his fretted ribs, and in his eyes a curriculum of abated life. He reached out to touch her but she didn't want anyone but Maurice to touch her. That was the truth of it.

– I can't do this, she said.

– Do it!

– Maurice, I want you to take me home.

– No. Kneel down and fucking suck him.

He went behind the tripod camera.

Mary went to leave.

He slapped her.

He wouldn't let her go.

When she cried he slapped her again.

She did some things with the boy but she hated it. Maurice took Mary home. She guessed he dropped the boy somewhere in the city, which was what he said he was going to do.

She didn't see Maurice after that, not for a long time, not until she'd been married to David for a few years and then he came back. Just like that, he found her, and he made things different all over again.

13

The faux Georgian gold clock on Mary's mantelpiece chimes 1 p.m. A large woodlouse scuttles over the marble-top, comes to the edge and turns sideways. Sunlight slants through mint venetian blinds onto the beige patterned carpet. Traffic drones by outside. A car alarm on an adjacent side street is an insistent and unrelieved distortion. The clean ashtray remains where Sheila left it the night before. The louver doors to the dining room are drawn back. The dining room window facing out on the garden is closed except for the upper rectangle which has been levered out to allow some air to freshen the room. This too is Sheila's doing.

Smith lies curled in his favourite spot on the red settee. His deposits of shed hair are balled in clumps. Mary must have forgotten to turn off the radio before she left as there is the distant sound of voices. The rakish sound of the car alarm continues.

Smith's attention is alerted by a new sound. On the lip of the open window rests a robin, its bright, unruffled breast in full winter plumage. The cat looks up; his eyes darken intensely, his small body becoming immediately rigid. The robin looks down to the concrete paving outside and then into the seductive expanse of the room. The car alarm stops, prompting the bird to launch itself forward. Almost immediately it panics, flying circularly about the room, then against the window. Stunned it rests on the windowsill, its breast palpitating. Smith has slithered on his haunches to the end of the settee. The robin flies up against the window; for a moment it appears that it might source its sole exit, but it does not. Smith bigcats his low-slung body across the carpet and under the table. The robin senses his presence but cannot see him, inducing a new flurry of chaotic battering against the window. Smith leaps towards the sill but misjudges and clings on with his gimpy claws before falling down. He leaps again almost immediately. The bird stops dead. It has no defence. Smith clamps his claws on its back and manages to gather the whole bird in his tiny mouth. He appears not to know what to do with it and is temporarily immobilised by victory. He jumps onto a side chair, bird in mouth, and from there onto the dining-room floor. The bird might now be dead, from shock if nothing else. Smith seems unable to determine what to do, and so drops the robin unscathed onto the carpet. The robin stands and perhaps for the first time understands the nature of its fate. It opens its wings and a game of sorts ensues. Smith stops its wings with his paws then takes them off again. The bird hops to one side, flutters. Smith pins it down until blood begins to speckle the ornate carpet. The bird's last valiant effort takes it to the venetian blinds. It clings impossibly to the topmost slat while Smith clambers up and takes it for a final time. With the robin dead Smith appears dismayed and tries to loft it physically with his paws into the air. Unrewarded by this, he eats its head off.

The telephone rings. Still on speaker from the night before, Mary's short message sounds out. Smith looks up attentively.

– If you've taken the trouble to ring leave a message.

A long pause.

–You shouldn't have called the police, Mary. That was a bad move. You see, I know everything. I saw you last night lying on top of the bed, breathing. That will have to stop.

The voice laughs.

– I don't like it. It brought back memories. You'll remember me when I want you to remember me. This is my life you're living, remember that. I hope you're beginning to grow fond of me. That's how it should be. I hope you like my calls. But I won't call again. Not in this way at least. Bar your windows Mary, lock your doors. I like windows, they're so transparent. That is the delicious thing.

14

Her meeting in Brooklyn over Mary returns to the city. Walking along Third Avenue she looks up and feels dismayed by the fog-depleted buildings ghosting above her. The light is darker, shallower. People's eyes are downcast, their skin greyer and more turgid, their movements joyless, guarded. The cabs, buses and cars muscle along slowly as though they are on some nether river of dark tar.

A group of tall Algerian men have gathered on the polished concrete pavement outside a major department store to sell their facsimile bags and watches. Two women stop to examine the merchandise. A black woman in a grey puff coat covers the sloppy shit of her charge – a West Highland terrier – with a plastic bag, which she then pockets.

It is lunchtime. People are eating sandwiches, wraps, burgers, pizza. Mary stops and leans her back against the cut stone façade of a public building. Her cell phone rings. Work-related. She forwards it to message. She looks at her watch. One-fifty-two. She walks down a side street. There's the smell of stale beer around the base of the brick wall. She looks for excrescences. There are none that she can see, but then the vilest things, she thinks, are not always apparent. She puts in D and selects. The ringing tone at the other end of the line seems to go on indefinitely. She's about to press redial when someone picks up. It's a woman's voice.

– Fuck! mouths Mary to herself.

Mary's tone is abrupt.

– I want to speak to David please.

There's a long pause. Jill, the woman at the other end of the line, turns away from the phone and calls up to David.

– David! Guess who? says Jill.

Mary imagines David upstairs. He's probably in his studio, working on a new piece. She visualises what he might be wearing. She wonders if he still favours cords. She's sure he does. He's thinking about her now, as he's walking down the stairs he's thinking about her. Who's to say that he hasn't thought of her already that morning, but for sure, right now he's thinking about her. Jill interrupts Mary's visualisation.

– You've got a nerve you know that? Why don't you just leave us alone?

– I don't want to speak to you, says Mary. Put me on to David.

– I suppose you know the police were around here. You'll be sorry to hear your little scam didn't work. But let me tell you something, if you make one more accusation like that we're going to sue for defamation, and one more phone call like this and I'll report you for harassment. Is that clear?

– Shut up you stupid, stupid cow! screams Mary.

– What is it? says Jill. What is it that's really getting to you? Is it that David has finally found someone who cares for him, someone who doesn't want to control his every movement, someone who loves him? You're a sick person, you know that, a really, really sick person. I feel sorry for you.

– You're the one who's punishing David because you know he still loves me. Every time he fucks you he loves me more.

– How dare you! How dare you!

Mary rants mantra-like in an effort to drown out whatever she might say.

– He fucks you and he loves me more.

He fucks you and he loves me more.

Mary stops suddenly. She can hear David's voice in the background, so cool, so cool.

– Here, let me talk to her, he says to Jill.

He comes on the line.

– What do you want?

Mary talks rapidly as though she has to get everything in, in one go.

– David I have to see you. I'm sorry about the police. I don't know what made me suspect you. I'm frightened, David. I just need to talk to you. Five minutes, that's all I ask.

– What good would it do? says David. I can't help you Mary.

– How can you say that? Don't you feel anything? You've no idea what I've been going through. Whoever this guy is he's threatening to kill me. To kill me, David! Don't you care?

– I'm sorry Mary, I really am, but I'm not the one to help you anymore.

Mary has begun to cry. There is something in David's tone, a care, even though he says there is no care, she hears a care, a softness, she knows his softness, she craves it. She feels lonesome for the want of it.

– All I'm asking is to see you, she says through her tears. Just for a little bit.

– No, says David.

– I love you David. Don't you understand that? You're the only one. If you've ever loved me, help me!

– No.

– Please David I'm begging you.

– No.

There's the sound of the receiver at the other end being put down.

Mary's palm, which has rested throughout the telephone call on a jagged piece of protruding metal, presses down on it. The metal pierces her glove and almost comes out the other side of her palm. All she can think of is that she has been denied three times.

15

Unnerved by the morning incident with the little girl Mary decides to leave work early and take the subway home. Near the subway entrance she stops and joins the rear of a small group of people watching a mime artist at work. Normally a spectacle such as this would detain her for a moment or two and she would move on, but there is something different about this one, a strange composure in the figure, an aura of power, or disdain, or mesmerism, that compels her to remain, that compels a kind of rapture.

The mime artist, whom Mary guesses is standing on some kind of dais, is dressed in a full-length silver gown, and over his shoulders is draped a yellow-lined silver cape held together by an amaranthine studded clasp. His hands rest on the hilt of a sword and he stands Zen-like over everyone. Waif-thin and slit-eyed, with cheekbones visible beneath the silver pancake makeup, the artist maintains a trademark stillness. When a mother and child go up to the artist and deposit some coins in the tray at his feet he motions the sword upwards, shafts it slowly and fluently through the form of a pentangle then finally allows the sword's tip to alight on the crown of the little boy's head. He withdraws the sword, points it down, while his free hand pivots delicately, delving and reappearing from a seam of cloth near his heart with a tiny roll of paper, parchment-coloured and vermilion-ribboned. He presents this to the boy, who takes it, and moves on.

Mary watches as a man presents himself and the routine is exquisitely reprised. She moves forward and stands before the artist. His kohl-defined stare catches hers. She feels in this moment movingly and memorably connected, she feels known, accessible, open. He sets the sword in motion before her. She cannot take her eyes off him. What she sees through the confusion of movements is the afterglow of trace lines and his eyes deeply and profoundly fixed on her own. The sword tip alights on her head and she feels that something is transferred, something ineffable yet real. She opens her palm and accepts the tiny roll of parchment that is offered to her. She walks down the subway tunnel somewhat dazed and only slowly comes to her senses.

As she waits for her train she wonders if the opposite of what she thought was happening has occurred. Rather than something being gifted or invested in her, has something instead been divested from her? Wasn't that how they did it, the avatars and gurus? They touched the crown of the acolyte and subtracted their spirit, their soul, and crumbled dust or something else at their feet in return. Mary opens the little roll of paper and reads it.

IF YOU LOSE YOUR HORSE DO NOT PURSUE IT

She reads it again but it discomfits her. It feels negative, meaningful. It hints at a world of loss, at the ache of inevitable separation. She crumples it up but does not discard it.

The subway ride home is longer than usual. With nothing to read she is forced to look either at her mirrored reflection or at the other passengers. She looks at their feet. She reads the advertisements.

PSYCHICS LIVE
WE KNOW EVERYTHING IS POSSIBLE

CORPORATE DRESSING UNIFORMS
Create a 'first impression' to achieve a personal look for your business
MEMORY EXPANSION

The graphic is of a woman's silhouetted head and a white question mark over her brain. She figures it's one of those intriguing first-base promos with more to follow.

There's a subway poem. She reads it unwillingly.

Giddy Andromeda

You thought yourself composed of stars –
A hundred billion single points of light
Comprised your body.

No one, on meeting you,
Could tell you just how fast you were going.

No one, on watching you move,
Could pinpoint exactly where you were

Or know how you suspected
That your suns were going out
Not singly but in clusters.

Even you could only
Guess how many regions of yourself

Were dark already,
Or how long you had left.

Nothing to be done but dance
As slowly as you could
Towards the exit.

The image of slow movement towards a bleakly illuminated exit stays with her. The aftertaste of relinquished hope depresses her.

She almost misses her stop, just managing to jam the subway doors with her foot. On the platform the train's piston effect flays her hair upwards into untidy wings.

Outside the subway station the fog is almost impenetrable. She stops at the local supermarket and buys the makings of dinner and a decent bottle of red Burgundy.

The house is dark when she gets there. She'd expected as

much. She'll do dinner. She's happy to do dinner. Sheila doesn't owe her anything after all. The house feels cold, damp. She turns on the light in the living room and notices something awry. Then she sees it altogether, individual blinds twisted, bird shit on the sill below them, feathers, some blood, and Smith purring lightly on the settee. She feels a kind of pride and sadness all at once. She likes birds, always has. She remembers the pair of binoculars her father gave her when she was six, the tan leather case, the olive green cloth inside, the sachet of crystals to absorb moisture, the bird hides they went to. She truncates the memory there, and thinks of something else.

The room is a mess, the window, the carpet, even the settee. She puts the groceries in the kitchen, checks the timer on the heating, and gets the blue scoop and brush from under the stairs.

She pokes the robin's headless body with her foot. Stiff as…David. She imagines his penis as a bird inside her. She laughs at herself for having such an image. Then it passes. She notices the message light pulse green on her phone but doesn't listen to it. The feathers she picks up by hand, the body of the bird she rolls onto the edge of the scoop so that she can examine it more closely. She searches briefly for the head but doesn't find it. Instead she locates the foul spot behind one of the armchairs where Smith has vomited. She scoops it all up and flushes it down the toilet. Smith is at her for food so she feeds him. She notices the open window and closes it. Rather than fix the blinds she draws the curtains across. It all makes sense, the open window, the bird, the death. That is how these things happen. There is an inevitable symmetry. Death and chance, the arbitrary eventualities, the threshold fall into or out of grace.

Mary is on her knees in the living room scrubbing away at the stains in the carpet when Sheila comes in carrying a plate of cinnamon buns.

–You're home early! I thought you said you wouldn't be home 'til seven.

– Did I? I almost killed a little girl this morning even though she was wearing a pink anorak. I should have seen her.

– Is she okay?

– She's okay but I was shaken. Maybe I was going too fast. I don't think so but maybe. The whole thing really shook me! I decided to leave work early.

– Where's your car?

– I couldn't drive. I just wasn't up to it.

– No, of course not. You're as well off. I mightn't take the car tomorrow. The fog slows everything right down. It's quite depressing really. I wouldn't have thought it would be but it is. There are no shadows, or nothing but shadows. Do you know what I mean?

– Completely.

Mary feels a sudden solidarity with Sheila, the echo of a similitude that made them feel like sisters or lovers years ago.

– Your neighbour gave me these.

Sheila puts the buns down on the living room coffee table.

– Inquisitive isn't she! remarks Sheila.

– You didn't tell her anything?

– About what?

– About my life.

– Nothing she didn't already know. She's worried about you.

– I don't think so. She's just worried that she doesn't know *everything*.

Sheila looks at the basin of soapy water.

– Did you spill something?

– Smith killed a bird. You must have left the window open.

– Sorry!

Mary holds the dead bird up in her plastic pink-gloved hand for Sheila to see.

– It's an instinctual thing. I guess it's in all of us somewhere, says Mary.

– Maybe.

Sheila looks over to the telephone.

– Any more calls?

– I don't know. There is a message. I didn't check. I think it's him. I don't want to know.

– You should call that Sergeant if it is. You've got to keep on top of this, Mary.

– No.
– No what?
– I don't want to call him again. What can *he* do?
– Did you change the number?
– Yeah.
– Do you want me to listen to it?
– It's up to you.
Mary gives the carpet a final rub and rinses the cloth.
– By the way I'm going to put some dinner on.
– What's on the menu?
– Chicken chasseur!

Mary lifts up the basin and walks out of the room down towards the kitchen. Sheila hovers for a moment then picks up the phone and listens to the message.

16

Sheila takes a second helping of dinner. Mary admires her appetite. She imagines all of her appetites are healthy. She's always had one man or another on the go. What must it be like to have the confidence to know that you can achieve love when you need it?

– I don't know why you won't let me contact the police again. They should know about this, says Sheila.

– I don't want to talk about it anymore. The reality is you either protect yourself or you die.

– It doesn't have to be as extreme as that. You see things in such a polarised way Mary. Besides how are you going to protect yourself?

– I have you, don't I? No one is going to attack me with you here. You're my guardian angel, right?

– I panic in a crisis, let me tell you that right now.

– Have you ever felt threatened? asks Mary.

– How do you mean?

– With a man.

– What woman hasn't? says Sheila.

– What did you do?

– I got over it.

– Did you report it? asks Mary.

– No.

– There you go, says Mary.

– This is different. When bad stuff happens you deal with it. Waiting for the bad stuff to happen is the killer, no pun intended. You know what they say about torture victims, it's hearing the screams of others and having to wait knowing your turn is coming. What puzzles me is how he got your number.

– I don't know. There are loads of electronic devices now, aren't there. You can buy them on the high street. Also the window was open. Maybe more than the bird came in. That's what he said, wasn't it? Something about windows.

– God I'm so sorry Mary. The place was so clammy this morning. I didn't think. Did you check upstairs, see if anything was missing?

– What, panties or something?

Mary laughs.

– Let it go Sheila. You know I'm actually beginning to be ok with it. It makes it easier, you being here. We should go out.

– Maybe another night. I'm whacked.

Mary gets Hilda's buns and puts them on the table with some butter.

– What if he came, says Sheila, and mistook me for you?

– They say you almost always know your attacker. Somehow I don't think there'll be any mistake.

Mary finds that Sheila's growing fear calms her in an odd way.

– We could sleep together if it'd make you feel better.

– No. Can we change the topic, or are you trying to make me a bit nervy?

– Sorry!

– The fog doesn't help, says Sheila. It's like it's permissive. Maybe it allows people to derange or skew a little bit. One of the women at work was saying how someone had been pushed into the river over by Sisley and drowned.

– It's like the fog chums up with death, sanctions it in a way.

They finish clearing up. Mary wraps the leftover cinnamon buns individually in bright aluminium.

– Do you mind if I get a nightcap? asks Sheila.

– I don't know if there's any whiskey left but there's some port. The key is in the cabinet. There are glasses inside.

– Want one?

– No thanks.

Sheila gets her drink and goes upstairs to her bedroom. Mary can hear her moving about, the old oak boards, her flat footfall. Mary rinses her hands and takes the knife with the onyx handle out of the drawer. She checks that the kitchen door is locked. She pulls back the curtains slightly so she can see along by the window to the outside passageway. She holds the knife level with her belly. She goes up after Sheila. She knows what it feels like to want to kill. Talking to that stupid woman Jill on the telephone, she could kill her. Mary switches off the stairs light, then the landing light. The door to Sheila's bedroom is slightly open. She can hear her inside mooching about.

Sheila takes out her earrings, releases her hair, slips out of her shoes and unzips her dress. Her room looks out onto the back yard. There's a fire escape going up past the window. She wishes she'd brought a transistor or something, other voices would help to mock the silence. A chill runs down her spine. She's standing in her pink panties. Mary stands behind her in the doorway, looking at her intently, the knife pointed towards her. Sheila senses a presence and turns. She gasps.

– Jesus Mary! What do you want?

Mary looks at her a little too long.

Sheila covers her breasts with her arms.

– Mary! Do you mind!

Mary speaks as though she is drawing herself back from some other space.

– I wanted to give you this.

The knife is still pointed threateningly towards Sheila. There's something skewed in Mary's approach. Sheila backs away. As Mary approaches she turns the knife inwards and presents the onyx handle to Sheila.

– It's my favourite knife and the best protection I can think of. Just in case.

Sheila takes the knife.

– Don't do that again. Don't come up on me like that.

– No.

– I'm serious Mary.

– I know you are. I'm sorry.

Sheila makes some pretend slashes with the knife.

– Just try it Silvino, she intones in an Italian accent, I fuck you up. I fuck you up good.

Then in her normal voice.

– What we need here is a man, one of those regular manly men, until this whole thing blows over.

– They're not so easy to find. You sure you don't want to sleep with me?

Sheila puts on her fake coquettish voice.

– O you Marys are all the same. Just one thing on your mind.

Mary walks away.

Sheila calls after her mutely.

– Nite.

17

Mary stays up a while before getting into bed. She makes an attempt to separate out the clothes on the floor but ends up dragging them with her foot into one pile. She feels anxious not sleepy, still trying to process the events of the day. She turns off the lights and tries to ease herself into sleep. She goes through her pre-sleep routine. She breathes a kind of yogic breath which almost always fails as she becomes too aware of her heart and the fragility of her stake in existence. Always the same question: does she breathe or is she breathed by some force, some energy outside herself. She ends up either not breathing at all, or taking short hectic breaths which almost induce a panic attack. She has to stop herself reaching for a paper bag to breathe into in order to retrieve some equilibrium. She believes she would never put herself in the position of cancelling her own breath. But this in itself comes as a surprise; only this morning she had thought of doing just that. She thinks of turning on the light and trying to read. She tries to read but cannot concentrate.

She hears Dr Lavender's instructional advice. "Take a routine act. It can be anything at all, washing the dishes, going for a walk in the neighbourhood, re-enact it in all its minute phases."

She had filled the car with petrol the previous day. She takes that. She sits into the car, ignition, gears, clutch, accelerator, rest footpad beside the brake, radio on, pedestrians, lights, supermarket, beyond that the garage, blue Mercedes in front, the wait, biting of a nail, fingering of eyebrows, looking in the mirror, sight of the woman in the long violet coat returning to her car, movement of the car, the inching forward, clicking of the release catch, turning off of the car, buzzer signalling that the lights are still on, turning off of the lights, getting out of the car, closing the door, twisting off the gas cap, checking the price per gallon, filling the tank, the smell of petrol, droplets of petrol, rubbing them on her neck, filling the tank, sense of it rising, replenishing, this volatile thing, seductive and so –

Then she's gone. Was it the filling of the tank, the soporific smell of the petrol, or the banality of the re-enactment that did it for her? She never questions it too deeply; so long as it works she doesn't care.

Then the nightmare comes. Not the same dream, not the same nightmare, not this time. It is a new one, out of the blue.

I am in the house, the same house I have always lived in, the house I have always shared. I am standing naked in the hallway. I can hear someone crying. The cries sound like those of a little girl. I go through the house looking for the little girl, trying to source the crying which has become louder and more hysterical. The longer it goes on the more frantic I become. I come to the stairs off the second floor. Streetlight illuminates the upper two steps and part of the door. I pass a bucket near the window full of a dark liquid which I imagine to be treacle. I know the child is close, I understand the complete terror in its cry. On the windowsill is a large key which I take in my hand. I place the key in the lock and open the door. Flames pour out. I can hear the child inside. I run back down the corridor to the bucket and pour the liquid over my head. It is not treacle but resin. Covered in resin I run through the fire. I find the child standing by a mirror, flames all about her. When I look to her reflection it is not there. The little girl reaches up to me as to a saviour and I carry her out in my arms. The door shuts automatically behind us. We descend the stairs. The little girl turns into a rock, grey, pulpy, pitted. I cannot stand the feel of it close to me. Screaming, I throw it instinctively through the window. Fragments of glass spatter back against my body but I watch as the rock falls into the garden creating a crater-like hole which seamlessly covers over.

She is still calling anxiously when Sheila rushes in and holds her.

– It's all right Mary. It's all right, says Sheila.

Mary looks to the window.

– Is the window broken?

– No everything's intact. Do you want to tell me about the dream?

Mary tells her about the dream.

– Can you stay with me…please?

Sheila climbs into bed. She wishes Mary had chosen to wear a nightdress or something. She dislikes the feel of her hand against her skin but she continues to hold her all the same.

18

In her office next morning Mary stands by the window looking down on the small park area in front of the entrance with its maples and beech trees and the long rectangular water feature in the centre. It is mid-morning and the usual assemblage of people, animals, and traders has gathered. She feels depressed suddenly by the regularity of it all, by its immateriality, its inconsequentiality. The sun has largely burnt off the fog but a light mist still shimmers in the distance. The city looks alleviated.

There's a woman feeding slices of stale bread to a flock of black-and-grey pigeons. The area around the woman is already fouled. One of the pigeons lands on the far corner of her window ledge outside Mary's 4th floor office. It drops the piece of bread it is carrying. Mary watches as it falls to the ground below and is immediately swooped on by another bird. Mary thinks of carrier pigeons, of encoded messages. She repeats to herself the cipher from the previous evening *If you lose your horse do not pursue it*. What does it mean? That the effort made to regain the thing of perceived value will ultimately imperil you? Accept that what is lost is lost? She applies it to her own life but cannot identify her symbolic horse.

Mary's intercom lights up.

– Jim McDonald, line 1, says her secretary.

Mary gathers herself.

– Hello Jim. Thanks for getting back to me. I was wondering if we could reschedule our lunch arrangement.

– Sure. If something's come up that's okay.

– It's just I'm under a bit of pressure today, says Mary. But I've had the contracts drawn up. I'll courier them over to you this afternoon. We can meet to iron out any issues at your convenience.

– That's fine Mary. Just one thing, do we have clarity on the inclusion or otherwise of the lift trucks and attachments?

–Yes, they're included in the sale.

– Great. I'll have my folks look over the contract and get back to you tomorrow.

–Thanks Jim. All the best!

Mary puts the phone down.

Her secretary comes in with a folder for her to look over.

– Grace, I'm going to work through lunch and take off around three. Courier these contracts over to Jim McDonald. You can leave a message on my mobile if anything important comes up and I'll get to it first thing in the morning.

After Grace leaves, Mary opens the drawer beneath her desk and takes out a photograph of her and David. She wonders about her capacity to joy in life, to find pleasure in a given day. She feels that there is a part of her story missing, a distortion in her past that impinges on how she lives her life. She hates her complicated abnegations of life. In the photo David does look happy, that's the thing, she made him happy, or he made himself happy with her. That's what she misses, the sense that she could complete someone else if not herself. David's hand is around her waist. He is facing towards camera, smiling. She is looking at David, her head in profile. Her fingers appear to be holding the edge of his trouser pocket. She can almost feel the pressure of his hand on her back and the comfort gifted from being touched so supportively. And to think that she had always railed against the idea of emotional dependency, not knowing then how it would scaffold her breath, her very being. Now its absence assails her.

Another memory surfaces of a trip taken with David into the mountains upstate. It was spring, maybe even around this time, and they had rented a log cabin on the shores of Lake Minnewaska. She remembers the rose curtains in the bedroom that caught the eastern light and filled her eyes when she awoke, and the weight of David's arm across her breasts. Kissing him awake. Kissing him deeply and without restraint, every kiss a kind of ballast, every rock of the sex that came that morning motioning them forward into a quiescent, and more present love than she had known.

Later that same morning they had walked through linden and alder trees to the lake shore, then rowed to the island at the lake's centre, and stood silently in the circle of high elms they had found. If halcyon has an image for her then it is that elm-green shade, that bed of wild garlic, David as her love-enamoured companion, her strongest connection to life itself.

She looks at the photo again and feels overwhelmed by images of what she has lost, and by the desire to re-achieve that essential alliance in love. She puts the photo back and closes her eyes.

By three-thirty she's driving through the gates of Wyncomb Alternative Healing and Psychotherapeutic Centre, a few miles outside the city and on the other side of the river. The afternoon light is beginning to fade. The building, an imposing nineteenth-century redbrick colonial-style house is a place of obvious retreat. Although Mary is early for her scheduled group therapy session the car park is almost full. She locks her car and stands for a moment looking towards the paddock. There's a mare in foal nudging bits of hay around with her nose. Mary walks to the fence and leans towards the horse, her arm outstretched, her red tailored suit starkly resonant amongst the leafless forms around her. The mare takes a long piss and Mary watches as the yellow liquid pools in the muddy earth. She likes the obvious looseness and fecundity of the horse. Mary makes a neighing sound in a studied attempt to attract the horse's attention. The mare scents her from a distance and draws close. Hopeful of some tidbit or other she nibbles the sleeve of Mary's jacket. Mary has nothing to give her, and in a moment of negativity this is how she frames it.

– I've nothing to offer you.

Then in an effort to alter this image she bends and pulls up a handful of rough grass. The mare takes a few strands, allowing the bulk of it to fall to the ground, then turns away and walks to the centre of the paddock. Mary loosens her pinned-up hair and shakes it out. A gust of wind jostles wooden chimes hanging from a large oak tree. She hears some more cars drive up the lane. She looks for a moment at the outline of the city from this vantage point across the river. She checks her watch. She has time for a bowl of soup before the session begins at four. Unexpectedly she feels a flow of blood in her crotch and a sticky coldness in her panties.

– Damn!

She looks through her handbag. No pads. She can't believe it. This hasn't happened to her for so long. It makes her feel so inadequate.

Maybe she can borrow pads from someone in the clinic. She enters through the glass doors, brass handles gleaming. The most striking aspect of the building is its absolute whiteness, white marble tiles, wonderfully plush white sofas in the reception area, sprays of lilies, soft lighting, immaculate finish. The receptionist greets her familiarly but not by name.

Mary clears her throat.

– I hate to do this to you but I'm afraid I've been caught short. Do you know if there are any sanitary napkins in the clinic?

The receptionist looks up at her.

– We don't stock them as a rule but one of the therapists may have some.

Mary sits down on the sofa. For a moment she imagines seeing herself from the far side of the reception area – her neat red suit, her blonde hair, her sheer legs. Then she sees the stain. What can she have been thinking? She jumps up and is afraid to look down at the dimpled mark her bottom has left on the white sofa. Is there a fleck of blood? Initially that's all she sees. She takes out her handkerchief and begins to rub at the imagined mark.

– Mary, what are you doing?

She looks around. The man standing in front of her is Sergeant Gerry Keaney, but that is not what she calls him.

– Maurice!

She doesn't want to talk to him. She feels flustered. He takes her arm.

– What are you doing? Has something happened?

Mary looks towards the swing doors and then to Maurice.
– Is there blood on the sofa?
–Why would there be blood on the sofa Mary?
– Just tell me.
Her eyes are pleading.
– No there isn't. Now get a grip.
The receptionist returns. Maurice separates himself from Mary and goes towards the counselling rooms down the corridor to the right.
– See you in there, he says
The receptionist comes over to Mary and hands her a white paper bag.
–This should get you through.
– I'll replace them next week, I promise.
–There's no need, really.
Mary walks behind the reception area down a curved corridor which takes her to the toilets. She walks faster, hugging the matt white surface of the wall. She hears footsteps. Maurice, she whispers. She looks behind. Nothing. But she imagines she sees a trail of blood spots on the floor. The toilet door is just ahead of her. She goes into a cubicle, pulls down her knickers, cleans herself and attempts to get as much blood as possible off her knickers. How could she have been so stupid? She reels off a wad of tissue, washes her hands, returns to the corridor outside and begins mopping the figmentary droplets of blood.
She hears the chimes for four o'clock.

19

The group therapy room is large and square. The long windows which look out on the paddock have an opaque white curtain drawn across them. There are twelve people standing around in small groups. Dr Mowbray and Dr Lavender, the therapists who facilitate the session, are there too.

– Ah Mary! says Dr. Mowbray, you're here. We're ready to begin so.

The padded leather chairs have been arranged in a circle. Clients and therapists move to take their habitual seats, except Maurice. He is already sitting where Mary usually sits. She thinks he's sneering at her. She can't but be impressed by the difference in his appearance from the man who came to the house in uniform. His blond hair is floppy, expensively coiffed, and he is wearing an elegant orange wool jacket and cotton trousers. Mary hovers over him for a moment. On another day she might make a point of getting him to move but not today. She sits beside Emily who loses time to five other personalities. One of them is a clergyman who screams obscenities, and rants about God.

Dr Mowbray joins his fingers then opens them like a book.

– Good afternoon, says Dr. Mowbray, and who are we today?

He laughs. Dr Lavender does not, nor do any of the patients except Timothy Leddy, who titters nervously then stops abruptly.

– Just a little joke, says Dr Mowbray. Just a little joke.

He continues more seriously.

– I have a story for you today. Listen carefully, please!

Once upon a time there was a little boy who had a dress for every occasion. Then one day his sister, who had been very cruel to him all his life and had abused him terribly, announced that she was getting married. The little boy thought long and hard about what he would wear and tried on lots of dresses but none them seemed suitable for the day in question. As time passed he grew more and more anxious as it didn't seem possible that he could resolve the dilemma over what he would wear in time for the big day. Then he happened to be walking down a side alley parallel to the main thoroughfare in the town in which he lived when he saw a little butcher boy's suit in the window of a butcher's shop. He went inside and the butcher asked him why he was wearing a dress. Didn't he know that little boys wore suits? The little boy couldn't remember exactly why he wore dresses or why he couldn't find one for the occasion. He bought the butcher's suit and wore it home. When his sister saw him she told him that he looked ridiculous. Take it off immediately, she said, and stop pretending to be something you're not. He did as his sister told him but that night he put the suit back on and butchered his sister. He never wore a dress in public again.

Dr Mowbray allows his hands to rest in his lap. A long pause follows. He looks around. Some of the patients shuffle uneasily in their seats.

Katherine expressing Kerry, lets out some yips and squeaks a la Tourette's or pseudo Tourette's syndrome. Dr Mowbray takes up the slack.

– I believe in my patient's ability to absorb, consciously or otherwise, complex experiential personality and psychic states which they cannot fully objectify. The little boy was condemned to present in a persona alien to his primary self, and ultimately released through an act of sororicidal violence to come into a state of accord with that self. The story is not an apologia for violence but an example of the necessity of defining the best self for the realisation of one's ascendant goals.

However, don't worry if you either don't understand this or cannot relate the anecdote to your own experience. Remember! No one personality is good enough for any of us, so we search around for one that fits the dynamics of our interior psychic situations. The challenge is to develop an integrationist feel for the self that most capably secures you in the world.

Dr Lavender turns on a recording of Amazonian mood music, opens his A4 pad and prepares to take some notes.

Dr Mowbray talks over this.

– …the brain blocks the pain, the body image alters, CHANGE, the dynamic self is lost. Of course we all, in moments of anger, hurt or joy, we all get stuck in one personality or another for a time. But in the face of challenges to the self, we originate other coping or deflector personalities. The reason why we have exaggerated shifts and why they remain unconscious is because there is a failure of memory, and remember, trauma is the cause and the only way we can understand the present is through the past. Knowing this we must reconstruct a single personality to contain the changes.

Dr Mowbray scans the room and fixes on Maurice.

– Maurice, you've listened to what I have had to say. Would you like to share anything with us from the week just past? Just to get us started.

Maurice looks up, his eyes trained on some point above Dr Mowbray's balding head. For over thirty seconds he doesn't say anything. It seems to go on forever. Mary touches her crotch, pressing the pad hard against it.

–Yesterday, says Maurice, I cried for most of the day!

There's silence followed by an audible Ah from someone else.

– My brother died.

Everyone looks at him. Those closest turn to him consolingly.

– It was very traumatic. VERY traumatic!

But life is traumatic, as we all know. I am in constant negotiation with that fact. It's hard – life is – so I take it in turns. I don't know if that's why I cried but it probably is. Life hits me hard so I take it in turns. I was so sorry. I had the idea that I wanted to quantify my sorrow so I placed two blue eye cups to my eyes. I was crying terribly you understand. I cried until my eyes drained empty. I wanted relief from the pain I was feeling but I also wanted evidence of my sorrow, otherwise who would believe me? I poured the tears from the eye cups into a clear bottle and I was surprised both by how much there was and how little.

I took a photograph of the bottle against a background which showed exactly how much was in the container and then I drank the contents. I drained my sorrow so to speak and that certainly felt good. I felt empowered, relieved and empowered. Reified!

Maurice stops at this point and makes eye contact with Dr Mowbray.

– Of course you realise, says Dr Mowbray, that your brother didn't just die. I have to say this Maurice. I have to confront your denial of the truth.

– I thought you would say that, says Maurice, but you cannot deny the photograph.

Maurice reaches into the lined pocket of his jacket and pulls out a print.

– Here! Look for yourself. Here is the evidence of my tears, of my sorrow. I was sorrowful because I imagined my brother was dead. The tears in this instance were evidence of my love. They are evidence of the pain of imagined loss – a pain no less real to me. I didn't enjoy the virtual pain of knowing someone so close to me was dead. But I enjoyed seeing the evidence of my love. Knowing that I am capable of love perhaps in consequence I am also liable to be loved. Perhaps I am capable of anything.

– One simple question Maurice. Do you have a brother? asks Dr Mowbray.

– No, says Maurice, but that doesn't invalidate my sorrow. If I had a brother and he died, this is how I would have cried.

– Pre-emptive sorrow. You're better off coping with the life you have. Limit your realities.

– If I cannot limit my pain or my desire for pain then I cannot limit my reality. Pain is the only thing that structures my reality, to live is to be in pain and vice versa. What I want, what we want, is someone to die for.

– I'll take that as a positive statement. However, with regard to your story, the truth is you lied.

–The fact, says Maurice, is I cried. With regard to your story Dr Mowbray, the truth is the little boy had someone to hate. It was his suit that became the true mirror of his subverted persona. Only when the injustice and violation became clear could he act. Signifier and signified as one.

Some of the others smile in recognition of Maurice's effrontery. Mary however remains stony-faced.

– Maurice, says Dr Mowbray, do you think you know better than I?

– Than me, says Maurice, better than me.

20

The session ends up some two hours later after everyone who has wanted to share has shared. Dr Lavender and Dr Mowbray remain behind, going through their notes. They stand by the long window, the weighted net curtains drawn back. The view in darkness is out over the lit lawn and car park. Dr Lavender watches as Maurice makes his way over to Mary. He describes Mary's body language to himself as submissive.

– I'm worried about Mary, says Dr Lavender, and about Maurice's influence on her.

– Maurice is toying with us all.

– What other personalities is he presenting with in therapy?

– Maurice is unusual, says Dr Mowbray, in that he has almost total recall of the transitions between personalities and of his constituent selves. So there is something of the fantasist about him. Basically he's into control, which is his connection, I think, with Mary. How much pain either of them can feel is open to question. To be honest I'm not convinced how valid the DID diagnosis is with regard to Maurice. I'm not convinced of the integrity of his alters.

– What worries me about Mary, says Dr Lavender, is that she is no longer presenting her secondary personas to me in private session. At the same time there appears to be a regression to a more juvenile self.

– Perhaps she's allowing her periods of dissociation to subvert naturally, says Dr Mowbray. Perhaps you've healed her or helped her heal herself.

– One of my triumphs, you mean!

Dr Lavender shakes his head.

– I don't think so. Sometimes Bernard, I wonder if group

therapy sessions like this don't reinforce therapeutically originated selves or fantasy projections.

– Don't go there, Orin. There are enough people knocking the diagnosis and incidence levels. Paper upon paper is rubbishing the classification of this as a syndrome. They're saying these people are just hysterics. But let them say what they like. I'm in no doubt that we help those who present to us. Maybe they don't resolve their constituent personas but what the hell, they get to live a life!

–There's no chance that we're leaving ourselves open, is there?

–To what, being sued? asks Dr Mowbray.

– Memory structuring, accusations of malpractice, says Dr Lavender.

– I don't know about you but I've validated it to myself and the methodology that proves it.

– But isn't that the problem or the potential problem, that we're naming sources of trauma and positing a resultant fragmentation.

– It's possible, but it all goes into our retirement fund, so don't knock it, says Dr Mowbray.

Dr Lavender's attention is drawn to a black Jaguar XJ series, which has just pulled up in front of the clinic.

– Nice car, he remarks.

– It's Maurice's mother, Helen Halliday. She pays the bills and a substantial amount extra for an exhaustive monthly report, says Dr Mowbray.

– And patient confidentiality? says Dr Lavender.

– She just gets the standard material any parent in a situation like this gets.

– Does Maurice know?

– No.

– Be careful, Bernard.

– I'm not really in a position to challenge the situation. I have an expensive wife, an expensive life don't you know.

– A lawsuit will very quickly make that life untenable.

Bernard resents this ticking off from his older and more eminent colleague but says nothing. Orin Lavender continues to look out over the lawn at Mary and Maurice talking together off to the side of Helen Halliday's car.

Maurice leans into Mary.

– Enough of this shit! We have to meet. It's been too long.

– I can't, says Mary.

– Why?

– I can't…because I can't stand it anymore.

– You fuck! You must! Don't disobey me in this!

Meet me tomorrow.

– Maurice, I can't do it anymore.

– Can't. Won't!

– Either way.

– I'll tell David.

– No.

– I will.

– All right.

– All right what?

– You know.

– I know all right. Tomorrow lunchtime. Say it!

– Tomorrow lunchtime.

Helen's chauffeur, a large, barrel-chested man in full uniform, cap tilted down, walks towards them. He nods to Mary, speaks to Maurice.

– Sir, your mother wanted to enquire if you'd be much longer. She has another appointment.

– I'm coming now.

Maurice fixes his eyes on Mary and then walks towards the open door of the black jaguar. Helen Halliday, a classic blonde, well maintained, looks out to Mary, her head turned slightly, a demure but frigid smile only barely corrugating her features.

– She looks just like me, says Helen to Maurice. Fancy that!

– I don't, says Maurice. Now can we go?

– So touchy and after a session too. You'd think the vitriol would be all spewed out of you.

– Shut it mother. I'm not in the humour.

– I love it when you talk rough like that. Your daddy all over.

21

By lunchtime the following day Mary has accomplished almost nothing in the office. She feels anxious. She checks her planner to see the date for her next scheduled appointment with Dr Lavender. Not for another four days. She looks at his emergency number and contemplates calling it but can't formulate in her mind what she wants to say. She listens to the others in the corridor talking about a football game the previous night. She envies them their easy camaraderie, the commonality of their shared interests, their shared language.

She remembers what Dr Lavender said to her once. "What you have, Mary, is a bit like an infected wound. Opening it up again and again to clean it out and apply antibiotics is very painful, but it is the only way to heal."

Mary wants to hide, she can hear another voice inside. She goes to her bag and takes out her nail file. She rolls up her sleeve and begins to chafe the skin along the edge of bone until it reddens and frays. Then she prods her upper arms until the tip of the file goes in and she gouges out a bit of her flesh. She wants to scream. That's what she wants, just to scream.

She puts the file back in her bag. There's a packet of cigarettes there, but she doesn't smoke. She can't remember how they got there.

One of her colleagues looks in.

– A few of us are heading down to The Locust for lunch. Care to join us?

Mary looks flustered. She imagines her arm is visible, or if not her arm then her sick instincts. Normal people don't behave as she behaves. What he will see when he looks at her is her abnormality, her gross, distended abnormality.

– Sorry, have I interrupted something?
She gathers herself as best she can.
–Tom…No…I can't…not today. I'm sorry…I'm sorry.
– Hey no problem! Catch you later.
He closes the door and she slumps down into her chair.

How long she sits there she doesn't know but when her keys slip to the floor she glances at the wood-framed clock on the wall opposite, sees that it is one-fifteen, and panics. Grabbing her fur-trimmed green leather coat she leaves the office and takes the elevator to the basement where her car is parked in the usual spot on level two. She counts the steps from the lift door to her car, looks at the thickly painted arrow lines, avoids obvious cracks in the concrete, and breathes shallowly. She feels like a child, unattached, creating patterns to help forestall the worst of fates.

As Mary drives along by the river, groups of old women and men saunter along the riverfront pathway or sit on the wooden slatted benches looking into the still water. She turns up towards Inwood and a neighbourhood of elegant houses near Spuyten Duyvil Creek. The fog has begun to descend again. She slows down and pulls into the curving white gravelled entrance of a large detached granite-fronted building with a broad lawn and centre circle of pruned roses, and further back the partly visible mesh-enclosed grass tennis court. She pulls around to the side of the building and parks in front of a small mews house, windowed to the front on both levels and with a cantilevered wooden balcony to the rear looking out over the orchard and the river. Mary glances over to the main house. She sees a figure standing in the main bay window to the right of the door. Mary looks away embarrassed, goes to the rear of her car, opens the boot and retrieves a small leather carryall.

There are some small birds in the branches of the ash tree overhanging the mews. She half expects Maurice to be there at the back door to greet her but he is not. She goes through, takes off her coat and hangs it on the brass coat rail in front of the utility room. She calls out Maurice's name but there is no reply. She goes into the main ground floor room which is spacious and sparsely furnished. The drawn yellow curtains fill the room with a warm vivifying light. In fact the whole room hums to this deep yellow light streaming through the curtains onto the wool carpet. There's a large plaid chair in front of a bank of wall shelving, a sofa near the window and a long mahogany table diagonal to that. She is about to call out to Maurice again when she hears his voice upstairs.

–You're late! Get changed!

She goes into the bathroom and changes. She can hear him plodding downstairs as she does so. She looks at her nails. They appear to be perfect. She remembers the last time she was here. She tries to connect with those feelings. There is an image that she goes to. She is standing in the kitchen with a large pyrex mixing bowl levered in snugly against her womb. She begins to beat two eggs into the butter-and-sugar base. The yolks, initially perfect, turn sloppy but finally bind the mixture together.

– Come out! commands Maurice.

The door opens and Mary walks out. Maurice tells her to sit down. He places his hand on either side of her head and stares directly at her. He moves his hands down the side of her head and instructs her to close her eyes

– When you open your eyes you will be who you want to be, who I want you to be. You'll be Sally.

Mary opens her eyes. She stands and walks around. She looks physically transformed. Dressed in a short, fluid, yellow camisole, her blond hair flowing freely, she appears loose-limbed, confident, sexy.

– Hello Sally! says Maurice.

– Hello, says Sally.

– Very good, says Maurice, sit down!

Sally looks to the sofa, walks across and sits down.

– Not like that, says Maurice, put your legs underneath you.

Sally lifts her legs and tucks her calves and feet under her bottom.

– Do you think I enjoy this? asks Maurice. Making you do things. You think I'm not demeaned by the demands I make on you, you think I'm not demeaned by you?

– I'm happy to do this, says Sally.

–You're happy to do everything I say! That's great! I have your best interests at heart. You're a good girl Sally. It's a relief to talk to you. If everyone was as understanding we wouldn't be so hard.

Maurice takes a toothpick and a small pill out of his pocket. He gives the pill to Sally.

– Swallow this.

She does so.

Maurice begins to clean his nails.

– Now then, when you were a little girl, when you were four years old what did you want to do? You can tell me everything.

Sally doesn't respond.

– Don't you remember? Your fourth birthday. Think of that!

–You're sure I can remember. It's all right?

– Didn't I say it was?

Maurice calms himself.

– Pull your top down, he says. Your knee is upsetting me. I'll close my eyes for a moment.

Sally, her eyes glazed, readjusts her camisole so that her knees are covered though it pulls the camisole taut from her breasts across her belly.

– Go on, says Maurice. You're four!

– I always wanted to prey on things.

– That's right, you always wanted to prey on things.

– There's a creature inside, says Sally.

– Inside?

–Yes, says Sally. When I want to shit I go to the tiny slanted room underneath the stairs. I squat down and watch the concrete sludge with gockgocks. The gockgocks is tinged with blood. It's the creature that's bleeding, not me. I poke at it. Does that seem strange to you?

– No, says Maurice.

– It feels okay to me too. It feels like the past.

– The creature must be wounded. Or is it bleeding you?

– Bleeding me? Maybe. I feel rotten, but when I think of what happens to other people, I feel okay.

– Only because you've no idea what's truly happening to you. Tell me about your hero.

– Keith Richards. My hero! What age is he now?
– I don't know, says Maurice.
– I have photos of him all around my room. He goes to Switzerland to get his system cleaned out. Everything can be bought. And there is no end to it.
– What?
– Blood. He uses his blood up and then he changes it. Blood is like fire.
– Is he like a kind of saviour to you because he survives his blood?
– I don't know.
– Where does all this garbage thinking come from? What are you looking for?
– Contact! I think about the way air transforms blood into something scabby. It's ironic! Air to breathe, blood to live, but outside the body the two together turn black. Contact changes things.
– Aren't you talking about something else now?
Sally looks at him.
– Don't look at me! he shouts.
– Feelings, you mean? says Sally.
– Go on, says Maurice harshly.
– Some days I have no idea of what lies ahead. There's no fear, not even the fear that I will have to return.
– What are you talking about? says Maurice. Return where? I told you don't look at me.
– To who I truly am or should that be whom?
Maurice looks at her derisively.
– You say that as though you know who you are.
– I do.
– I know who you are. You don't, says Maurice, because you don't remember. You aren't the real you. If you were, you would know why you feel as you do. Bring your hair over you right shoulder.
Sally changes position slightly, and draws her blond hair across the top of her shoulder.
– If you didn't confuse me so much I might, says Sally.
Maurice rises and stands over her.
– There's only one way to get you to remember. You have

to abuse your position. You know, inflict love, inflict your will.

– What do you want me to do?

– I want you to hurt me, says Maurice.

– Why do you want me to hurt you? asks Sally.

– Pain exhausts me. Pleasure exalts me. I want to be good. What are you in love with?

– I'm in love with your desire to save me.

– Very good. We'll ride the dark horse together.

Sally loses concentration as he is saying this and begins to fiddle with her hair and to bind it in little finger-curls to her head. She appears tranced, dissociated.

– If I hadn't shat the creature might have stayed put, but he kept coming out and all because of what I did…

Maurice strides over to her and slaps her across the face. She freezes. No cry, no anger, just a sense of her being stunned. She stands and grabs a paper knife from the mahogany table and lunges at him. He parries her thrust and flings her against the wall. She flops to the ground. For a moment it appears as though he is going to kick her but some other thought intercedes and he walks away.

– Remember where you are! says Maurice.

Maurice goes over to the curtains and opens them slightly. He picks up a lipstick and smears some over his lips roughly. He returns to where Sally lies slumped on the floor. He reaches down for her hand and pulls her up.

– Do you trust me? he asks.

Sally has been pulled close. She can feel his breath on her cheek.

– I don't trust anyone, she says. Do you?

– No.

He lets go of her. Sally walks around the sofa and around the table, trailing her finger over its polished surface. She imagines his eyes staring at her ass.

– Do you find me attractive, she asks.

– No, he answers.

She feels a kind of heat in her groin.

Maurice walks over to Sally. He stands in front of her with the gold canister of red lipstick and seems to be about to try and push it into her mouth. Instead he streaks her face with it and circles her eyes. Sally touches her lips. He lifts her camisole and scrawls a + and – on either thigh. Sally accepts this.

– Where's your uniform from the other night?

– That's none of your business.

He slaps her across the face again.

– Sergeant Keaney! Sergeant Keaney! taunts Sally.

– You're a bullshitter Sally, a fucking bullshitter! Now do you want to have sex?

– You're meant to say fuck.

– I think there's another word we should use?

– Go on, says Sally.

– Do you want to fucking sex?

– You're weird!

– I'm like you Sally, that's why we're doing this. No one else understands.

Sally takes off her yellow camisole and bra, but leaves her black panties on and goes over to her carryall which is on the floor. Maurice continues to talk to her as he strips off.

– I'm the key for you Sally. You're damaged goods. You'll continue to damage everyone until you fucking sort yourself out. I am the key. Use me.

Sally takes a white dildo with waist and butt-straps out of the bag and puts it on. She touches her nipples and wades towards Maurice.

– You're not doing this properly, says Maurice. What about your lines?

– Do I have to? asks Sally.

Maurice nods.

Sally says it quietly, almost inaudibly, at first.

Sally had a turgid cock
Her cock was white as snow
And everywhere that Sally went
Her cock was sure to go

– Again! says Maurice.

Sally pushes Maurice back onto the sofa and turns him round so that his ass is there in front of her. She kicks his feet apart and begins to lubricate him with Vaseline.

She continues to repeat her rhyme.

Sally had a turgid cock

Her cock was white as snow
And everywhere that Sally went
Her cock was sure to go
She enters him.
And repeats.
Sally had a turgid cock
Her cock was white as snow
And everywhere that Sally went
Her cock was sure to go

Sally's momentum increases. Maurice is about to come, when his cell phone rings. It distorts the atmosphere.

– Leave it, says Maurice. Fuck me!

Sally leans down and grabs his trousers. Still fucking him, she reaches in to his pocket to get the phone. It's gone into messaging. Sheila's number comes up. She puts the message on speaker.

– What are you doing?

– Listening to your fucking message.

– Bitch!

Sally rams into him again and again. He is swamped by his need to get off.

Sheila's voice comes on.

Sally's momentum begins to slow almost immediately.

– Hello Sergeant, this is Sheila Deane. There was another call two nights ago. Mary asked me not to phone but I felt you should know. Frankly I'm worried.

Mary's rhythm has slowed.

– Keep going! screams Maurice. Keep fucking going!

Sally starts again but is clearly fracturing on some level.

Sheila's message continues.

– Could I meet you somewhere after work? I'll be at 61457775 until four then I'll be at Mary's. I need to talk to someone!

Sally can hear a note of coyness and sycophancy in Sheila's tone, and a note of duplicity and treason. Sally stops altogether and Mary goes towards the bathroom.

– Come back here! screams Maurice.

He bangs the plush sofa.

– Come back here!

Hearing the bathroom door lock he grabs his dick and jerks off.

22

By five o'clock, darkness has fallen. It is an oppressive darkness that overshadows the city. Sheila walks towards the intersection at 10th Street just up from Mary's. She thinks about going into the Briar Patch for a drink but decides against it. She counts up the days she has been away from her own place: four days, seems like longer. She thinks about going home, she longs for it. Give it a week, she thinks, that should be more than enough. She doesn't think she could stand anymore. The previous night really freaked her and having to sleep with Mary brought back the wrong kind of memories. She goes into the supermarket and buys a packet of cigarettes. The cashier asks her if she'd like to support the local school by buying a raffle ticket.

– What's the prize?

– Trip for two to the Costa Blanca with five hundred cash spending money.

Sheila buys two for twenty. She puts Mary's name on one and her own on the other and uses Mary's address for both.

As she walks up 8th Street everything appears to be in slow motion: the people, the cars, time itself. The fog induces a kind of fatigue. She wonders if Sergeant Keaney will call. There was something about him that she liked, a lethal beauty, a strength she found attractive. Besides she'd never been with a cop before. She sensed he liked her. That was enough to be going on with.

A strong wind would clear this weather, she thinks. She takes out the key for Mary's place and lets herself in.

There's a musty smell coming from somewhere. She's smelt it before, that was why she had opened the window the day that Smith killed the bird. She'd learned her lesson and not done that again. But there is a smell, not getting stronger but not diminishing either, like something fouling, maybe drains or sewage or a smell peculiar to this house. She can't remember it always being there and God knows she's been coming here for years, on and off.

She goes down into the kitchen. She feels aimless like there's nothing for her to do here. She lights up a cigarette and thinks about going outside to smoke it and then thinks, fuck it, some privileges should accrue. She opens the back kitchen door a little as a kind of tokenism then carries the ashtray around with her as she moves from the kitchen to the hallway. She looks at the photographs pinned to the corkboard which runs the length of the corridor. They span Mary's life pretty much. The ones of her childhood are mostly of Mary with school pals on trips away or with her aunt Emma who became guardian to her after her father died. There's one with her mother. They're standing in snow on the edge of a forest somewhere up north. Mary is dressed in a red anorak, with a teal scarf bulging out under her chin and a multi-coloured cap plopped on her head, holding her mother's gloved hand and smiling weakly to camera. This is one of the few photographs of the two of them together. Mary's mother Geraldine had died shortly after the photo was taken and even in this one there is a ghostly aura to her presence. There are a few of Mary's father, John, a tall, blond, good looking man – soft smile, kind eyes – holding a pair of binoculars. Sheila notes to herself what she has noted before, namely the resemblance between the two, all the greater as Mary grows older, the same jawline, the same refinement in the features. Her mother was coarser, darker.

Sheila goes upstairs, thinking to lie down for half an hour or so before starting dinner. Mary's dressing gown is on the floor of the bathroom. She picks it and some other pieces of clothing up and returns them to Mary's room. The place is still a complete mess. Sheila doesn't understand it. She drapes the dressing gown over the end of the bed and places the other items on the armrest of a corner chair. Mary's red dress, which Sheila has admired many times, lies in a crumpled pile near the wardrobe. Sheila holds it up to herself. It's the one thing of Mary's she could see herself wearing. She thinks about trying it on but grabs a hanger instead, one sticking out from amongst some boxes on an upper shelf. It doesn't come loose at first so she yanks it, toppling a cardboard box in the process. Some of its contents spill out onto the floor.

– Shit!

For a moment she thinks about leaving them there. But she doesn't do that. She bundles the bits and pieces back into the box. In the bottom of the box she sees a pair of handcuffs. Her immediate thought is that they are of the toy variety. Her interest is piqued. She picks them up. They're heavy, real. This is a first. What the hell is Mary doing with real handcuffs? She opens them up with the small key dangling from a piece of string. She clicks it around her wrist. Tightening it to its smallest point she still has room to move her wrist around. It's hard enough to open it up. She has to twiddle the key a few times before she manages it. She's curious now. She picks out a few more objects, mostly leather stuff. Tacky, high-street S&M gear, whips, red nylon rope, collars, whip, gags. Sheila's surprised, she can't even disguise that to herself. It's not what she's into, and it's certainly not what she had thought Mary was into. She's not sure what it explains or what it really tells her about Mary. The fact that she's a little kinky is her business. Besides, it may have been something she dabbled in when she was younger. She's in the process of replacing the box on the upper shelf when she hears the phone ring downstairs. She pushes the box in. She's in no particular hurry. Then she wonders if it might be the guy who's been calling. She has predicted this as an event and already thought of what she will say. She will scream out a diatribe of obscenities. She'll be strong in a way that Mary could never be. She makes it to the phone before the call-answering kicks in. She braces herself.

– Hello!

– Mary!

Play along. See if he exposes himself. Her heart is beating. She wants to let go of some of her rage, but she holds back.

–Yes.

– Mary is that you?

–Yes.

It's not the voice she had imagined or remembers, not the tone.

– I just got your e-mail.

–Who is this?

– Germain, Germain Kiel.

–Who?

– I can't say this bodes very well…Germain…from the dating site.

Finally it clicks with Sheila.

– Ok! I'm sorry, Germain. It's been one of those days.

– Sounds like I might be just one of a multitude you've written back to.

– No. It's just that you caught me at a bad time. I was expecting to speak to someone else.

– Another respondent?

– No.

– But you would like to meet?

– Definitely!

– It was hard to gauge from your email.

–What?

–Your interest.

–You rang didn't you?

–You're right I did.

– So, where do you want to take it from here?

–You make it sound quite functional.

– Listen, I'm definitely interested, says Sheila, but I'm afraid I've got to go right now. Can I call you back later this evening?

– Sure. I'll be out for an hour or so but any time after nine. Do you have my number from the phone?

–Yep. By the way I like your voice. It's sexy!

– Hmmn! That's a good start. Somehow I didn't expect you to be so forward, but forward is good. So you'll call me later.

– I will. I definitely will.

Sheila stands holding the phone, smiling to herself. She hopes she hasn't messed things up for Mary. What the hell, get her off on the right foot. Still, better tell her the truth, more or less. She's just too uptight, unlikely to even get past first base with this guy.

Then she recalls the gear upstairs and all of her evaluations become just a little bit more uncertain.

23

Sheila wanders back upstairs. She stops by the window on the second floor landing and looks down onto the street below. There's a flotation of pearl light from the street lamps, some distant barely discernable cars, the flat grey planes of office buildings to the left, and a scatter of people visible under the canopy of a corner café. She cleans one of the window corners of cobweb, rolls it into a sticky ball then tries to shake it off. She feels a mild sense of trespass. In the moment of thinking this, she hears the sound of glass shattering. Just below her a car has skewed into a lamppost. The car is deep blue, its bonnet crumpled, its blank headlight altered upwards, staring at her. She kneels on the windowsill to get a better view. It's awkward. She has an image of herself falling, the twist of her body, the crumpled somersaulting, the loose angle of her unstructured hand. She adjusts herself then tenses at the sound of something downstairs. She cocks her ear, straining grades of noise. Mary's voice calls out.

– Darling I'm home!

The old wooden sill breaks under her knee and she falls, clutching the shutter panel. The sundering reverberates through the house.

– Fuck!

Sheila brushes herself down and examines a cut along the inside of her palm. She shuffles downstairs, rubbing her scuffed knee and intermittently applying pressure to the open cut on her palm. When she gets to the first floor Mary is walking past her bedroom door.

– Did you hear a door banging?

– It was just me upstairs. I broke the windowsill in the front room.

–You okay? asks Mary.

–Yep. The car that just crashed, what happened?

– Dunno. I heard someone say an ambulance had been called. It doesn't look like anyone was hurt though. I didn't hang around. You should do something with your hand. There are some plasters in the bathroom cabinet, and some antiseptic cream.

–Thanks. Good day?

– I had a session with my therapist. Sometimes I wonder if it's doing me any good.

– Do you want to talk about it?

– No. I'm ok.

Mary takes off her jacket and begins to unzip her skirt as she walks into her room. Sheila stands in the doorway.

– I left some other things on your bed. They were in the bathroom, says Sheila.

–You were in my room?

– I was just putting things back.

– Did I ask you to put anything back?

– I was just tidying up a bit. Is there a problem? asks Sheila, pulling her shoulders back defensively.

– You know I value my privacy. I don't like people foostering about.

– I hate to tell you this Mary but I slept in your room last night. How private is that?

–Yeah but when I'm not here.

– I'm not going to be here much longer but when I take a shower I prefer not to be standing on your stuff. That's all.

Mary doesn't respond. Sheila watches her throw the rest of her clothes on the bedroom floor. Sheila stands outside for a moment, listening for Mary to see if she goes to the wardrobe. She doesn't appear to. Sheila is anxious. She wishes now she had left well enough alone, not looked in the box, not satisfied or half satisfied her curiosity. She looks at her bleeding hand and catches a droplet of blood before it hits the floor.

24

Sheila is sitting in an armchair in the living room reading an old book she had found upstairs called *Redemption*. She can hear the TV on in the kitchen. She's wearing Mary's red dress. It's really a little too dressy for the night that's in it but Mary offered and, she didn't want to refuse. It's a little tight around the bust but it shows off her cleavage. Mary comes towards her with a glass of wine.

– Thanks, says Sheila. Is that the end of the bottle?

Mary bends down and kisses Sheila gently on the lips.

– Not quite.

Mary gets her own glass from the dining room table and sits opposite. It's odd seeing Sheila in her own dress, the kind of narcissistic echo that stirs attraction.

– Thanks for being here, Sheila. I know I don't show my appreciation very well but I don't know what I would have done without you. *Merci pour tout!*

– It's not over yet, or is it?

– How do you mean?

– This business with the caller. He may not have been in touch but how do you know it's over?

– Just a feeling.

– What if you're wrong?

– If I'm wrong at least I have a sense that I can cope now.

– What's changed?

– I think I have it more in perspective now. Until it becomes something more than a threat, more than an occasional phone call, I think I can manage.

– Do you want me to leave?

– No.

– That sounds like *Maybe*.
– No.
– Has something happened? Have I done something wrong?
Mary can see no chink in her friend's defiant subterfuge.
– I suppose I'm used to being on my own.
– Is this because I was in your room?
– You were just putting back clothes. That's what you said.
– Was there something you didn't want me to see?
– Everyone has something to hide, don't they?
– Relax. I didn't find anything. I wasn't interested in finding anything.
– OK.
– OK then. Let's finish that bottle.
Mary gets the bottle of red, tops up her own glass then refills Sheila's, giving her the last drop.
– You get the luck!
– Thanks.
Sheila returns briefly to her book but with Mary just sitting there picking at some loose threads on the armrest of the chair, Sheila decides to put the book to one side.
– Before I forget, says Sheila, someone called shortly before you came in. I wasn't sure about answering it. The only reason I did was I thought it was *him*, so I pretended to be you.
– Why?
– I was going to give him a piece of my mind on your behalf.
– And! Was it him?
– It was Germain, your polio infatuation. I said you'd call him back later.
– So he thinks you're me, is that it?
– That's it.
– He'll get a surprise. What else did you say to him?
– Nothing much. I asked him if he could do it standing up.
Mary smiles.
– Actually he sounded kinda nice. You didn't tell me you'd written back to him.
– Nice. You mean weak.
– I don't know about that. Anyway I said I'd call him back later or rather you would. I told him his voice was sexy.

– Sounds like you told him a lot. Maybe you should talk to him some more seeing as you got on so well.

Sheila finds it kind of hard to read Mary's tone. There's a criticism in there somewhere. She chooses not to respond.

– I'll have to balance this benign image that you've projected. I don't want him to think he's dealing with some sloppy romantic.

Mary resents the way that Sheila makes her feel inadequate when it comes to all these shitty negotiations with men.

– Sloppy romantics have the best fun, didn't you know?

Mary drains her glass. Sheila follows suit.

– Jesus I should go easy.

– What time are you heading uptown?

– Around eight-thirty.

– Anyone I know?

– Just an old friend from college.

Mary hates it when people lie to her. It makes her feel stupid. What do they take her for, some kind of retard? She can feel herself getting angry. She's gotta watch that, it's a sure sign. She's learned to watch for signs. She's got pretty good at it.

– I told a lie today, says Mary looking directly at Sheila.

Sheila shifts her gaze slightly.

– It was the strangest thing, says Mary, I cancelled a lunch appointment. I told this client that two of my teeth had fallen out and that I had to go to the dentist to have them re-implanted. In fact I met David.

– Two of your teeth! What made you say that?

– I don't know. Teeth have to do with decision making, don't they? I guess I was thinking about that, being at sixes and sevens. Does that make sense?

– Not really. So you met David. How did that go?

– Really well. Neutral venue. The museum over by Saint Patrick's. I apologised for setting the cops on him. You were right about that one. He had nothing to do with it. It was just my paranoia. God I'm fucked up!

– You're not the only one.

– You just hope you're going to get past it, get to where things even out. Maybe I need to get away. I saw that brochure on Sicily on the back seat of your car. Now there's a place I'd like to return to. Do you ever think back to that time we spent in Cyprus? I still have the video. We should watch it together some time.

– No thanks. That's ancient history. I thought we'd agreed never to talk about that again.

– Don't you think you'd find it erotic?

– No.

– It's nothing to be ashamed of.

– I'm not ashamed of it. But I was the one who was used. At least that was how I felt. Besides I think I'd just find it embarrassing. Was that why you kissed me?

– Maybe. I think about it sometimes. It seems so out of character for me now, don't you think?

– I don't know what to think. I don't know why you brought it up.

– Hey like you say it was a long time ago. It was just the talk of islands made me think of it. I haven't upset you have I?

– No.

Sheila stands up and puts on her heavy coat.

– Maybe my memory of it is a little different than yours. Anyway I've got to go. See you tomorrow sometime.

– Sure. You have a good time now!

Mary watches Sheila go. She pets Smith. Trusting people is hard, she thinks, one of the hardest things in the world.

25

Midtown is quiet, even for a Wednesday. The subway gets her in early so she takes her time checking out the fashions. There's a window dresser in Greenwood's Department Store. He's filling up the background with felt flowers. It's a spring look, lots of greens and yellows. The mannequins are naked and turned away from the window. Sheila wonders about the women they're modelled on. She indulges the fantasy of being such a model and of coming upon her body in a strange city; of observing her model self being the object of public scrutiny and desire; the idea of being both ideal and real. She moves on and stops again at an electrical store. The stainless steel units, she knows, will be passé in a year or two. There's a coffee maker though in green enamel which takes her fancy. It strikes her as odd the alliances she makes with objects. She strolls along until she realises her shoe has stuck to some gum. She goes to the kerb and tries to scrape it off. It frustrates her and she finds herself internally ranting against the detritus people discard. She hates this random rubbish, she hates the delinquency and casual filthiness that degrades the world.

The Sophix pub is their rendezvous point. Sheila has been once or twice before and would probably have opted for somewhere a little less trendy had Sergeant Keaney not been as decisive as he was. She likes the fact that he got back to her almost immediately. Even though the whole thing was set up on the pretext of talking about Mary, she is sure he knows that she is interested in him. She doesn't want to get there too early although she has brought the *Francis Stuart* book with her, just in case. When she thinks about Mary she feels immediately angry. Bringing up that stuff about Cyprus! Why or why now? It's not that she's into me. It's her own displaced frustration and paranoia, just because she thought I was prying. Sheila sees it as passive aggressive positioning. She shunts it to one side.

Sheila admits to herself that maybe she was wrong to invade Mary's privacy. But if Mary had been more open with her she wouldn't have been so inclined to root in the box, or toy with the gear. Sheila convinces herself that the trespass came on foot of what had become an essentially distrustful relationship with Mary. But what had she found? Some pretty innocuous sex stuff. Maybe the friendship was dead, maybe that was the truth of it, and maybe things should have been left as they were. Same old mistake Sheila, she chides herself, a failure to broach or accept the truth of the situation. If Sheila was honest with herself she would acknowledge that she had had her own reasons for letting the friendship slip. But she and Mary had a long history, and some part of Sheila was disinclined to definitively inter the remnants of their friendship.

She walks by some more clothes shops and a furniture department store. She can see the pub across the road. She looks at her watch. Eight thirty-five. She goes to the traffic lights at the cross-street. The pub has a pale wood veneer, gold lettering on the window, shiny brass plates. Couples sit at high round tables in the window. She had hoped one of them might be free, public enough to make the whole thing potentially diverting if it didn't go well, or if she and Gerry just didn't click. She presses the button at the traffic lights and waits. She watches a man go into the pub. He has blond hair, is about the right size. Could be him, she thinks. She has a moment's anxiety wondering whether she will recognise him in civvies or not.

She enters smiling and scans the bar left to right. She takes in the whole scene, flash image by image, before the door falls closed. Music blares out, *In a trailer park in Seattle*, curly haired attractive middle-aged woman, nice eyes, *They're waving candles in the rain,* warm smile, bias-cut brown cord skirt, *Mis-spent youth doing battle*, thin sable man, head shaved, *Over what is and isn't there*, wool collarless jacket, oddly shaped skull, next table, slim woman, late twenties, honey blond, expensive clothes, *And trying for the clincher a girl tries to explain*, with older man, very expensively dressed, big watch, soft stomach, *How Jesus lived six years longer than Kurt Cobain*, barman, black jacket and white shirt, tea towel slapped over left forearm, the chorus reprised, *And Jesus' Hair was longer,* can-I-help-you smile, *And Jesus' Arms were stronger*, turn left, abstract paintings mostly red, orange and yellow, *And Jesus' Thoughts were truer*, bank of soft leather seating, various circular and rectangular tables in front, *And Jesus' Eyes were bluer*, leather armchairs in the corners, *And He will take you higher*, can't see him, can't see him, see him, *Through the rain and through the fire*, nod, affirmation, *And the truth was in his hands*, smile from me, smile from him, walk over, *And the truth was in his hands,* stands up, open palm, *And the truth was in his hands,*

– Good timing, says Maurice.

He takes her coat and hangs it up.

– Thanks, Gerry. You look different. Good but different.

Sheila has watched him eye check her boobs.

– Great dress! Looks familiar somehow. What can I get you?

– I had a glass of wine with Mary before I came out. Maybe I should have a coffee.

– Oh go on, have a wine! *I'm* going to.

– Oh! Okay. Red. French if they have it.

– Excellent!

Maurice gets the drinks and brings them back to the table.

– Did you tell Ms Reid you were meeting me?

– No.

– Probably just as well. She might think we were going behind her back, which I suppose we are. Still, we have her best interests in mind.

– I was worried. I tried to get her to call you but she didn't see much point.

– I must admit we don't always have the manpower to devote to stalkers and nuisance callers so they tend to slip under the wire. Maurice pauses. I hope we're not going to talk about her all night.

He touches her hand. Sheila doesn't remove it.

– To be honest, continues Maurice, I don't think the calls

are such a big deal. Obviously you know her a great deal better than I do but it strikes me that she has some deep personal issues.

– What makes you say that? Not that I'm saying you're wrong, but I'm just curious.

– Well she rang the station a day or two ago. She was questioning my credentials. The duty officer felt that she was a little unbalanced.

– I don't know about that, says Sheila. This past while has been difficult for her. She's struggled to cope at times. The phone calls were just the last straw. That's why I'm staying with her. There are times when we all need a rock to hold onto until the tide abates.

– That's a nice way of putting it but I hear so many hard-luck stories that I really believe there comes a point when you have to take responsibility for your life.

– I think she is trying to take responsibility for her actions. I mean…and this is strictly confidential…

Sheila looks to Maurice for his agreement.

– Sure, it won't go any further, I promise.

– Well, Mary *is* in therapy. I don't know why I'm being so secretive about it, I'm sure she'd tell you herself. A Dr Lavender. She's been seeing him for years.

– That's interesting. Although I'm not convinced therapy is the best way forward, and I'll tell you why.

Maurice pauses and takes a gulp of his wine.

– Let me show you something. Do you have a piece of paper?

Sheila clangs around in her bag but doesn't come up with anything.

Maurice tells her to leave it, goes to the bar and comes back with a napkin. He takes out a pen and writes in big block letters the word THERAPIST. He shows it to her, then folds it, and tears the napkin. Sheila is intrigued.

– You know, Sheila, I was in therapy once myself when I was a teenager, nothing major, just the usual stuff. It's not even that it didn't work for me, or that I didn't respect the therapist, but I felt there was something else going on, something that I didn't trust, implicitly, emotionally. Then one day I was looking at the word and I saw it in a completely new way, but one that made complete sense.

Maurice lays the two pieces of paper down in front of Sheila.

THE RAPIST

Sheila just looks at them. Somehow, she finds it shocking.

– I don't care if it is an old joke. It just came to me. I didn't read it anywhere. Seeing it laid out like that, says Maurice, I've never been able to think of therapists in any other way. It's like they rape the psyche. They fuck your mind up. Excuse my French! I'd never let one of them near me again, not really.

– Why would you? You seem great to me, really sound you know. I think that's what I like about you.

– You know what I like about you? That you're impulsive. Not many people are, not really.

The pub fills a little more as closing time approaches. There's a group of guys in the far corner who are out on a stag night. All of them are dressed in pink T-shirts, each with a large screen printed photo of themselves as babies on the front. Sheila, although she doesn't really want another drink, offers to buy another round.

– I like a woman who keeps her end up; so many women don't.

– Do you want a shot to go with it?

– Only if you join me.

A waitress brings the drinks to the table.

– She's really pretty isn't she? comments Sheila.

– To be honest, I prefer women with a little more *up front*, something to hold onto when the waves break.

– Very funny!

What might be an uncomfortable silence in other circumstances just becomes part of the flow of time between them. Sheila, sensing his ease, determines a big question.

– So who are you, Sergeant Keaney, aside from being a *big* guard?

– Who am I? You sound like a therapist now. What do you want to know? asks Maurice.

She finds it hard to gauge his response. Is he being dismissive? Was her question trite? She feels momentarily insecure.

– Listen I'm not trying to pry.

– No go ahead, there's very little I wouldn't tell you. I'm not threatened by questions.

– Do you have a girlfriend?

He eyeballs her.

– Straight in there, huh! No, I don't have a girlfriend.

– Do you want one?

– Are you offering?

– It's just a question.

Maurice leans back, opens his legs.

– To be honest, I've kind of shied away from women these last few years. Two years ago I went bankrupt. My marriage broke up as a result.

– There were no other problems?

– Why do you say that? asks Maurice.

– I didn't mean it to be critical.

– No, of course not.

– What kind of company?

– I had a security firm that went under. I'd been a cop before that and I used my contacts on the force to get my old job back. I began rebuilding my life.

– Where's your wife now?

– Canada. I haven't seen or heard from her since.

– I'm sorry, says Sheila.

– Shit happens! I'm stronger now because of it.

Maurice flexes his arm.

– Feel that, he says.

Sheila touches his arm.

– You've got an unusual sense of humour, says Sheila. I like that.

– I like you Sheila, it's as though you have the right *temperature* for me.

– That's an odd word to use.

– Another one of my theories, says Maurice. You see I believe everyone's blood boils at a different temperature and yours and mine are compatible. Of course, I say that without knowing you very well, but I'd like to change that.

26

Mary sits watching a documentary about polar bears. The presenter is some naff young English guy with an array of brightly coloured parka jackets which he wears and which ring the changes over the month-long period he spends in the Arctic tundra. After a summer of virtual starvation, she watches as the bears encroach on remote settlements. The rangers who trap these bears, anaesthetize them, tag them, wrap them in a large net and helicopter them to safety. Mary identifies with the bears, with their desperation, their panicked efforts to scavenge, their confusion in a world of loosening and unknowable co-ordinates.

She listens as the presenter defines the problem, the sea icing over later and later each year, how much harder it is for the bears to hunt and to feed their young. He doesn't really sound that perturbed, even though he's mouthing that the bears will be virtually extinct within thirty or forty years. Some other scientists on the programme talk about ancient viruses locked in the ice and the danger of them being released at some future point. She sneers at their overblown names, *Pandoravirus* and *Megavirus*.

Mary recalls reading an article in the weather section of the *The New York Times* only a few days before, about the apocalyptic worst-case scenario, how with no corrective action, the rise in average global temperatures could reach a catastrophic six degrees, causing the deaths of billions with only a few breeding human pairs remaining in the very place where the polar bears now struggle to survive. In the nightmare that would follow, knowledge systems would be lost, brute survival would be the order of the day. She believes she would kill herself rather than be a part of that sordid progression.

Mary turns the TV off and pours herself another whiskey. She can't get her mind off Sheila and the fact that she is with Maurice. She visualises them colluding somewhere, talking about her. This is betrayal. They damage her. Her store of secrets unfolded and betrayed. How could Sheila do this to her? No friend loyal to the drama of her needs would do such a thing. No friend in good conscience would undermine her in this way. There's Sheila prioritising her own crass needs. Feigned support, feigned loyalty. Mary feels alone. The image of her isolated and traipsing some desolate space comes to mind. There is no one and nothing to appeal to. But this realisation gifts her a sudden or momentary strength. She feels emboldened by her appraisal of her friends' shallow partiality and disloyalty.

Mary goes to the back door and lets the mewling Smith in. She gives him milk and a shake of dry biscuits. Taking the phone and whiskey with her she goes upstairs. She undresses and examines her naked body in the mirror. There's a small bruise on the right side of her bottom from where she had pummelled herself. She presses the bruise and feels a slight, warming pain. She picks up her orange-and-green silk dressing gown from the floor and puts it on. Sitting at her vanity mirror she chooses a short dark bobbed wig, settles it in place and combs it out. She applies deep rouge lipstick then paints her nails a deep green. She shakes her hands to dry the varnish, tilting her head coquettishly from side to side. She puts mascara on her eyelashes and pencils her eyebrows a deeper brown. She thinks she looks like some 'forties film star, Merle Oberon perhaps, in the kiss scene from *'Til We Meet Again*.

From the lower side drawer in her vanity dresser she takes out a length of fishing line with multiple unbarbed silver fish-hooks trailing off it. She presses the hooks variously into her belly and chest, wiping away the small emissions of blood with a piece of tissue. Looping the line around the fingers of her left hand she tugs on them gently.

She plumps up her pillows and settles back. Opening up

her laptop she looks at Germain's photograph and profile on the dating website. She picks up the phone, scrolls through received calls and rings the number.

Someone picks up.

– Germain!

– Speaking.

– This is Mary. You were talking to my housemate Sheila this afternoon.

– Can you just hold the line a minute? I want to transfer to the other phone?

– Sure, says Mary.

Mary takes a slug of whiskey and waits.

– Hi. So I wasn't talking to you this afternoon? Your friend led me to believe…

– I know. She's like that.

– Like what?

Mary can sense that he's up for a little banter. She likes that.

– She didn't mean any harm by it. She was just trying to protect me. It's a long story.

– Why would you need protection?

– I don't. It sounds like she ended up being a bit frivolous.

– Intriguingly forward, would be how I'd put it. Are you implying she set the wrong tone, created the wrong expectations?

– I don't know, I'm more serious, more disciplined maybe!

– Ok. That conjures up all kinds of things.

– Like?

– Control.

– That's always the fear isn't it? But then we're all into control, aren't we? Becoming slightly demented when we don't have it. But we want to even things out a bit. Why else would we be doing this, having this conversation?

Mary tugs on the hooks and utters a restrained groan.

– Actually, says Germain, I don't think like that. You make it sound like we're all malfunctioning types, desperate seekers, screwy loners. That normal folk don't do sites like this.

– Normal is pretty abstract, for me.

– Join the club!

– Why do you say that, because you're a cripple?

– That's not exactly PC. I hope I'm not getting a cripple fetishist vibe here?

– So what should I say… otherly abled?

– I'll let you figure that out all by yourself. Am I in left field here or do you have a problem with this?

Mary tugs again on the hooks and keeps the line taut.

– I have absolutely no problem with you being the way you are. I'm just trying to build a picture is all. Out of curiosity are your crutches steel or wooden?

– Why would you care?

– I've upset you haven't I? How come I always manage to say the wrong thing?

Mary takes another slug of whiskey. She can feel her tongue getting loser. Does she care? Not really.

– You tell me.

– You are upset!

– If the fact that I need to use crutches occasionally, is a problem, then you need to say it, or if you're into it on some other level you need to say that too.

– How did we end up here? The bottom line is that I'd like to meet you.

– I was beginning to wonder. Actually, we've met before.

– I know.

– I met you with David?

– I've been trying to place where it was.

– David and I did a two-hander in a Gallery on the west side a few years ago. We met at the opening.

Mary sits up and stops pulling on the hooks.

– And what, you fancied your friend's wife, is that it?

– Sure why not. Anyway you've picked me out of the pile this time, and you do sound interesting even if you have some cripple issues.

– You're wrong about that!

– Well I'll reserve judgement for the moment, if you don't mind.

– Anyway I think you sound nice too.

– Too as in?

– It was something Sheila said.

– Nice! It's a bit anodyne isn't it? Can't you do better than that? I have my dark side.

– A dark side! Yes, I believe you.

Mary pulls too hard on one of the loops and the hook rips clear through her skin.

– Fuck! says Mary.

– Something the matter?

– I just spilled something. I'd better go.

– So do we have an arrangement?

– How about Thursday, eight o'clock?

– No not Thursday, says Germaine. How about tomorrow?

– Tomorrow. Wow! Ok. I can come by your place if you like?

– No need. I'll come and get you. I know where you live, says Germaine.

– Of course you do.

– Tomorrow at eight so. I'll be sure to bring my best crutches!

He hangs up, leaving Mary holding the phone. She untangles the fish line and stares glumly through the black window.

27

The barman calls last orders. There are a few couples aside from Maurice and Sheila still finishing up their drinks. Sheila is listening to Maurice while peeling silver foil off an aluminium cap with the tip of her nail.

– I'm sorry, says Maurice, would you mind not doing that. It hurts me here.

He taps his forehead.

Sheila looks at him, her eyebrows arched, surprised.

– You're a difficult one to figure. You don't fit the mould somehow. I like that about you. It's always good to preserve a little of the enigma, don't you think?

– I wouldn't like you to get the wrong idea about me. I'm a pretty ordinary guy. I'm not trying to hide anything. I'm not trying to gloss what isn't there.

– Don't you think we all hide something? Don't some parts of us always remain mysterious, enigmatic?

– I've never given it that much thought; I just try to be open with people.

Maurice touches her hand. Sheila doesn't pull away. Maurice traces the thin bones on the back of her hand.

– Women's hands look so soft and innocent, yet they do such crude things. I always think of them as deceptive somehow. Do you think we could go back to Mary's place for a nightcap?

– That might be a problem, says Sheila, you see I told her that I was meeting an old college friend. She might think we were in cahoots, aside from the fact that I lied.

– Oh I'm sure she's lied plenty of times.

– We could go to my place, says Sheila. It's on the other side of the city but –

–You wouldn't want to leave her alone. What if something happened? Neither one of us could forgive ourselves. If it's a problem I can sleep in another room. We don't have to have sex if that's what you're worried about.

– No it's not that. What the hell, maybe it'll be all right.

– Of course it will.

As they rise to go Maurice leans over and kisses her.

28

Mary stands before the bathroom mirror taking off her makeup. She can hear the low hum of the boiler downstairs and then silence as it clicks off. She'd set the timer for twelve-thirty a few days ago so that Sheila wouldn't feel the cold. She wonders if Sheila's even noticed. She tries not to think of where she is. She had half-expected her to call. She gives herself a quiet mental reprimand. It was foolish to have expectations of people. If they came good in the end then fine, but you couldn't count on it. She walks across the hallway to her bedroom, consciously avoiding the loose floorboard that she has assiduously avoided all her life. She thinks of it as a kind of distortion, a corruptive sound that chills her. She makes it to her bedroom and eases her body between cooling sheets. She thinks about Germain. His connection to David intrigues her. The art world was such a small, close-knit jealousy of talents. They all knew, or knew of each other. She had met him, there was common ground; it would make it that much easier. She had looked up the catalogue of the show he and David had done together. Most of Germain's work had to do with polio, which he had contracted at nine, and his experience of being in an iron lung in an isolation ward. There had been lots of sea references and a strange audio soundtrack, which had been in part an *homage* to the German artist Kurt Schwitters. She remembered that it had made her feel quite queasy.

She begins to drift off, tucking her legs up to her belly, and is about to reach out to turn the light off when she hears the front door open and close loudly. She looks at the digital clock on the bedside table. Twelve forty-five. She hears voices, she's sure of it, more than one voice, muttering, giggling. She feels invaded. She pushes back the quilt and steps out of bed in one movement, throws on her dressing gown and pads softly out onto the landing. She can hear them, it is *them*, more than one, ascend the stairs. She peers over the banister railing and sees Maurice shepherding Sheila up the stairs. Sheila stumbles. Maurice grabs her under the breasts from behind and pulls her to her feet.

– There's a good girl, he says. Are you all right now?

A vomiting reflux fills Mary's throat. She swallows the bile and retreats quickly to her bedroom. In the face of this obscenity she panics. Closing the door to her bedroom she jumps back into bed and pulls the quilt over her head. She names it immediately for what it is: revenge. This is his punishment of her. Were she stronger she would tell them both to leave, right now. Get the fuck out! Get out of my fucking house! She hears them stumble into Sheila's bedroom. The walls are thin. She has forgotten how thin they are. There is a memory from the past but it has been so long since anyone… She cannot block the sounds out so she throws the quilt back.

– No Gerry, put me down!

Then the sound of Sheila body flumping heavily onto the bed. Mary can hear Sheila's voice, half-terrified, half-excited. Maurice rips something, bed-linen or garments. Then he starts giving orders.

– Take off your knickers. I'm going to fuck you. What are you going to do?

– What do you want me to do?

– I want you to cunt me till you prick.

There's silence for a few moments then Sheila screams Jesus! She screams it again. There's pleasure and fear in her voice. They start to fuck. It's a theatre of macabre sounds. Mary thinks it will stop, any moment now it will stop, but it doesn't stop.

– Turn over, Maurice tells Sheila.

Sheila comes loudly.

Mary feels like she's being crucified. Like some part of her core is being extracted. Finally it stops. No post-coital chat, no fawning affection, no words at all. Spent, they merely sleep. Mary remains awake and in her anger determines that this will never happen again. This is the beginning and end of it. She will change her life.

29

Through a night she thought she wouldn't endure, she endures. Mary is in the kitchen waiting and not waiting, holding on to an anger she fears might dissipate. She cannot afford to let it ebb, this tide of pain, this gross insult and degradation of her. She fears that she will rename her anger as irrational. After all what was so bad about what they did last night? They came back, they fucked. They came back, they pissed. They came back, they shat. So fucking what! Get a grip!

There's a pot of coffee on the stove. She refills her cup and stares out through the kitchen window at the fog-shrouded apple tree struggling to survive in the paltry patch of yard dedicated to soil. If she had time one day she would make a proper garden: plant flowers, dahlias and fuchsias, and a water feature somewhere with fat goldfish like the ones she'd seen years ago in the gardens of the Alhambra. There's movement upstairs. She checks the clock. Seven-thirty. They'll be down soon. Sheila at least. She's got work. As for Maurice, he can do what he likes. What if Sheila calls in sick? Will Mary go up to the room and have it out with them? She feels outnumbered, she knows that Maurice will deride her. This is his revenge on her, she knows that.

She hears them coming downstairs, the two of them coming downstairs. Anxiously she empties the cup of coffee down the sink and begins scouring the insides and rim of the cup. She will have her back to them when they enter, she will say what she has to, without looking at them directly. Maurice's eyes might flay her and reduce her to a kind of stupefied blubber. Don't look at him, speak your truth then the worst will be over. She feels like an old woman, dark and interrogatory. She looks for the kernel. *I don't like the way you make me feel*. That's legitimate, isn't it? This is what Dr Lavender is always telling her. Believe in the integrity of what you feel.

They enter and she turns. The best plans corrupt. She grabs the stained tea towel and begins drying her hands. Sheila is dressed in the same skirt and blouse she'd worn the day before. She is sheepish, her head bowed. At least she has the decency to be cowed. Will Sheila blame it on the drink? Will she beg forgiveness? Maurice on the other hand is unshaven, shirt open to his navel, like a bit of rough trade. Mary's voice catches when she sees him. His eyes inveigle her into the game. She can feel the weight of his duplicity, his knowingness, his control.

Mary waits.

– You won't believe this Mary, says Sheila, but I ran into the Sergeant at the pub last night and well…one thing led to another.

Sheila smiles forlornly.

Maurice pours some cereal into a bowl.

– Miss Reid, Mary, I can call you that, can't I? We meet under different circumstances. Life is full of the strangest twists don't you think, and there's no point in feeling guilty over something innocuous. Better to save that for the serious stuff. By the way I hope we didn't keep you awake last night.

– I may have asked for surveillance but I didn't expect you to be fucking my friend in the spare bedroom. I want you out of my house, both of you.

– I think you're forgetting why Sheila is here in the first place, and as for me I'm afraid I can't do that. I mentioned your case to the inspector. Apparently you're not the only woman in the area who has been receiving these calls. He recommended in the strongest possible terms that I station myself in the area. This house is as good as any so unless you have a particular objection…

– That's crap! There is no threat.

– There's always a threat. Policing is a two-way street. Unless we get co-operation everything becomes more difficult, and by difficult I mean difficult for you. Do you understand what I'm saying?

– Go to hell! And I won't be threatened. Not by you, not by anyone.

– *You're not hearing what I'm saying*. You have a choice as to whether to co-operate or not but you run a risk if you don't. You need to assess that risk Mary because what we're talking about here is your life. Don't worry, I won't be here all the time, but I feel that Sheila's presence and mine will be a boon to you in the end.

Sheila interrupts.

– Mary if you want me to leave I'll leave.

– Sheila that would probably suit all of us but it's not the right option, says Maurice. We need to hold this together and safeguard each other until the danger has passed. What might appear to be an accommodation will I'm sure turn out to be much more than that.

Maurice pulls on his jacket.

– I'll leave you ladies together. I'll be back this evening.

He takes Sheila's key.

– I'll get another one cut.

He kisses Sheila and grabs her ass.

Maurice turns to leave.

Mary turns to Sheila.

–You stay here!

Mary follows Maurice into the hall and out to the front door. He turns on her suddenly, grabs her shoulders and drives her up against the wall.

He presses his knee into her groin.

– What do you think you're doing? Don't you understand all of this is for you?

– I don't want you mixing things up anymore, says Mary.

–You sound like a fucking baby! Can you hear yourself? *I don't want you mixing things up anymore*. You can't tolerate the world without me so don't accuse me of mixing things up. You don't exist. You barely know what to fucking think without me.

– But you get to fuck my friend, is that it?

He slaps her across the face.

– Don't be crude. My truth Mary is I act, and I manage the fucking consequences. You bought into this, you play by the fucking rules.

– I don’t know the rules.

Mary tries to turn away from him, to walk away from him, but he draws her back, pulls her close.

– Don’t think that you can just choose the masks you like. Life isn’t a fucking Mardi Gras.

Maurice leaves, banging the door behind him. Mary stands there deflated, useless, like she’s lost in a place where everything is familiar yet unknown. She kicks her foot through the stained-glass panel beside the hall door and for a moment is stuck. She pulls her leg back and slashes the skin along her calf. Blood begins to pour down her leg. She should feel something; she feels nothing.

30

When Mary returns to the kitchen Sheila is sitting with her back against the wall by the pine table, a pint glass of water in front of her, and a pack of paracetamol tablets in her hand.

– You've got to go, says Mary.

– He wants me to stay. I think I should stay.

– I don't know how much more clearly I can say this. I WANT YOU BOTH OUT OF HERE.

– You don't have to shout Mary. Besides I don't think you're in any fit state to make a decision like that. You heard what Gerry said, this is happening to other women too, you have some responsibilities.

– So, this is all about me, not about you meeting your selfish fucking needs.

– Are you really that upset about what happened last night?

– Yes.

– We only made love, for Christ sake!

– It's more than that and you know it. I could hear every groan. It was like listening to someone going to the toilet. How could you? It just doesn't make sense, you being with him.

– Listen Mary I hate to break it to you, but making love is a pretty natural thing to do, and whether I fuck my dog or the president is none of your business.

– You think I don't know what you're doing. You think I don't know why you're trying to undermine me.

– I'm not trying to undermine you. Mary sometimes I think you're getting really paranoid. It's time to take responsibility and get healthy.

– That's easy for you to say. You're not listening to your fucking friend. You're not getting the phone calls. You're not the one being threatened. You think you know this guy, you don't. He's not even a cop.

– What do you mean he's not a cop?

– Keaney, Gerry Keaney! That's not even his real name.

– Who is he then?

Mary suddenly feels herself on the brink of a fall and is afraid. Offer it all up, tell your truth, but she cannot.

– Ask him yourself.

– You know Mary the more I think about it, the more it seems like jealousy to me.

Mary takes a piece of white bread, slathers it with butter and piles lumps of coarse-cut marmalade on top, before folding it over in two and taking a huge bite. Mouth full, her voice sounds like it's coming from under water.

– Next you'll be telling me all I need is a good fuck to sort myself out.

Sheila's whole demeanour softens; her voice when she speaks is conciliatory.

– Listen, let's take a step back. Maybe it wasn't the right thing taking him here last night, but I honestly didn't think you'd mind. I'd have brought him back to my place but I didn't want to leave you alone. You were the one who was feeling vulnerable.

Mary joins her hands like a little girl in prayer.

– He's sick. Can't you smell it on him? He has an appetite for suffering. He'll fuck you up.

– This is all over my head. But I'm a big girl Mary. I think I can handle it. Now I have to go to work. We can talk about it later.

Sheila stands up to leave.

– I know what he really wants to do, says Mary.

Sheila remains looking at her.

– He wants to put on his favourite dress. He thinks he's in control now.

– Whatever!

Sheila leaves then comes back in with the mail.

– You've got a broken panel outside.

Mary makes no response.

– Do you want a hand to clear it up?

– No, that's something I can do all by myself.

After Sheila leaves Mary phones in sick. She roams around the house, aimless, disconnected. An image comes to her of the house filled with stones – a barricade against the onslaught.

31

It's 2pm. Clinton Park on the west side of the city is full of students and fitness types, stay-at-home fathers wheeling strollers at an A-to-B kind of speed, a few old folks, and a few motorised-wheelchair users. There is a bit of blue sky, a bit of sun, the grass looks lush enough for this time of year. Sheila sits on a park bench, the ground in front of her sloping down to a small lake with a central island where some ducks and migrant birds have gathered on the shale shore. To her right is the children's play area, climbing trellises, whirligigs, swings. She glances at her watch, looks towards the park's side entrance and to a bronze sculpture of a horse and a general. She opens her handbag and breaks a couple of chunks off a bar of plain chocolate.

– Sheila!

She knows the voice. He's late but at least he's here.

– David!

He leans down to kiss her on both cheeks.

– Good to see you. Thanks for coming, says Sheila.

– You sounded upset this morning.

– Yeah. I'm okay now. Sorry to drag you all the way over here but I just needed to talk to somebody.

– No problem. At the moment anything that gets me out of the house seems like a good idea.

– Why?

– To be honest the police coming by and all that has made Jill a bit nervy. She's convinced Mary is trying to break up our relationship. Jill's a bit in her head about it. In fact she wants to move.

– Where?

– Somewhere up north but I'm hoping it will pass. I'm happy where I am.

– For what it's worth I tried to stop Mary from involving you. You know I've been staying with her this last while?

– Yeah she mentioned it in one of her many calls to me. I don't know why I just don't change my number.

– That's what she's done.

– It's not that I don't feel sorry for her, I do, but there's nothing I can do, or want to do.

– She said she met you yesterday.

– Did she indeed? Well, surprise, surprise, she didn't.

– Why does she do that?

– What? Lie? I don't think she even thinks of it like that. It's just part of her weird fantasy life, or part of her personality misalignment. I don't know anymore.

– It's all a bit extreme.

– She is extreme. Maybe it's part of her attraction. I gave up trying to sift out what was true a long time ago.

– You'd think with all the therapy she's done she'd be better.

– I never thought it did her much good. She's happier being a victim, or being an enigma to herself.

– It's understandable in a way given what she lost.

– I know.

– It's strange in all the years I've known her, and you, I've never *really* understood what actually happened. It's always been off-limits. Sure I know the basics...

– What do you mean? asks David

– The basic stuff of her past. I know she was close to her mother, not that she ever talks about her.

– She doesn't have a clear memory of her, that's why, says David.

– One thing about the car accident. Was she in the car with her sister?

– No, she managed to open the door. Sally was strapped in. They were both only wee things. Mary six or seven. Sally three-and-a-half.

– And the mother was dead by that stage? asks Mary.

– Yeah.

– And the father?

– He died in the house fire.

David picks up a handful of loose stones and begins flicking them one by one onto the grass verge.

– How has it been staying in the house these last few days? asks David.

– It's okay, a bit dreary but I'm there to support her, not redecorate. Did you ever use the top floor?

– Not really I had thought of adapting it for use as a second studio at one point, but the stairs up was too steep and narrow. I always liked the feeling up there and the view. After the house was re-roofed it was left largely unused. As far as I know when they were kids her parents used the rooms up there as guest accommodation.

– And he died in there?

–Yep. The body itself was badly burned. I don't even know if they were able to make a positive ID at the time. Apparently Mary didn't speak for more than a year after the fire.

David looks at his watch.

– Are you in a rush? asks Sheila.

– Not particularly but I need to pick up some supplies. So how did we get onto that? Presumably your upset this morning had something to do with Mary.

– It did but that's not why I wanted to see you. I guess it's all related but there was something I specifically wanted to ask you. You don't have to answer if you don't want to.

– Go ahead.

– It's about your intimate relationship with Mary.

– What there was of it.

– Yesterday I was putting some clothes of hers back in her wardrobe. Anyway a box fell down from the upper shelf and some things spilled out onto the floor.

– You never could resist an opportunity like that, Sheila!

– Just listen to me for a moment. You know as well as anyone I'm not a prude, but well they were S&M things, whips, handcuffs, leather gear – the whole bit.

– And you're wondering if they're a relic of my antique sex life?

– Like I say you don't have to answer if you don't want to.

–Thanks. The straight answer is no. I didn't realise she was into that but in a way it makes sense.

– You see it might explain something. If she's had some casual affairs it might explain the phone calls. Maybe she's too embarrassed to say anything about it, says Sheila.

– Maybe. The thing about S&M is that it's usually just playful fantasy games and I very much doubt that there are any more weirdoes involved in it than in straight sex, whatever that is. But I suppose you're right, it is a possibility given the circumstances.

– So how do I handle it?

– I don't know.

–You wouldn't think of talking to her yourself, asks Sheila? You never know it might help.

– It would be a mistake Sheila. I know her; it would only create in her mind the possibility of our getting back together. I don't want to do that.

– OK. I understand. Anyway I'd better let you go and I'd better get back to work myself.

– Sorry I couldn't be of more help.

They both get up.

– By the way are you seeing anyone yourself these days?

– A policeman, believe it or not.

– So you won't be needing Mary's handcuffs.

Sheila smiles.

– I hope everything works out for you and Jill.

– I'm becoming fatalistic about relationships, which is probably fatal.

32

Mary feels guilty about having called in sick. It makes her feel sick. She can't decide whether to get dressed or not, so she doesn't get dressed. There's so much that she could be doing around the house, vacuuming Smith's shed hairs from off the sofa, scouring the oven, cleaning the presses, but she does none of these things. Instead she goes upstairs into Sheila's bedroom. Sheila's bedroom! The fact that she even names it as such disappoints her. The bed has been dressed. It looks neat, untrammelled. The room doesn't echo their pleasure. Pleasure evaporates. She pulls back the duvet. The stain is there where his semen has seeped out of her. She throws everything onto the floor and pulls off the lower sheet. She smells the stain. She wants them to know. To let them know she has touched their dirt. She dresses the bed again with clean sheets and plumps the pillows. She sits in the armchair by the window looking at the bed. She visualises how they will be. How they will prepare, how they will act, how they will finish. She imagines being a part of it, not being left out, not being cancelled, being a kind of guardian eye.

She goes downstairs and from underneath the sink retrieves the grey plastic toolbox. Everything that she needs is there. For the first time in days she feels coherent. She takes the drill upstairs, fixes the drill bit, marks her spot and, from her side of the wall above the bedside table, drills a hole. She punches through, goes into the other room and sands down the corrupted flares of wallpaper. She checks to see what she can see. Nothing. She returns to Sheila's room and tilts the vanity mirror by the far wall at a slight angle. She shifts Sheila's bedside lamp so that it obscures the hole from almost every point in the room. She goes upstairs and from a cardboard box in the junk room on the second floor, takes out a couple of old soft animals she'd had as a child. She places the bunny and the teddy in a fucking position on the bed and returns to her room. In daylight she can see everything and wonders whether this will be compromised at night by the lamp. She replaces the bulb with one of a higher wattage, fearing at the same time that their attention will be drawn to it, or that it will create a glare in the mirror opposite. Before she leaves, she places the bunny and the teddy nestled up, one against either pillow.

There is one other thing she has to do. She goes back upstairs and from another box retrieves a bunch of old videos indexed with name slips of the places she had vacationed in over the years. She roots through them until she finds Cyprus, dusts it off on the sleeve of her dressing gown and returns to place it on the bed between the teddy and the bunny. She draws the curtains slightly and drags the armchair opposite the end of the bed. It's almost as though there is a narrative at large in the room already, a story complication of her making, an investment in the room and by implication in their lives. She feels empowered by this intercessory manipulation, like a celebrant at the altar bed of desire.

Downstairs she gets the vacuum from underneath the stairs and flicks on the TV with the remote. She has the sense now of being in a state of defiant readiness. Let things unfold as they will. The images on the TV are of mudslides in the Philippines. The mud-splattered bodies of the rescuers are almost indistinguishable from the dead bodies being dragged and heaped for burial or burning. The terrain looks ugly, the people too. If it were more beautiful, or if *they* were more beautiful, she might feel something; as it is she feels nothing. A number flashes on the bottom of the screen appealing for donations. She could give something, money has never been an issue for her, she has more than she needs, but she cannot valorise it as a useful act, it is merely placatory, a sop to conscience. Besides, these people have a different attitude to life and death; a sense of inevitability colours their acceptance of the chaos. Expectation of loss, she believes, enables their survival.

33

Evening. Mary sits by the window waiting. Neither Sheila nor Maurice has returned. She feels almost disappointed. She figures they've gone to Sheila's place. Everything that Maurice had said was just a sham – empty veiled threats, empty promises. She expects Germain to arrive early. It's already seven-forty. Hilda's place across the road is lit up. Mary has never been inside, though not for the want of invitations. Tonight she is feeling benign, even towards Hilda. Some days just turn themselves around; maybe today would be like that. She looks at her nails – red. It was either that or purple, and the red suits her dress. She had thought about wearing a wig, the blonde one that comes down to her shoulders, but she had washed her hair instead and straightened it so it looks almost as good.

The rush hour traffic has died away. A few doors down, on the opposite side of the street, a neighbourhood dog pisses against the front wheel of a silver Ford. She guesses that Germain will approach from the midtown end of the street unless he's driving. They could do that couldn't they, cripples? Specially adapted small cars and all that. Who knows, he might be more vigorous than she thinks. She's about to get up and mix herself a whiskey when she sees him. The street light makes everything softer but he looks good, handsome anyway. The crutches are aluminium, the hospital kind. He uses them not so much to swing as to support his body, which makes the total effect a lot less ostentatious. She moves away from the window; the idea of her waiting, watching, is too pathetic. She can see his face now. Early forties she figures, good hair, he moves his fingers through it and across his brow. He touches the inside pocket of his coat, checking for something, his wallet perhaps, what else? Is he shorter than her? Maybe. No taller anyway. She checks herself in the mirror above the mantelpiece. She presses her lips together and touches her breasts. The bell sounds. She doesn't answer. Why would she? The scene suddenly appears as being extraneous to her life, or not of her life. It's such a juvenile scenario. What was she thinking? There's no reason to extend it any further than this. He came, he left. He presses the bell again. She feels a kind of panic, a kind of entrapment, she wants to run. If only there were a sanctuary, or a person to run to. There's the bell again. Will there be a fourth ring? No. She waits a few moments then returns to the window, peering out, just to see his retreating figure. It is a disaster evaded, the self intact, uncompromised. She steps closer to the window. The dog opposite is still wandering around. When she is sure her visitor is gone she will head out somewhere for a drink on her own. She's all dressed up isn't she? Who knows what might happen, this is just the kind of situation that might work in her favour. You give up on one thing, and another thing takes its place.

Mary slowly realises that there is someone standing before her on the other side of the window, looking intently at her, smiling with his lips but not his eyes. She tries to move to one side but she's stuck. He's pointing towards the door moving his finger backwards and forwards slowly like a bolt. She feels faint, clammy, bungling. She could still go upstairs, close the door and wait, but as directed she moves towards the door and opens it. The last thing she thinks before she is forced to speak is that she has nothing to say.

– Do you want me to pretend that I'm not thinking what I am thinking, that you don't want me here, that you think this is a bad idea and you want out?

Mary doesn't answer.

- Listen, says Germain, if it stops here, that's fine by me.

His directness confuses her.

– I was upstairs…

– No, don't go there. Do you want me to leave?

She hesitates and he turns. He's careful of the steps; they're difficult to negotiate. Her instinct is to help him.

– No.

He stops for a moment.

—You're right. I was having second thoughts.

Strangely, she's empowered by the admission.

– So, what do you want to do?

One question after another.

– Come in. I want you to come in.

Mary opens the door. He stands before her in the hall, rests his crutches against the wall and takes off his overcoat.

– You can put them somewhere if you want. I don't need them in the house.

– If you want to go into the living room?

– In here?

—Yeah. I'll put these down in the kitchen.

Mary gathers up the crutches. When she comes back he's standing in the dining room looking at an old painting David had given her.

– Not one of David's best!

– I like it, says Mary.

– Have you seen his recent work?

– I don't go to galleries much anymore. Not openings anyway.

– I've got a show coming up. Maybe you'll come to that.

– Maybe. Do you want a drink? I'm afraid it's whiskey or whiskey.

– Straight is fine with some water on the side if that's not too much trouble.

Germain bends down and pets Smith.

– Great cat! Bit of an aberration like myself.

– I suppose.

– You're good at this, good at ameliorating other people's self-deprecation.

– I didn't mean to offend. I looked up that show you did with David online. I remember your work. It was strong, or it had a strong impact on me.

– Strong is good. But it was four years ago. My work has changed.

– Four years is a long time. *I've* changed, says Mary.

– I found you attractive then. I still do.

– I wasn't fishing for compliments.

– But you accept them graciously when they're offered.

– And I don't like sarcasm.

– Why do I get the impression that we're working with a rulebook here? What I'm meant to say, how I'm meant to behave.

– I'm sorry I just don't like people being false.

– But I do find you attractive. Is that so hard to believe?

– Listen, let me get you that whiskey. I'll be back in a minute. Sit anywhere. Smith will keep you company.

Germain sits down. Smith twines himself between his legs. He notices a framed picture of Mary and David on top of a lacquer cabinet in the corner. He goes over and picks it up.

When Mary returns she places the whiskeys and water on the glass-topped table near the sofa.

– Where was this taken? asks Germain.

– A little village in the Luberon in the south of France. We were staying with a friend of David's, Patrick le Haye. Maybe you know him?

– Can't say I do. Nice photo though. You made a handsome couple.

Germain returns to sit beside Mary on the sofa. Mary notices that his fingernails are chewed down, the fact of them belies the coolness and detachment of his persona.

–You're very relaxed, she says, I didn't expect that you would be.

Germain swallows half the whisky and leans forward.

– How do you mean?

– I expected…I don't know what I expected really.

– Expectations are a funny thing. Do you have any? asks Germain.

– Of you? Not really. I'd like not to be bored!

– That should be easy. You're resourceful after all.

Mary scratches the inside of her palm, then pulls her dress down closer to the knees.

– Do you have a plan? asks Mary.

– For tonight? Nothing firm. I thought a film might be a good idea. Something conveniently neutral.

– I was thinking of a meal. I haven't eaten, have you?

– No.

– I should have checked with you, but I went ahead and reserved a table for two at the Holywell.

– Sounds good. I don't know it though, says Germain.

– It's uptown. We can take my car if you like. I had thought about somewhere more local but this place is good, something of an indulgence. But what the heck!

– Should I consider myself an indulgence?

– Definitely! It'll be my treat.

–What time is the reservation for?

– Nine. It won't take us more than twenty minutes to get up there. But we should probably go.

Germain grabs his coat and gets up to leave. Mary catches him checking his image in the mirror. He touches his nose a number of times and then his chin.

Mary gets his crutches.

– Do you mind if I try them?

– Go ahead!

Mary swings herself to the end of the room and back.

She hands them to him.

–You'd think they'd have devised something more beautiful by now, more colourful, says Mary.

–You're right, aesthetics are important.

Mary looks at Germain.

– You know I'm glad you persisted, says Mary. Others wouldn't have, and life's too short.

34

8.45pm.

Smith stirs when he hears the front door open and eases himself carefully down off the sofa. Maurice enters carrying his police uniform and black baton. When Smith brushes against his leg and meows Maurice kicks him to one side.

– Get the fuck out of my way you cunt.

Smith flees into the dining room and hides.

Maurice throws the uniform over the back of the armchair, returns to the hallway and calls out,

– Sheila! Sheila!

He checks the kitchen looking for Mary. He figures they've gone out, colluding behind his back. He checks upstairs. When he sees the bedroom he recognises Mary's hand in the arrangement of the details. He takes the soft toys, opens the window and throws them out.

– Stupid bitch!

He looks at the video and takes it with him, then checks Mary's room and returns downstairs.

He sees the two glasses on the table, sniffs one, gets the bottle from the cabinet and fills a glass. He downs it quickly, puts the video in the player and sits down. The remote is to his side, the corded string of the baton looped around his wrist. It's a holiday video, grainy, random, disjointed. The opening shots are of Sheila looking ten years younger, gesticulating to camera, smiling, hands on hips, and then pointing out to sea from the top steps of some amphitheatre or other. The shot switches to Mary eating a sandwich, a map open on the car bonnet, a winding mountain track and a signpost for the Trudos Mountains that she points to. Maurice fast-forwards through more scenes of bathing, boat trips and then a restaurant pub scene with long tables of assorted tourists and locals. Mary has her arm around one of these locals and is kissing him, then she turns back to camera, eyes wide, eyebrows arched. There's a blackout for a few seconds then the interior of what looks like a hotel bedroom. Mary in her bra and knickers is unzipping the guy's fly. She pulls down his underpants and releases his floppy dick. Sheila comes behind him. Her bra is off. She drapes herself over his back and starts kissing his neck. Maurice has the baton in his hand now and thumps it into his other palm. Mary sucks the guy's dick until it's rigid; she squeezes his balls. Blackout. Maurice fast-forwards. They're fucking now, all three of them. The guy fucks one for a few minutes then the other. Then it's Sheila who's being fucked. She's on her knees, her arms are tied to the headrest, and the guy is fucking her. Mary is underneath her. Sheila turns to camera, pain on her face. There's no sound but she appears to be pleading with them to stop. Mary gets up on Sheila's back like she's some kind of cowboy and rides her.

The doorbell rings. Maurice pauses the video and goes to the door.

It's Sheila.

– Hi, she says, I had to work late. I tried to reach you on your cell phone.

– Oh yeah! Come in here!

–You ok?

– Just get in here.

Maurice lets the video run on. Sheila is being fucked brutally. The guy comes, pushes her ass off to one side, gets off the bed and goes to the bathroom.

Sheila can't quite believe what he's watching. For a moment she's transfixed by the image of herself on screen.

–Where did you get this?

–What the fuck does it matter. It was on the bed upstairs. Mary must have put it there.

–You watched the whole thing?

– I've seen enough.

–You'd no right to do that.

– Fuck you! I'll do whatever I want.

– I'm leaving.

– Get the fuck back here.

Maurice grabs her by the arms, pulls her back into the living room and throws her on the sofa.

– Who are you?

– I'll ask the questions, I'm the fucking policeman.

– Stop it Gerry, please, you're scaring me.

– You're nothing but a cunt, a fucking cunt!

– Listen Gerry, I'm sorry you saw that video. That was something that shouldn't have happened; it happened a long time ago. We all make mistakes.

– That's your excuse is it? *We all make mistakes*. So what other mistakes have you made? Am I a fucking mistake?

– I just came back here to get my stuff, I'm leaving.

– You're not fucking leaving.

Sheila grabs a glass and throws it at him. It smashes into pieces against the wall. He strikes her across the face with the back of his hand. She's astonished and then as her face begins to redden she cries. Through her tears she says,

– I know you're not a cop. There's a Gerry Keaney on the force all right but you're not him. I checked. That's what I was doing. That's why I'm late.

– Well, bully for you! Aren't you the smart fucking wank? You're right I'm not a cop, I'm a therapist.

– Stop lying!

– No it's true I'm a fucking therapist. I help people remember. Did Mary say something this morning?

– No.

– Liar!

He hits her again.

– Did she?

– Please Gerry!

– It's all right Sheila, I'm here to help, that's all I want to do, help you remember. Now did she fucking say anything?

Through her tears Sheila tells him.

– She said you weren't who you said you were, that you weren't a cop.

– See how easy it is? I'm fucking gifted amn't I. Answer me!

–Yes.

Sheila tries to stop crying.

– I'm just going to go upstairs Gerry and get my stuff. We can meet up later.

– You're frightened aren't you? Why are you frightened? WHY IS EVERYONE SO FUCKING FRIGHTENED? You know if I could do one thing in the world, just one thing, it'd be to make people stronger, to get them in touch with the limits of their fear and go beyond. It's another one of my theories. What do you think?

– I think you're right.

–You don't do you? You're lying again.

He begins slurring his words.

–You're a bad fucking lying fuck!

Maurice stands over her and beats her with his fist and with the baton. She screams. He hauls her up, puts his arm over her mouth and beats her again.

35

9.20pm.

The restaurant is upmarket Italian, red walls, discreet lighting, framed pictures of the mountains above Bolzen and Miran in the South Tyrol, some family portraits and memorabilia behind encased glass cabinets. An ebullient, German-accented waitress in a crisp white shirt, black trousers and dust-red apron, leads them to their table. Mary looks sinuous, beautiful, her red dress startling against her pale white skin, a sparkling-white-and-orange glass necklace resting above the merest hint of cleavage. Germain looks dull by comparison, sartorially unprepared but confident enough in himself to manage the discrepancy.

– Would you like an aperitif? asks the waitress.

They order two gin and tonics then peruse the menu.

– What's good here?

– I usually have the fish, says Mary.

– There's a variant of steak béarnaise here that looks interesting. Do you want me to choose the wine?

– If you feel up to it.

– Do you have a preference?

– Red.

– How about the Barolo?

– Sure.

The waitress arrives with a basket of hot bread and spiced oils. She takes their order.

There's an awkward silence. It feels like their true conversation should begin. Mary feels panicked again and is tempted to go to the bathroom. She forwards a question instead.

– Do you still see David?

– That was my question.

– You remind me of him in some ways.

– Is that the attraction?

– David was strong in lots of ways, is strong in lots of ways. Although when I think about it that's not really true. He wasn't strong enough for me. He didn't have enough faith.

– In you?

– In me, or maybe in his love for me.

– I was never really that close to David, professionally maybe, but never privy to the machinations in his personal life. Did your relationship with him end badly?

– Of course.

– And now?

– Now what?

– Can you see him? Do you see him?

– No, he doesn't want it, I don't want it.

– So it's over, no residual feelings?

– No residual feelings? I don't know about that. We had some good times. When I think about those I can't help but feel a sense of loss, and there's a fear, I guess, that I won't find it again with anyone else.

The waitress comes with the wine.

Germain proposes a toast.

– To residual feelings!

Mary looks at him.

– Do you mind if I call you David?

He looks at her incredulously.

– What?

– You should see your face, says Mary. I was only joking.

– There's always been a competitive thing between me and David – art wise. It goes with the territory.

– And now you think you're going to have his woman, is that it?

– Am I?

– We'll see.

– I'm curious, why did you choose me?

– The competition wasn't great.

– Thanks.
– Compliments don’t come easy to me. Sorry.
– But something attracted you.
Mary looks at him directly
– I liked your face.
– That’s it?
Mary takes a sip of wine.
– I thought I could talk to you.
– So *talk* to me.

36

Their main course arrives. Most of the diners from the earlier sitting have left or are fixing up their bills. Germain cuts into his steak, releasing the juices in a red pool to the side of the plate.

– Do you always eat your steak that rare? asks Mary.

– I enjoy the fleshiness of it. It makes me feel more alive. I had a girlfriend once who ate raw mince. It's not uncommon I believe – dangerous but not uncommon.

– Women are strange! Was that your last relationship – the mincemeat girl?

– No, I've had quite a few since then.

– Have you indeed! You make yourself sound like quite the lothario. How many is quite a few?

– Are you sure this is a good idea?

– It's a reasonable question.

Germain looks distinctly uncomfortable.

– Three or four.

– Surely it's either one or the other. Are you having a problem defining what constitutes a relationship?

– Why, do you have a definition?

– You're the one who named them that way.

– Three then, I guess it's three.

– In how many years?

– Ten or so.

– Why did they leave?

– Now *you're* making assumptions.

– I'm just trying to talk to you.

– It's beginning to feel more like an interrogation.

Germain places his knife and fork down and looks directly at her.

– I'm sorry.

– The truth is I put my work before everything else and in the past either what I or they had to offer, just wasn't enough. Now your turn. Why did you and David split up?

– David doesn't really like women, so relationships diminish him.

– So you never had a problem with him isolating himself in his studio for long periods?

– That was never an issue. I like my space too. Sure, sometimes he was emotionally unavailable, too wrapped up in some etherised world or idea. But I suppose he offered me enough when he was available.

– As far as I know David has never been out of a relationship, he just seems to move seamlessly from one to the other.

– He uses women, and he emotionally abuses them, so he's compelled to be around them.

– You don't still love him?

– I hate him, which is the next best thing.

– I suppose, or the inevitable next thing. And you haven't been involved with anyone since?

– It's interesting that you phrase that in the negative.

– Well, have you?

– No. I almost feel like a virgin.

Germain looks at her, his eyes smiling.

– I've never had a virgin.

37

Sheila's bloodied and battered body lies on the sofa. Maurice comes in from the hallway holding a fresh roll of grey duct tape. He puts it down on the table and begins to fold his uniform into a neat pile. He places the baton on top, and the duct tape beside that, and carries them upstairs.

– I'll be down in a minute Sheila. Don't move now!

Sheila's eyes flicker open for a moment then close. She remains immobile, awkwardly arranged.

In the bedroom Maurice draws the curtains closed and switches on the bedside lamp. He gets some towels from the airing cupboard in the bathroom and places them and his uniform on the floor beside the armchair. He takes out some deodorant from his wash bag and sprays it liberally around the room. He looks at himself in the mirror, takes out a comb from his back pocket and combs his hair across his scalp from a side parting. It gives him a country gent kind of look. He should have brought his diamond-patterned pullover and camel-coloured slacks. He notices a fleck of blood on his shirt. It gets everywhere. Still, no point in soaking it now, although he wishes he had some of his mother's magic stain remover or even some salt. Oh well! Looking at the bed, nicely dressed and so forth, he actually thinks it was a good idea now on Mary's part to arrange things anew. It feels like a fresh start, a point of departure so to speak, a fresh room to journey in, a room in which to meet or dare he say it, to confront one's destiny. Every moment was replete with such possibilities and opportunities; you just had to know how to see them, how to take advantage of them. The success or otherwise of one's life was all in the true seeing of things, in perception, apperception, clarity: these were the determiners. He knew above all else that he was singularly advantaged in seeing things for what they were and in winkling out the corruptions that distorted others in the full realisation of their lives. It made him feel alone though. So many people lived blindly. To know the truth, to see the truth and to act in complete alliance with that truth was a responsibility he took seriously. The problem for most people was that they couldn't see, let alone analyse the obvious. Here he was, a being of lucidity and acuity, in true alignment with his insights and desires, acting with authority and justified impunity. There was after all a hierarchy of souls, and of acts. That he should satisfy his soul's needs with passion was utterly appropriate.

He thinks he hears a sound from downstairs.

You try to help people, you tell them what to do, what not to do, you give them patterns of behaviour to act within and affirmations when they function well within them, and you hope that they can expand their potential outwards from these narrow parameters. But when they disobey it's important to reprimand them, to marshal them back between the lines determined for them, until they begin to resolve themselves. This is what works. This is what he knows works.

When he gets downstairs Sheila is crawling on the floor towards the telephone. You have to hand it to them, he thinks, the recalcitrant persistence of some people.

He unplugs the telephone at the socket and goes over to Sheila. He grabs her by the hair and pulls her up onto her knees.

She blubbers pleeeeeassse or something like that. It's hard to make out. Next thing her lies are going to be unintelligible. That'll be the last fucking straw.

–Time to go upstairs, Sheila.

He hoists her to her feet and has to help her to the bottom of the stairs. The things you end up doing for people. Surprisingly she makes a pretty good stab at getting up the steps on her own. The odd prod moves her on with a little more alacrity. He avoids the droplets of blood falling on the carpet runner. Mary's not going to be happy with her about that. They're in Sheila's bedroom in no time at all. When he looks at her straight on he has to admit she is in a bit of a mess.

– Why don't you clean yourself up? There's plenty of hot water.

– Gerry…

– Oh you can stop calling me Gerry. My name's Maurice. Maurice will do from now on.

– Maurice can you call Mary and ask her to come home. I think I need some help.

– You just go ahead and clean up. Mary will be back soon enough.

He watches her go out onto the landing and across to the bathroom. She locks the door.

Maybe that was a bad idea, he thinks. I hope I'm not going to have to expend undue energy and break the stupid thing down. Be calm, he thinks. No need to be hasty, we've got all the time in the world.

38

Mary and Germain drive through virtually deserted city streets. Between First and Second Avenue, City Council workers are out repainting road markings and doing emergency repairs. There are queues outside one or two midtown clubs.

– I need you to give me directions from here, says Mary.

– We're pretty close. If you hang a left here, then take the third right.

Mary is feeling a little light-headed after the Barolo. She shouldn't really be driving, but hey!

– You don't drive? asks Mary.

– I do, says Germain, but I've no need of a car. I'm a city boy. If I go out of town I fly.

Mary drives down a street of low-rise apartment buildings.

– Okay this is good, says Germain.

Mary thinks about turning off the engine but keeps it running.

This is the awkward bit, she thinks. Still, she wouldn't mind seeing him again. He suits her.

– I enjoyed tonight, she says, without looking at him directly. I'll see you again if you like.

– Suits me.

– At least I know where you live now. Actually it's not too far from David's place, says Mary, if I have my bearings right. Do you bump into him much?

– I used to quite a bit but I've gone through an anti-social phase this past year or so. Last time I saw him he was with Sheila. I guess they're still together.

Mary turns towards him, instantly perturbed.

– Sheila!

– Sheila Deane I think her name was. I never knew her myself. I understood she was the woman he left you for.

Mary has gone rigid, unable to process the information, wanting to close down, unable to do so. It's clear to Germain that this is new information.

– Shit! You didn't know.

–You saw them together?

– Listen Mary, I think I've said too much already.

– Did you see them together?

She's almost shouting.

– I did. Listen Mary, why don't you turn the engine off and come up. We can have a chat.

– Get out!

– Come on! It's not my fault. I'm sorry if I spoke out of turn there but I figured you knew. Anyway if you can't handle it maybe you shouldn't be here.

– I told you to get out.

Germain struggles a bit but eventually swings his legs out onto the pavement and stands up.

– Good night!

He slams the front passenger door shut and goes to open the rear door to retrieve his crutches when Mary drives off. He gesticulates and calls after her but she's gone. He takes out his keys and shambles towards the lobby entrance, cursing.

39

1.30am.

Mary closes the door to her house. She's shaken, distraught. She throws her car keys onto the hall table and allows her coat to fall to the floor. She sits down on the stairs, her eyes blank, unfocussed. She tries to tease out the information offered up by Germain. Certain things make sense to her now: Sheila's decision to remove herself from Mary's life, her decision to have an affair with David, her decision to take him away from her. Whenever they had discussed David in the last week or so there had been a tone in her voice, a knowingness around what he was or wasn't capable of, an unacknowledged intimacy and regard, a kind of yearning or love. It was the one thing she had never believed Sheila capable of – duplicity, betrayal. They had known each other for half their lives; there was trust, there was an unspoken loyalty; at its best it was one of the closest friendships Mary had managed to foster, and now it was over. That one other person that you needed, that everyone needed to deliver truths of self to, to expose to, to listen to you, to support you intelligently if not unconditionally – was gone.

The lights were on upstairs. Sheila's car was outside. She was with Maurice now. Mary wondered if Sheila had ever truly been her friend. Mary was such a fool. Why did the same lesson have to be reinforced over and over again? The hope you held out for others, the faith you placed in them, betrayed, over and over again.

Smith gimps towards her from the living room and coils around her feet. They hadn't even had the decency to put Smith to bed in the back kitchen. No courtesy. She finds she doesn't even have a tolerance for the animal's fawning attentions and instinctively wants to push him aside too, but cannot. She picks him up and holds him close. She feels instantly tearful. She goes into the living room to turn the lights off.

The condition of the room shocks her. There are patches of blood on the sofa and on the floor, the armchairs tumbled over, and by the door a clump of blood-saturated hair. She picks it up and lets it fall again.

She understands and doesn't understand. Everything happens for a reason. She feels suddenly exhausted by the complexity of dishevelments in her life and space. Everything and everyone is at fault.

She walks upstairs as though tiptoeing through an alien environment. It no longer feels like a place she occupies and yet she is a part of its transgressive identity. She will go to bed and she will wake. She will go to work and she will return. Routines to normalise extremes. Patterns to revoke the chaotic. She knows how to survive, and that survival can be validated as its own revenge. Peace is concordant with nullity. This is desire. This is what she knows from the past and this is what she now returns to.

She steps on the blood spots and cancels them. On the landing she sees the toolbox she had used earlier and the sundered lock on the bathroom door. She stops briefly outside Sheila's room and hears muted voices inside. As she moves towards her own room the floorboards creek and her whole body trembles in expectation of a fall, as though the floorboards are a signal prelude to the abyss opening beneath her.

In her room she turns the key in the lock, pointlessly. The too-bright overhead light exposes the capsizing shabbiness of her room. She feels contained, empty, gross. Unable to take off her clothes, fearful of turning off the light, she crawls under the blankets and stares at a circlet of mould on the ceiling. The noises from next door become more intense. She can hear Maurice shouting, one defiling cluster of words after another. She listens too for Sheila's cries and hears them. She thinks of going up to the next floor to sleep, but she feels suddenly leaden, incapable.

She tries to withstand the noises, pressing her fingers against her ears, humming atonally, but there is an inner echo of the noise she cannot block.

She forces herself to get out of bed and places her eye beside the peephole. You can never cancel what you see, she thinks, though you can deny it. She can see Sheila kneeling on the floor, naked, her wrists tied by lengths of terrycloth to the end of the bedstead. The duvet has been pulled off and the lower sheet is stained in blood. Maurice is talking but she cannot see him. Then she sees him. He walks over until he's standing beside Sheila. He is wearing the blonde wig Mary had almost chosen to wear earlier that evening. His body is covered in shaving foam and as he continues to shave off his body hair, rinsing the razor periodically in a bowl of soapy water, he talks to her like a benign friend or guiding guru.

– Think of these moments Sheila as the most intense of your life, unforgettable moments, moments to be relished for what they are, always. I know that must seem strange to you, being asked to value intensity for its own sake, but I think in time you will realise that you have lived more completely in these past few hours than at any other point in your life, and that surely is a godsend. Life passes so unextraordinarily, we deserve the enrichment of drama. I say that as much for myself as for anyone else, this renews me, you renew me. It sounds like a love paean and it is. We are bonded in a way that so few are, in the finite joy of acts. When you think of your pain you must think of it as a vehicle to sublime self-realisation. That's how I think of it. Your pain purifies me. The imagination authors, and the mind wills the extremes of being that define us. In defining your memory I define myself. You know I didn't expect this clarity, when I thought of what it would feel like I thought there would be less poise, less control, these are the surprises of reality.

Sheila lifts her head up from the soiled sheets. She is barely recognisable, her skin broken, her face bruised and puffy. She manages to turn her head part way towards Maurice.

– I'm dying Maurice, I don't want to die. Please, please don't do this to me.

She urinates.

–You're just a fucking piss artist.

Maurice takes the baton and pushes it between her legs.

Mary cannot watch anymore.

She cannot tolerate the cries. She turns on the radio. It's an old disco hit by ABBA, *Waterloo*.

Through the walls, through the music, through the pain, Mary hears Sheila call out for her.

– Mary!

That's it, nothing more.

Perhaps she didn't hear anything. It might be that there was no cry.

She does nothing.

Perhaps there was nothing to hear.

Perhaps she will remember that she did nothing.

But another truth is that she did nothing to occasion this. She may not be fated to contradict this, or they may be fated to enact this. It comes down to what you can withstand, and witness, and survive.

Mary does nothing but she feels more entwined in it now. She is a presence in Sheila's consciousness. As audience to the pain she becomes conscience of the act.

The night wears on in interludes.

Mary lies on top of the bed, her body tucked up into a ball, her dress maddered in sweat. The horrific sounds, the imagined acts, have stopped. She thinks that whatever had to happen, has happened. It is over. The consequences are not hers to deal with. She is innocent. Then the doorbell rings. Her first thought is that the momentum of justice, the hammer weight of retribution has come, faster than anyone could have expected. The doorbell rings again and again and again. She gets up finally, her legs barely supporting her; she unlocks the door and clambers downstairs. Standing before the hall door, she imagines that when she opens it a river of water will flow through and carry everything away. She will be swamped. She will surrender. She clips the chain lock on and pulls the door back. It's Germain!

– Jesus! What happened to you? he asks.

Part of her hears the question, part of her understands, part of her wants to answer.

– What do you want?

– My crutches! You didn't hang around. I had to get a taxi here.

Mary is confused. She answers as though in a trance.

– They're in the car.

She grabs the keys off the hall rack.

There's a sudden scream from upstairs.

– What was that? You sure everything's okay?

– Here are the keys.

She lets them fall to the ground.

– Drop them in the letterbox when you're done.

– You mean you're not going to drive me home. The taxi's gone. What do you expect me to do?

– Mary closes the door and begins to make her way slowly back upstairs.

She hears Germain mutter *fucking bitch* a few times but it doesn't leave much of an impression. He bangs a couple of times on the hall doorframe, then stops.

40

Dawn breaks through the fog, pear-flesh light, light, relieving and new. Relief always comes in one form or another, it is an eventuality not predicated on anything. Mary stares at the window. A robin lands on the sill. She imagines for a moment that it was its mate that Smith killed. Now it too is alone. From the adjoining bedroom she hears the sound of Maurice levering himself off the bed. A few moments later the door opens and he goes downstairs. Mary gets up. The robin flits off. She pulls on her dressing down and unlocks her door. She listens for movement downstairs but can hear nothing. She hugs the wall and hovers outside Sheila's door. She knocks. Why would she knock?

There is no reply. What does she expect? For a moment she thinks about returning to her own room. This is their business. She has no right. Then she opens the door to Sheila's room and enters. The curtains are drawn. Her eyes adjust. The blood is hard to discern at first but it is everywhere, even on the walls. With Sheila's blood Maurice has scrawled over and over the words:

The RAPIST
THERAPIST
The Rapist
TheRapist
The Rapist

T
h
e
r
a
P
i
s

Therapist
TheRAPIST
THE RAPIST
The RAPist
THE RAPIST

Sheila remains slumped and tied to the bedpost. Mary kneels down beside her and runs her hand over her hair. She becomes aware that Sheila is breathing. She is alive. Mary unties the bonds around Sheila's wrists and allows her to slump into her lap. Sheila manages to open one of her eyes. She feels small in Mary's arms, dwindled almost to nothing. Mary draws a sheet over her body. She whispers to her.

– You shouldn't have taken David away from me. I don't understand why you would do that.

Sheila turns her face towards Mary. Her voice when it comes feels ancient, childlike.

– Mary… he's going to kill me. Help… me!

Mary cradles her face.

– Don't you feel any remorse? I trusted you.

Mary gets to her feet and helps Sheila to a sitting position on the bed. She gives her a sip of water from the glass on the bedside table.

– I told you he was sick. But you wouldn't listen.

Sheila's hand pressures Mary's leg.

– For God's sake Mary!

Mary gets her to her feet and begins to guide her towards the door.

She picks up the onyx knife lying on the vanity beside the basin of water full of Maurice's body hair. They make it down the first set of steps to the landing. Mary can see the car keys on the hall floor underneath the letterbox. Mary's whole body is adrenalated and hugely attuned to hear the slightest noise from downstairs. She expects Maurice to appear at any moment. They make it to the bottom of the stairs. They're almost there. It doesn't have to descend into madness. Things are retrievable. Everything can be cleansed and rectified.

They are inching their way towards the hall door when Maurice suddenly appears.

He is holding two cups of tea.

– Mary what do you think you're doing?

He puts the cups down on the hall table.

He looks at Sheila and touches her face gently.

– I was just making Sheila a cup of tea. Poor thing looks

like she could really do with one. She's completely tuckered out, don't you think? I'm sorry I didn't make one for you. I thought you were asleep.

– Sheila has to go, Maurice. She's not afraid anymore.

Maurice looks at Mary.

– I can't believe that. So soon!

He sniffs around them like a dog.

– I'm sure I can smell some fear.

There's a kind of laughter in his voice.

– MAYBE…maybe it's you Mary.

He sniffs around her. Mary braces herself. He turns to Sheila.

– So you're not afraid anymore! I think you are, and remember the only way to get rid of fear is through pain. I have told you that, haven't I? You have to ride roughshod through your pain and it *is* painful but in the end you'll find release from it. But you're right in a way; you're nearly there.

He turns to Mary.

– Now, let go of her.

Mary holds on.

– I said let go of her.

– No. We're leaving.

She slashes Maurice across his right arm and chest with the knife. It's like a kind of magic. Blood forms in the slash line and begins to seep down.

He half pirouettes and slumps against the wall. Mary leans down and picks up the keys. She has one hand on the door lock, the other arm around Sheila, and then all she feels is Sheila being wrenched from her, and a fist pummelling her stomach. She doubles over and crumples to the floor. He pulls back his foot and kicks her again and again. Then he turns to Sheila and lifts her into his blood-soaked arms like a baby. Mary watches as he walks upstairs; she hears the door close and lock.

Mary wanders back up stairs. She sits by her vanity. The noises from the next-door room reach a kind of crescendo, a whirlwind of thuds and slaps. Mary takes her dark bobbed wig and fixes it on. She applies her make-up carefully, deep red lipstick, eyeliner, mascara. She hums a song as she does so, a simple nursery rhyme in a childlike voice.

Miss Polly had a dolly who was sick sick sick
So she called for the doctor to come quick quick quick
The doctor came with her bag and her hat
And she knocked on the door with a rat a-tat tat
She looked at the dolly and she shook her head
Then she said Miss Polly put her straight to bed

Mary wakes having slept a little. She feels initially disorientated as though she is conscious of being within time but not alive within it. She touches her stomach, remembers, and wonders if perhaps one of her ribs is broken. But there is nothing you can do about ribs, just like there is nothing you can do about so many things.

41

Dressed in a tailored blue suit Mary gathers some loose papers together on the dining room table and places them in her briefcase. She returns to the kitchen and prepares a breakfast tray for two, some warmed rolls, pats of butter, local blueberry jam which she heaps into a glass bowl and into which she settles a tiny silver mustard spoon. She makes a silver teapot of fresh tea and, unable to remember whether either of them takes sugar she decides to put a small bowl of brown sugar beside the jam. As a final touch she goes outside into the garden and from her one rosebush snips a petrified yellow rosebud and places it in a narrow glass stem vase in the centre of the tray. Perfect! The night was terrible but it's over now. She takes the tray and goes upstairs. She knocks on the door. No answer.

– Are you two lovebirds awake yet? You kept me awake half the night, what with the noise you made. Anyway some of us have to go to work. I'll leave the breakfast here. You can get it in your own time. Cheerio now. See you later.

She pauses for a moment as though trying to remember something.

– O Sheila, can you give Smith something to eat around midday. Thanks a mill! Bye!

42

Mary drives along by the river front on the Brooklyn side near where the little girl lives. It is as though she has been unconsciously directed here, to this place of recondite normality.

Mary watches as the little girl comes out of the house, pushing her little pink bike, followed by her father who lifts her onto the saddle and kisses her on the forehead. He waves to her as she cycles off slowly down the footpath. When he has closed the door Mary starts up the engine and purrs alongside the little girl. Mary tries to remember her name but cannot. The little girl notices the car and in noticing loses concentration and wobbles a bit. Mary pulls into the kerb further up and stops. She gets out.

– Hi! Do you remember me?

The little girl looks up at her but doesn't stop her slow pedalling.

– Don't tell me you don't remember me?

– You're the lady in the car.

– That's right. My name's Mary. What's yours?

– I'm not meant to talk to…

– …Strangers? I'm hardly a stranger. Your Daddy knows who I am. Come on, you can tell me your name!

– Susan.

– What grade are you in Susan?

– Second.

– And who's your best friend?

– Jane.

– I saw your Daddy saying goodbye. He looks nice. He must love you a lot.

The little girl looks at her nervously.
– Did you get the chocolates?
–Yes.
– Is your bike ok?
– It's ok.
–We'll have to get you a new one, your Daddy and me.
Susan is clearly anxious.
– I have to go.
She cycles off.
– I'll be late for school.
Mary calls after her.
– I'm sure I'll be this way again. Maybe I'll see you.
Susan is joined by other kids on their way to school.
– Maybe we can be friends. Mary mutters to herself.

Mary continues to look at Susan as she disappears from view. She feels tearful yet resents the emotion.

– Damn! she says. Damn!

She returns to the car, writes out a cheque for two hundred, slips it into an envelope with her business card and drops it in the letterbox of the house.

43

Mary waits in the anteroom to Dr Lavender's rooms. There's a man sitting opposite who attends one of the other therapists. He worries a small blue thread falling from his suit button. He breaks it off then obsessively puts it in his mouth. I'm obscurely fucking sick, is what everyone's body language proclaims. Mary feels sick, like her real sickness is beginning to expose itself in her body. Her real sickness! What does that mean? Who names it for her, who names it for her if not herself? Here she is, after how many years of working through her selves, and what is she left with? She imagines all of the talk, all of the spewed-out talk gathered in a hairball bolus in her stomach, she wants suddenly to retch it up, finger it loose, and cast it aside. She has the courage for that, they all think she doesn't have the courage for that, the courage to come into her true life, to walk through the shadows, to stand unsupported, to walk unhindered to the wrested safety of her own selfhood, but she has. There is a space somewhere isn't there, where she can stand alleviated. She imagines her body in a desert, a light wind, the sun, her feet becoming as dust in the dust, her desiccating life flaking to a kind of mergence and subsumation. One death, another life. Another life, another death. Maybe you shouldn't feel so responsible. It all passes. All of the life, all of the pain.

The man opposite tries to say something then doesn't.

He never tries to say anything, why does he bother now?

Then he says – *It's a beautiful day isn't it?*

It's a beautiful day isn't it? echoes Mary to herself. But it isn't a beautiful day. He's beginning with a lie. He's beginning as he means to go on. Or is he thinking of something else?

What kind of day is he thinking of. Why would he say something untrue so casually? Does he mean, *it's a beautiful day* isn't it! Beautiful day isn't it! *Beautiful day Beautiful! Beautiful isn't beautiful, isn't beautiful, isn't beautiful....* She can't stop it. The noise! Just noise, or was it just...

Mary has forgotten that she hasn't responded. There is nothing to respond to. She forgets that she has forgotten to respond. She watches Dr Lavender's door. A woman will come out any moment now. Then her turn. She thinks of how she will begin. She cannot imagine how she will begin. Perhaps there will be no beginning as such. She tries to remember where they left off. They left off at what they left out. What did they leave out? They left out what they didn't know, knowing they would return to it, to what they knew they didn't know, some day. It was like that, they said, you returned to what you knew but didn't know, or didn't know you knew, some day. She tries to stop the noise but it's like trying to stop. But you cannot just stop, you cannot just stop the life, not by thinking you can't. You can't just think yourself stopped, it doesn't work like that, or maybe it works like that, or it works like that and you get to a different kind of end. She looks to her side for her bag of accoutrements.

The door opens. The woman passes by. Dr Lavender nods to Mary, anoints her with his eyes, ushers her in.

He closes the door and takes her coat. Always the gentleman.

– How are you today Mary?

Why does he have to start with such a big question? There's a smaller question somewhere. You'd think he could find it. He's so clever you'd think he could find a little bitty question, just to get things rolling, but no, he has to start with the biggest question of all. I'm sick of it, I'm sick of answering the big questions over and over. Doesn't anybody understand that?

–You seem absorbed Mary.

Absorbed. Absolved.

– I'm here aren't I?

– Yes you are. Take a seat. I have some Rescue Remedy here. Would you like to take some?

– No.
– I think you should take some.
She takes the dropper full of liquid.
– Would you like some water?
He goes over to the sink and fills a tumbler with water.
He sits down and strokes his beard.
– So, tell me about your week.
She imagines his beard hairs up against her cunt, his tongue slipping in.
– *My* week! It's funny to think of me being in possession of something.
– As against…
– Not being in possession of anything or being possessed.
– Stay with that. Who possesses you?
– I don't know.
– Is it Sally, or your father?
– Just because they're dead? My mother is dead too.
– Well, do you want to include your mother in that?
– No.
– Do you think about Sally?
– No.
– Think about Sally. I think you're losing touch with Sally and that's having an effect on you.
– Sally's dead.
– Is she?
– You know she is.
– The real Sally is but you know we agreed that some of the things you say seem to be in Sally's voice.
– I don't believe that anymore.
– You don't believe it or you don't want to believe it?
– I don't think it's true.
– What do you think is true?
– I don't think this is getting me anywhere?
– Where do you want to be?
– Where that isn't a question anymore.
– And how do you do that?
– I'm not to blame for what happens.
– What happens?

– People die.

– Mary I'd like to do a visualisation with you and within the visualisation I'd like you to focus on Sally. Can you do that for me? Perhaps if you'd lie on the couch.

Mary walks over to the couch. She picks up a tack from the floor and hands it to Dr Lavender.

– That could have been dangerous, he says.

She lies down then jack-knifes forwards almost immediately.

– Is something the matter?

– There's a smell of cologne!

– Relax! I'll get another one.

He goes to a cupboard on the opposite side of the room and pulls out another pillow and casing. He takes the old pillow and cover slip and puts them in a cupboard by the door.

– That better?

Mary lies down. Dr Lavender puts on a CD of gentle mood music.

– Listen to my voice. Relax into the rhythm of my voice. Feel it wash over you and carry you out to a deeper place. Visualise the scene I'm going to suggest. Be within it, carry it forward.

It's a beautiful sunny day. You're walking along a road. There's no one about but you can feel the warm sun on your skin. You walk for a long time, longer than you've ever walked before. You might have been walking all your life to get to this point. You are alone but you are not afraid. There is something or someone on the horizon. I want you to walk towards that point.

Mary doesn't pick up at first. The music plays on.

– You're right, the sun is warm. I've been walking for such a long time to get to this place. Blue sky, distant sea, no clouds. On either side of me are fields of corn and wheat. I can barely see over. I stretch out my hand and run my fingers through the stalks. I listen to the dry stalks rustle. Further on in a yellow field is a huge oak tree. I think about going over but I think I have been there before and there is no need to go there again. I continue to follow the road. It turns into a dirt track. If a car was on this, I think, it would raise clouds of dust, clouds of red dust. The dirt track rises upwards to a cliff face on the edge of the ocean. Now that I look in the dirt I can see there are tyre tracks and further up on the edge of the cliff a car. It is a red car with shiny hubcaps. I can hear the cries of a baby or a child. When I reach the car I can see there is a child inside strapped into a baby chair on the back seat. There's no mammy, no daddy. The car is on a slope not far from where the grass ends. The little girl doesn't stop crying when I try to shush her. I don't know why I don't lift her out but I don't. I can see her bottle on the driver's seat but the door is locked. I go around the other side and get in the passenger side. As I'm reaching for the bottle my knee cranks the handbrake off and then we're rolling. I look at the kid, but there's nothing I can do. I can't save her. I can only save myself. I say something to the kid, or want to, but nothing comes out. I fall out and tumble along by the wheels for a bit, thinking I'm going to be crushed by them. I'm sitting on my bum when the car goes over the cliff. It's like I'm watching a film. I can't hear the cries any more. I guess it's over. I can't find the track any more so I walk through the yellow field of rape to the oak tree. There's a man sitting underneath I don't recognise. He asks me why I killed the little girl. But I don't know the answer. He tells me that her life was the better life. He tells me I will be burdened until I die, no matter what. Then he vanishes and so does the tree. I can't imagine which is the right way to go to get me back to where I should be, so I lie down amongst the rape and stare at the sky until it clouds.

Mary begins to hum a little song.

– Mary did you recognise the little girl? Was it Sally?

– No not Sally.

– Was it you?

– No not me.

– Where is Sally?

– Asleep.

– Is she dreaming?

– No dreams only nightmares.

– Can she hear the sea?

– She can hear it crash.

– And your memory?

– Is full of blood.

– And your pain?

– Is all scrunched up.

– And your fear?

– My fear is for myself. I'm afraid I'm going to die.

– We're all going to die. Why are you afraid to die?

– I'm afraid of who will be waiting.

– Who will be waiting?

– Maurice.

– Mary, open your eyes. Mary have you been seeing Maurice? Is there something between you? Are you lovers?

– How can you say that? He hates me.

44

Mary sits on a high barstool at the end of a long mahogany counter. It's not a place she's been in before. She feels anonymous. That's okay. She's not drunk although drunk is maybe where she wants to be. She orders another double whiskey on the rocks and a bottle of still water. The barwoman is one of those women with *personality*. She tops up the double with a little extra for good measure and slides a bowl of nuts and crackers in front of her. Mary offers to buy her a drink.

–Thanks hon, I'll put it on your tab and have it later. Gotta keep a clear head! You need anything, you just shout.

She goes off to serve someone else.

The place begins to fill with a mixture of arty and business types and a group of women she figures are nurses; some of them look like Filipinas. Mary picks up one of the newspapers from a table underneath a painting of a small woman with a black dog in a green landscape. She brings the newspaper back to the counter and turns to the crossword, which has been partly filled in. She has some idea that she should keep her mind sharp. Only a few days ago she had read though a list of ten exercises to help keep your memory intact. She tries to recall them now but can't. There it was, the slippage you had to watch! Next thing you'd be forgetting your favourite, your favourite…… Then she remembers one, imagine walking around a known space. She thinks about doing that. She does that, closes her eyes, blocks out the bustle of the bar, takes a step into the dining room, feels the shiny wallpaper by the light switch, the long sideboard with the large yellow bowl resting on an antique doilie. She tries to see the scene on the bowl, church spires behind a copse of trees, and around the circular rim at the base of the bowl an iron ring that must have secured it to a wall at another time. She returns to the crossword and fills in the remaining gaps.

Discharged a debt. *Paid*

It's cast when light is blocked. *Shadow*

Broke free, got away. *Escaped*

Soulful or amorous idealist. *Romantic*

She tires of it quickly but finishes it nonetheless. What does it prove? It doesn't prove anything. But you have to prove something, day in, day out, or you lose out to yourself, lose yourself to yourself, lose your future to your past. She's *capable*. Wasn't that what Sheila had said? *One of the most professional people I know*. Better not to think about that.

She wonders who was sitting here before her, who will sit here after her, the lives, all of the lives that start and span and blur. Being. Being like this. Being like everybody else, that's ok. That'd be ok. Like everybody else. Everybody. The whole slam dunk body of souls that squeeze through the hoop. Day in, day out. Forged like everybody else through muck and blood. Here I am just like everybody else, having a drink after a hard day, unwinding, winding down. We all get sprung way too tight and for what? For no good reason, for no good reason that's what! Just jettison the bad stuff, jettison the day, let it go. Unwind and let yourself go.

She takes a swig of her drink. She imagines being in a soundproofed room, screaming, her throat opened, the big pipe down to her belly opened right up, not just words, sounds, like the sound of her mother crying, the sound of the windbreak, the sound of skin scales falling, sound of the word *stupid*, hardest word of all. She goes quiet after that.

There's not much to think about really. It's better that way. When you think of the things you want to think about, there's not that much, a few ugly thoughts, a few less-ugly thoughts, how the rain sounds against tin, how people fail in sadness and despair.

She orders another drink. She feels a little sloppy, but that's ok. There's a memory of her in the desert somewhere, the sand lifted up into a high stratum, a scarf pulled round her face, the delicious lacerations of her legs and arms. She felt like she was being eroded to nothing, she remembers that, blown to whiteness by the wind. There's a song echo. She begins to hum it in her head as soon as she thinks it.

She's aware of someone beside her, closer than you'd expect, closer than you'd like, sometimes. It stays like that for a long time, closer than you'd expect but nothing more, no chat, no move. She eye-checks the person. It's a woman in a pink dress, good figure, beautiful figure, talking to a man, a colleague. Mary guesses that he's not that special friend. Just the snippets of conversation or the body stuff tell that tale. Then the woman turns to Mary and says,

– Looks like you're hanging one on there sister?

– Gotta get happy, says Mary, in a drunken imitation of her tone.

– So aside from the booze what makes you happy?

– Cats. Katzz!

– That's it?

– You got something better?

– Everyone's got something better than that sister! I'll show you something better.

– O Yeah!

– Why don't you follow me into the rest room?

– Why would I do that?

– Because you're a thrill-seeker.

She touches Mary's arm just above the wrist.

– Don't be long now.

Mary watches her move, her legs, her ass, her class. She figures she won't follow, then she follows. She makes a poor job of slipping off the stool but she's OK once she hits the floor. She gestures to the barwoman to fill her drink and the one beside, finally holding up two separated fingers. She bounces her way to the toilets and has to take a moment to figure out the symbols. She gets it right first time. There you go. Pink dress is in the last cubicle of four, down by the end wall beside the hand dryer. There's another woman washing her hands. She dries them and leaves.

Mary wobbles a little as she looks at the pink dress with her back to her, a few lines of coke spliced out on the china top of the loo. Pink dress does a line then invites Mary to do the same. When the four lines are done the two women lean back against the walls of the cubicle heads lofted upwards as though witnessing something in ascension. The pink dress stretches out a hand and rubs Mary's left breast.

– Hmmm you've gone hard right away!

She runs her hand down and inside Mary's blouse. She puts her hands on Mary's other breast and pinches the nipple. She opens the pearl buttons and Mary's blouse flaps loose.

–You're beautiful!

She eases Mary's breasts out of her lace-frilled bra and begins to stridulate her turgid nipples. Mary feels it in her groin, the soft heat, the drugs, the booze, the scent of sex, the alien risk. The pink dress puts her hands on Mary's ass, tethering her nipples with her teeth, stretching them with her lips, pulling them off. Mary feels like they are going to burst, to ooze. The pink dress runs her hand under Mary's skirt and strikes her panties down.

– O I need to piss, says Mary. Fuck!

– Go ahead, do it for me, do it standing. Go on!

Mary steps out of her knickers and straddles the bowl. The pink dress hoists Mary's skirt up around her waist and watches as she squirts out the water in a dribbly stream. She doesn't let her dry herself but gets down on her knees and licks her, then licks her until she's wet again, her thumb in her cunt, the tip of her tongue teasing and flicking until she comes. Mary can hear some women in the other cubicles. The pink dress keeps fucking her with her tongue. She begins to feel queasy, not sick exactly, just overwhelmingly lost and unsecured. She becomes conscious of her disorientation, of a slippage of self she wants to retrieve. There is an urgency to flee, to fill her lungs with air, to clarify in space, to get out of this enclosed space. She pushes the woman's face away and looks for her panties. The woman in the next cubicle bangs on the partition wall. She can see her panties. She reaches for them and falls against the toilet bowl. She leaves them be and gets to her feet.

– What the fuck are you doing?

Mary flaps down her skirt and fuddles with the bolt on the door.

She runs, almost slipping on the wet tiles and stumbles out into the bar. She leaves some money on the counter beside the fresh drinks, grabs her bag and leaves. She runs into the coiled darkness of the city, running undestined, lost.

45

The river is the dark flow, a slow remorseless energy, carrying the unfiltered dirt streaming into it from lives eradicating in rooms, lives submitting to the inevitable, submitting to the calamity of being, to the attenuated life infinitely erasing, to the river carrying away the dross and deeply dying things of the world.

Mary looks down into the river from one of the high stress beams of the Brooklyn Bridge She stands on the edge of a platform overhanging the eddies and currents of muscled water. This is a just and necessary moment, this partuition, this separation. Every moment is a once, every once a moment of complete appraisal.

How many times can you do this? How many times can you approach an end, and fail your question, fail yourself. How many times can you fail to carry out the sanctioned act?

Mary stands on the platform, she imagines her life in the river, the river in her blood and bones, she draws close to the idea of correspondences in existence, people and things perfectly matched and mirrored. She cries, seeing herself as author and reader of the realities she has invented, the clotted auguries that have gathered since childhood, clusters of them now rising to wreck her. She takes off her coat and places it and her purse in a neat pile. She can hear the abysmal traffic on either side of the river and shallow voices on a far corner. She takes off her red shoes and finds an easy footing in the wrought-iron railing. She thinks she will be able to stand with her narrow feet on the topmost rail and balance momentarily, to stand in the ultimate moment of her life, caught between what is known and what is unknown, finally commandeering her life, orchestrating its quiescence.

But she is never in the moment completely, each moment is evasive, and the present of the moment is a memory of the past, the pink dress tongue, the toilet, the road, the oak tree, *stupid* and worse than *stupid*, fault and hate and love's negation. She never gets to stand, never achieves that moment of alleviating lightness, of acceptance, of surrender, of hope regained in the moment of relinquishment. No sooner has she placed her foot on the narrow ridge than her foot slips and skews and she falls achingly puppet-like downwards. The fall is like no other, it is a fall of staged stations of causality and clarity. For a moment she becomes her mother, her head blown asunder, particle to the particle world made mergence. The water when the water meets her makes a place for her. Some things accept you willingly, without obstruction, without resistance, places it would never have occurred to you that you would find a place, you find your place. She swims or she does not swim, she scrambles hopelessly. Then there are another slew of moments to decide within, there is an ease to claim, a final rapture to actively surrender to. This she does. Her arms stop moving and her body follows, and her breath follows that. The taste of the water is the taste of darkness and orange light; she imagines it mixing with her blood and with her spirit. She is lost in a transport of passivity and inundation. This is how it was meant to be. It is how it unfolds but it is not how it ends. She becomes aware of a halo of yellow light.

Mother of divine mercy. Mother of perpetual suffering.

Arms from behind, from underneath, her breath lost and regained, then the tug, the pull, the striving, the halo around the body, the body aboard the surface, the voices from the ether calling, the river holding on.

Lover of perpetual patience

Lover of divine justice

– I've got her!

– Pull her in!

– Someone call an ambulance!

A young man pulls her in towards slime-strewn steps. The

other young man swims alongside her. They labour between them to get her to the top of the steps and lay her out on the wooden balustrade running parallel to the river wall. One of the young men kisses her and blows, kisses her and blows, kisses her and blows. Whose breath is it now she breathes? A different breath, a different life. She vomits some water and then some booze and enzyme-degraded crackers. Someone retrieves her coat and shoes and purse. It has happened or it hasn't happened, she is where she is, where she was before, she is the same or she is changed.

–The ambulance will be here in a few minutes, one of the young men assures her.

– I'm okay, she says, I don't need an ambulance.

She has a memory of the fire and of the ambulance that took her away from the burning building, the water, the fire, the silence she has retained within herself ever since.

She does not thank them. There is nothing to thank them for. She walks away. One of them grabs her arm.

– Lady, you need help.

She looks at him, his blue eyes, his soaking clothes, his youthful propriety, his dutiful conscience.

– I don't need anyone's help.

She slips loose and does not look back.She walks down some side streets and out onto the main avenue which runs diagonally across towards Flatbush. She hears the ambulance in the distance, the awful drone, the hysteria and lights, and feels that she has escaped something at least.

46

She walks until her clothes are dry. She hears the bells of a remote church and walks towards them. It appears for a moment like a destination but it is not, it is merely a spur that prods her on, so she goes on, being in movement in lieu of not being in movement, being or not being, without choice. She evades the shopfront streets and walks north through the fog, through streets of four-storeyed apartment buildings, the lights in ground floor sitting rooms ablaze, or else flickering with the blue-white light of TVs through nylon curtains. When she passes the corner shop, now closed, where she bought the chocolates, she is aware – in a way she has no wish to be – of where she is. She crosses the street and stands outside the ground floor window of Susan and her father's block. She stops and peers in. Like almost every other apartment the TV is on. Susan is there in her pj's and in her father's arms. Both of them asleep on the green sofa. Mary has no memory of anything like this, but she has a yearning for it. She imagines being small, creeping in, crawling up beside them, curling up in their warmth and peace. She feels the fog on her face, the wetness of the night, the unassailability of loss, the ridicule in expectation. She walks away from it because she has no place in it. Part of her believes it is what she wants most, what she would have wanted most, with David. With David there was a signal hope, a possible life, the dreamed for magic of a child-compounded love.

At the bottom of the street she turns a corner and almost collides with a cluster of boys, all boys she thinks initially though there is a girl amongst them. They block her path. They meet her out of the blue and block her path. Why would they do that, why would they block her path? One of them slaps her coat.

– Fanceee!

–Would you like that Jess? he says to no one in particular but presumably to the girl.

– Hey boys will we do her?

–What the fuck, we may as well.

Just like that they whack her up against the wall.

– Mind the fucking coat! That's Jess's.

– I don't want it, says Jess.

One of them has his face pressed up against Mary's. His breath smells sweet, Chinese sweet-and-sour sweet. His hands are on her breasts, mauling them roughly. The only thing Mary can think of is that this is what she deserves. These kids are merely instruments. She brought this on herself. She is to blame. No one else. At those points at which she resists, she resists merely as a reactive, unstoppable physical gesture. She doesn't really care what they do to her, certainly nothing more than she wanted to do to herself. Although at least in that instance the beauty of it, and there was a potential beauty in it, was that it was a transfiguring act, an act to give her final purchase on life before her relinquishment of it.

– She's a fucking ride. Look at her; she doesn't care what the fuck I do to her. Let's fucking ride the fuck out of her.

– Leave her alone, says Jess.

–You can watch, Jess, maybe learn a fucking thing or two! This old bitch has been at it for years. You know all the tricks, don't you sweetheart!

He levers his knee up into her groin.

Mary can't help but smile. There's an echo of Maurice, the same gesture, the same hardness, was it this morning, yesterday morning? These are the framing symmetries.

They drag her down to a vacant lot. There are bottles strewn everywhere and some flattened cardboard boxes.

– I'm fucking leaving! says Jess.

–You're not fucking leaving, says one of the others, maybe her boyfriend.

–Take off your fucking coat.

Mary takes it off.

One of them hands it to Jess.

Mary is cast down on the cardboard. She is lost in a memory of falling.

– Why is she so fucking calm? asks one of them.

– Maybe she fucking likes this. Do you like this bitch?

The main guy opens his jeans and pulls out his dick. He pumps it a few times to get it hard.

– Look at that ! he says, acclaiming his manhood.

He straddles her and pulls up her skirt.

– For fuck's sake she doesn't even have any fucking panties on? Are you on the game?

Mary doesn't answer.

– Are you? he shouts.

Mary doesn't answer.

– Get the fuck on with it, says someone else.

He sticks his fingers into her, then his prick. He's finished in no time. They take her in turns. Mary's feels like she's bleeding semen.

When it's over they take the money from her purse and throw the rest aside. Jess throws the coat on top of her and rejoins the group. They vanish.

She continues to lie on the crumpled wet cardboard. She finds herself wishing she could see the stars, a small transport of lights, a world of worlds, a beyond to this, the quiet mystery of aeons and space she might appeal to. She picks herself up and wipes herself with a piece of newspaper. The cold banality of it all. She imagines the unimportant narrative of what just happened. It has happened a millions times before and will a million times again. The real strength, she thinks, probably comes in the imagination courted for survival. Maybe this will survive as part of her true story, her best self.

She walks across the lot. Why has she survived this night? There has been no guile in her survival, no real wish. Out of nowhere her legs break beneath and she falls to her knees. Crawl. Why? If your legs won't carry you, crawl. She crawls to the nearest wall and heaves herself up by a windowsill. She walks small step by small step until she reaches the illuminated corner. Without thinking what she is doing or why she is doing it she finds herself knocking incessantly on Susan and her father's front door. Bang! Bang! Bang! She can hear him coming down the hallway.

– What's with all the racket?

When he opens the door and sees her, his eyes perform a complex diagnostic, and all that he intuits in the moment is instantaneously graded. At the limit of this narrative lies the only question anyone can ask.

– My god! What happened to you?

He draws her inside. Susan is there, woken but sleepy, standing by the doorjamb to the living room.

– Susan, go to bed, there's a good girl.

– What's the matter with her Daddy?

– Off to bed now, the lady's had a mishap.

Susan wanders down to the end of the corridor, stopping half way to watch her father guide the woman into the kitchen.

– I'll be there in a few minutes to tuck you in.

He settles Mary in the kitchen armchair and puts the kettle on.

– Would a cup of tea help?

It's not really a question. He simply needs an activity, something to give him a moment to compose himself.

– You shouldn't have dropped in that check this morning. There was no need. The bike is fine.

Mary just sits there.

– You look as though you're in shock. Should I call someone for you?

Not for the first time Mary knows that there is no one to call, though she cannot deny that she thinks of David, but there is no one, not anymore.

– Were you mugged?

Even he knows it is a stratagem by which to take cover rather than an appeal for the truth. He has no right to the truth nor does he really seek it.

– Whatever I can do, he says. Do you need to get to the hospital, we could go to the emergency at *Brooklyn Hospital*, or to the police?

– No, no one please.

– Would you like to go home?

– They took my money too.

Funny that it's the *too* that tells him more than almost anything else.

– I can give you some money that's not a problem. You don't have your car?

She shakes her head.

– What would you like to do?

Mary just sits there. Then as he puts a cup of strong tea on the table beside her, she asks,

– Can I stay, please?

He's taken aback. He hadn't expected that. Why would she want to stay? She's got to feel vulnerable. Why would she want to stay in a stranger's house? It makes him suspicious of her.

– I live alone. I can't think of anyone I could go to right now, not in this state. Do you understand?

– I understand. If you want to have a hot bath? You're sure you don't want to go to the police. I mean if anything really bad happened tonight and evidence is needed, well…

His sentence trails off.

– Do you understand?

– I just want to get clean.

– But you need to take precautions.

– I will.

– Drink your tea, I'll run the bath.

He turns at the door.

– I'm afraid we've only two bedrooms. You can take my room. I'll change the sheets. I can sleep on the sofa.

– No, *please*. The sofa is fine for me.

There is no room for polite discussion around this. He simply accepts what she says.

– Okay.

As he closes the door, she thinks, the wish I least expected to be answered has been answered.

47

On the taxi ride home in the morning she feels like a woman in evasion from her life. Home! She has an idea or idealisation of what it constitutes in the abstract, she is no different from anyone else in that, but the home she returns to now is a confusion of people and happenings. It is not real. She thinks about Sheila, though she cannot really think about Sheila.

She thinks back to earlier that morning. She had woken in the tiny room with its clutter of photographs on the mantelpiece, its cheap furniture, its threadbare carpet, the smell of decency, the sanctity and security of it all. She had gone in to him in the kitchen after she had heard him moving about. The table was set for three and she ate her bowl of cornflakes with them both. All of the conversation focused on Susan. It was easier that way. And then he had given Mary some money and wished her well.

– Take good care of yourself.

She had felt in that moment a kind of mournfulness for the generosities placed before her, for his decency. He had a certainty about the life he inhabited. She envied him that certainty, that sense of a confirmed self. When she left she expressed her thanks and meant it.

The taxi pulls up outside Mary's house.

The lights throughout the house are still on. Hilda Wobbe is outside sweeping up in front of her building. Mary pays the taxi and tries to make it to the door unseen.

– Hey Mary! Mary! You got a minute for Hilda?

Mary stops dead, impaled.

Hilda crosses the street and stands facing her, sweeping brush in hand.

–You come home now?

–Yes.

– I thought you got a problem. Lights on all last night. Whole house all lighted up. That a waste!

– I must have forgotten to turn them off before I left.

–Your car wasn't der. It was strange. I going to call police. I knock on door, no answer but all these lights and I sure people inside, maybe that woman who come and go. I don't know so I figure I wait, see what happens.

– Ok thanks Hilda, I'll turn off the lights.

–You want I come in for cup of coffee?

– Some other time Hilda, please.

– Okay, no problem, I go now.

Mary opens the door and it feels like another life she is returning to, or not even a life, the after-image of a life. She half-expects everything behind the door to have an illusory quality, a shape-shifting insubstantiality, a mirror room of memories, a phantasm of rooms and decors that will persist for a moment then vanish. She will see its alter reality – white rooms, architectural space, enormous windows, light and shade, points of colour, roses in voluminous clear glass vases, beauty, elegance, peace.

She opens the door and her breath passes from her.

Blood and more blood, blood everywhere, on the stairs, pools of it on the hallway floor, streaks of it on the skirting rail, smudges on the walls. She turns away from it. It is all too much. More than anyone should have to stand, more than anyone can withstand. She remains trapped by the patch of clean space by the door. Unable to move, her eyes remain closed against the reality, her mind manifesting worse realities. She hears Smith's mewling come from one of the rooms. She calls him and he comes prancing out, sidestepping the bigger pools, dragging other bits with his paws. She picks him up and holds him close, leaning with her back against the door, wanting to scream. She should leave but she cannot without naming the truth of what has happened, or naming her part, or subtracting her part from the horror. As she walks down the long corridor to the kitchen a droplet of blood falls through the ceiling above. She screams, wipes it away, then wipes her hand on her jacket. She stops, then walks on. She can see Maurice dressed in his police uniform sitting at the kitchen table looking out on the yard, on the over-spilling garbage bins, the wormery, and patchy winter grass. The kitchen is full of steam from a continuously boiling kettle set on the hob. She should leave. For some reason she doesn't want to die here, or die here maybe but not by his hand, by anyone's hand but not his. She finds her voice and pushes it out like a projectile of vomit.

– Maurice, what have you done?

There is no answer. Perhaps there will never be an answer. She can concede that. She just wants it to be over, to be different. She turns the hob off and the steam subsides. The room begins to clarify. She places her hand on his shoulder and shakes him. Her voice breaks.

– Answer me Maurice. What have you done?

The head flips backwards, the whole throat cut, the gaping sluice gate of her life, cut back to the spinal bone.

– O my god! Sheila! O fuck! O god no!

She looks at her, Sheila's eyes cast open, her battered face, her lipstick-smeared mouth, her neck cleavered, her trachea like an animal's gut exposed.

Smith tries to jiggle from her arms. She holds him closer than she has ever held him. She walks amnesiac-like into the dining room and crouches down in the corner, rocking rhythmically, back and forth, rocking into a mindless, eyeless, blank, forgetful present.

It is mid-afternoon before she begins to slow her rocking down, conscious or alert in the moment as to what she must do. She forces herself to return to the kitchen and pulls a knife from a drawer. She returns to the dining room and pushes Smith away. She takes the serrated steak knife and draws it over and back across her wrist wearing the skin down, cutting the little veins, the bigger veins. She repeats it on her other wrist.

It is evening when she wakes, her veins clotted over, the blood flowing freely through them. She feels the pain.

She takes the knife and moves out into the hallway and up the stairs. She can kill the thing. She has done it before. The door to Sheila's room is open. She enters. Maurice is there sitting on the bed dressed in some of Sheila's clothes, combing a wig of long red hair taken from Mary's stand. The room is the same as it was before, the blood-scrawled words, the soiled sheets, the pools of dried blood between bed and door. When he sees her he begins to cry. Mary stands looking at him for the longest time. She puts the knife in her pocket. Her voice when it comes is almost soft.

– Why did you do that Maurice?

– It was hurting me, says Maurice. Maybe it didn't mean to but it was really hurting me. I had to stop it.

She sees he is lost. How can you kill a thing that isn't there?

– I'm going to phone your mother. Maurice, listen to me, I'm going to phone your mother. You have to go.

– Excuse me. You don't have any containers do you? Some little blue eye cups. All of this stuff is coming out of me and I just don't know what to do with it. If I could take a photograph…

Maurice smoothes his dress out with the palms of his hands and returns to combing his hair, the tears continuing to stream down his face.

Mary returns downstairs and makes the call. Maurice's mother tells her to keep him in the house until the chauffeur gets there, he will take him away, he will rectify everything. These orders are repeated.

Mary wonders if a baby will come from all the semen. Strange that she thinks about that now, all the semen from those young men in her insides. She thinks about something else and goes into the utility room where there's a medical freezer pack. She opens it up and takes out one of the vials of frozen milky liquid with David's name scrawled on a tiny yellow label. She lets it thaw then smears some of it as far up her dry vagina as she can manage. She thinks of it as a kind of protection against what might come, a plausible confusion for what might happen. If she gets a baby then maybe she'll be able to believe it's David's. She thinks of Sheila. She deserves some too. He applies to both of them, she can admit that now. She imagines it as a kind of cleansing, as a kind of retrospective ownership. David owns them both. The idea she could never have surrendered to when Sheila was alive, she surrenders to now.

48

Mary has fallen asleep in one of the armchairs, Smith lies curled on her lap. The doorbell rings. It's three in the morning. She wakes and slowly makes her way to the door. The chauffeur is there, tall, thickset, holding a carryall in his hand. The black jaguar is parked where Mary's car should be. He strides in.

– Someone got a bit messy here. You have anything to do with it?

Did she have anything to do with it? How can she answer that?

– Where is he?

– Upstairs.

– And the young lady?

– In the kitchen.

– Down this way?

– Yes.

He checks out the body, then the living and dining rooms.

– I'm going to take the body away now. There'll be some other people here shortly to clean up the house. They'll probably have to work through the night so if you want to go somewhere else.

– No I have to stay.

– Whatever. There isn't a back entrance is there?

– No. But there is one to the side of the house.

– Okay I'll back the car up to it. This happened last night?

– I suppose.

– You're all right with this, you're not going to flip or anything? His mother is concerned about things getting out. It's over now. We'll clean up, get your place shipshape and that'll be it. We clear?

– Clear?

– Listen to me. I'm only going to say this once. I know you and Maurice had a thing together. Maybe things got out of hand. That's okay. Shit happens, but it stays here.

– Where will you take her?

– Does it fucking matter?

– She was my friend.

– Okay, I'm sorry.

– Listen, we'll find somewhere nice, okay. Maurice's mother's got some ground. We'll take her there.

He begins to make his way upstairs. Half way up he turns.

– You got a spare key?

Maurice has. Ask him.

Fifteen minutes later he leads Maurice down, dressed in fresh clothes, the make-up gone, his hair combed flat. Maurice doesn't look at her but docilely allows himself to be shunted forward and into the rear of the jag. The chauffeur backs the car up flush to the side entrance and opens the boot.

In the kitchen he strips Sheila of the uniform and rolls her in a thin throw rug from the back kitchen. He black-bags the uniform.

– Make sure the guys who come to clean the place take this as well.

He hefts Sheila's carpeted body up into his arms.

– Turn off that outside light will you?

Mary turns it off.

For some reason it is this act that makes her complicit. If she wasn't a part of it before, she is a part of it now.

49

It is approaching dawn when the chauffeur scrambles the jag up a steep mountain track, forested on one side with spruce. Further on the ditches and hedgerows are strewn with discarded litter, plastic containers, and ripped-apart black bags. There is no sign of vermin. They are forced to stop about a hundred metres short of the edge of the illegal dump, the wheels beginning to spin in the sodden, mulched waste. The whole stretch to the edge of the pit is a mire of mud. The chauffeur eye-checks Maurice in the rear view mirror. Maurice is sitting there, pert and prim like a little boy, his hands joined in his lap.

The chauffeur gets out and opens up the boot.

– Shit!

Blood has seeped from the body onto the lining of the boot. He struggles to get the body out of the boot, his feet sinking and shifting in the mud and filth. Unable to make much headway he opens the rear door.

– I need a hand here.

Maurice just looks at him blankly.

– I need you to get out now and give me a hand.

He grabs Maurice by the arm and pulls him out.

– This is a horrible place, says Maurice, why have you brought me here?

– I want to get this bullshit over with as soon as possible, so take the legs.

– I'm cold.

– Don't give me fucking cold, just do as I tell you.

The sound of their shoes squelching calf-deep in the soft mud is mixed with birdsong.

– The sublime call of birds. It is a solace isn't it? says Maurice.

– What are you talking about?

– These songs are a solace for the world.

– O for Chrissake!

The chauffeur places Maurice's arms around the legs. He goes to the other end.

– On three lift, okay.

One, two, three…

Maurice actually manages to obey this instruction and Sheila's body moves over the rim of the boot. He can't hold on though and allows the body to fall through his hands into the mud.

– You fucking wanker! You think I want to be here. You get your shit together and you lift this fucking body.

They go at it again and make some headway up the incline.

– Keep fucking going. Don't think about it, just keep fucking going!

The mud becomes deeper. Maurice, walking backwards up the hill, fails to keep his footing in the sludge. Sheila's body slips to one side and Maurice falls face-down. The chauffeur begins to laugh. He can't help himself. He can't stop laughing. Then he too loses his footing and as he falls he grabs the end of the rug and Sheila's head is pulled clean off.

The two of them sit looking at the head partly stuck in the mud, Sheila's eyes staring up at the lightening sky.

The chauffeur stands as best he can, grabs Sheila's decapitated head by the hair and throws it in the direction of the car. He has another place in mind where he can fuck it in.

The chauffeur opens up the rug.

– It'll be easier if we just grab the body.

When Maurice sees her exposed like that he can't look at her. He lets out a cry and scrambles on his hands and knees clear of the body.

– Get back here, you fuck!

But he doesn't turn back. He doesn't come back.

The chauffeur stamps slowly to Maurice's position and begins to drag the body bit by bit up the final few metres to the sloping litter-strewn edge of the dump. He drags the headless corpse onto a boulder beside a stand of hazel with their winter catkins jittering in the breeze. The body is draped over the stone. There is something painterly about the composition. He stands to his full height on the boulder, surveying the woodland and the hedgerowed fields flecked with the diminutive forms of distant cattle. He pauses a moment then tips her with his boot down a ten metre drop to the bushes and detritus below.

50

Days pass. The hallway, the living room, the dining room, the stairs, the landing, the bedroom, are all immaculate, cleaner than they have ever been perhaps. Pristine! The house has an eerie absence, like all of the noise, all of the voices have been subtracted, and all of the echoes too.

Mary walks out of one of the topmost rooms with Smith in her arms and down the steps to the second floor. There's a stain on her trousers. It begins to morph before her eyes, becoming a grotesque gargoyle with lank hair and rabid teeth. She scratches at it with her nails until one of them breaks. Frantically she pulls her woollen green jumper down and hides it. She looks drawn, tired, absent.

In the kitchen she opens the fridge and takes out a tin of sardines in tomato sauce. She mushes the sardines up and spoons it into Smith's bowl. Smith sniffs it and walks away. Mary takes the bowl up angrily.

– I don't know what you want.

She dumps the mushed-up sardines into the sink, turns on the faucet full blast and squidges the little dead fish down the plughole.

She opens the fridge again and takes out a carton of eggs. She cracks one into the cat's bowl, sticks a fingernail in the yolk and lets it run. Smith laps it up hungrily.

Mary takes a half-empty bottle of whiskey from the kitchen table, grabs a glass and goes into the living room. The room looks different, more austere, whiter. The red sofa is gone, replaced by a soft, white, leather three-seater. The walls are eggshell, the floor now a polished pine. She switches on the TV with the remote and plonks down in the matching white leather armchair. There are the usual afternoon shows. She stays with one of the local channels for a bit; a voluptuous, big-chested blonde, simmering clementines for her clementine cake, making love to the food, to the camera, to herself. Mary looks at the woman's cleavage when she bends over the bowl to blend the ingredients, the dark inlet to her paps, the jiggle, the fulsome pressure. She stays with the show until the finished cake is finally produced, a flat golden slab; *it's a wet cake* she is told, *keep it wrapped in greaseproof paper and the flavours will only intensify*.

She has dozed off into a kind of stupor when the six o'clock evening news comes on. There's some stuff on car bombs, hostages, then:

Earlier today some hikers discovered the mutilated remains of Sheila Deane at an illegal dump site three miles north of Oakbridge. Ms Deane, a thirty-six-year-old chartered accountant, was last seen leaving work on the evening of the twenty fourth.

There's a picture of the dump site, the mountains in the distance, the dark oppressive trees, and yellow-black tape. Two of the forensic team, clothed in hooded, white plastic body suits are there in the background.

The police are appealing to anyone in the vicinity of the dump site who witnessed anything suspicious over the last two to three days. A confidential line has been set up at 088 2686800. The police are not thought to be working along any definite lines of inquiry and are appealing to the public for any assistance they might offer.

Mary is out of her seat, pacing back and forth, shaking her hands as though attempting to rid herself of some foul contagion, and at the same time trying to assimilate the information.

There's a police officer being interviewed now.

– When was the body found exactly?

– Earlier this morning.

– How long do you think Ms Deane has been dead?

– Initial investigations suggest perhaps forty-eight hours. We will have a more precise determination following the autopsy.

– Had she been sexually assaulted?

– I'm afraid I can't go into specific details.

– But you are appealing for help from the public.

– We are currently trying to trace Ms Deane's final movements so any assistance the public can give in that regard would be invaluable. We would also like to interview anyone who was either in the vicinity of the crime scene or witnessed anything unusual over the last few days.

Just to repeat, the confidential help line number is…

Mary turns off the TV then switches it back on again, flicking between channels for other news reports. It's on them all. She panics, aware that her armpits, her whole body, is wet with sweat. She fills her glass with the last of the whiskey and slugs it back. The doorbell rings. She goes icily calm. So soon! It accelerates so quickly. Her life, her freedom, compromised in an instant. She thinks of her mother and she feels shame. The doorbell sounds again. She tries to prepare herself. She walks in a fated way towards the door.

It's Hilda.

There's a kind of relief, but it's no relief really.

– You looks terrible! You sick?

She's in the door before Mary can stop her.

– Place look good, she says, looking around. I like this, she says, pointing to the new mirror above the hallstand. New?

– Yeah.

– Who all these strange people coming and going all time, day and night?

– Just some cleaners Hilda. I was getting rid of some stuff. They work odd hours, you know that.

– You should ask if I want some old stuff. Any condition! I repair things. You should see state some things I get. But something to do, you know?

– I didn't know. If I'd known…

– Sure, I understand.

Hilda barges into the living room. She sees the empty bottle of whiskey.

– You drinking?

– Just a little. You know how it is.

– You watch yourself Mary, it get into you. I know.

– I'll watch it.

–We watch out for each other, that's what we do.

– Sure.

–You good girl Mary. Me good girl.

She laughs at herself.

–We all good girls, ya?

–That's right, we're all good girls, says Mary.

–You eating okay?

– I'm doing fine.

–You need some food you call me, okay?

– Listen Hilda, I'm not feeling great at the moment. I just need some time to myself.

– Okay, Hilda's going.

Hilda makes her way back to the door.

– Place look real good. You give me name of cleaners, ya?

– Sure.

At the door she presses Mary's arm.

–You need a friend, you call me.

Mary wanders through the house aimlessly. The telephone rings downstairs. It's probably the office, she thinks. They had called earlier asking her when to expect her back. Or it could be Maurice. Would he call now? Would he threaten her? Would his mother? She goes downstairs, keys in her password and listens to the message. It's only her therapist.

Mary, you left me high and dry this afternoon. That's your choice, of course, but I've told you before if you want to cancel I've got to have twenty-four hours' notice at least. You know my feelings about this kind of thing and you will be charged for the session. That aside, I hope you're well and I look forward to seeing you next week.

Mary makes a call to the liquor store and orders two litres of whiskey and a five-litre bottle of still water.

As darkness falls, she thinks to herself, I should eat something. But she can't, she just can't.

51

The hours of night pass in a stupor of drink and pills, hours when the edges of her world deliquesce and enisle her, hours when there is no truth to claim, no sound that does not reduce you, hours when the weight of blankets is the weight of earth, where the smell of enclaved darkness is the smell of ash, hours when there is no mind rest or mind space, hours that flow into hours without end, into the girdling vortex of unstoppable mind, hours that river you to a bleak lake, hours that trammel you, that unstitch you thread by thread, hours like no hours before, where the worst thoughts come unbidden, where you walk blood step by blood step, where you list and fall, where you eke out breath wishing it would fail you, hours where you lose hours to hours without end.

The gaunt house speaks stone to mortised stone of the history confided to it, layerings of acts and voices, breathings it has registered and deposited to memory. The house does not call in its own time for anything to be corroborated. There is no conscience in matter, only the impact of occurrence. The house stands, declared and unknown; the house will walk in the shadow of space to an unreferenced and immaterial next space, and become part of the meaningless reality of another pattern.

The bleak day rises, leaden sky, limited horizons, limited eventualities. Mary lies in bed, thinking. There is a white snow in her head. She hears the doorbell sound and repeat, sound and repeat. When it does not stop, she stops thinking that it will stop, and she rises. She goes to the landing window and looks down to the street below. The bins of her neighbours have been placed out for collection and been emptied. The blue of the receptacle containers she finds too blue, almost hurtful. Everyone else gets rid of their shit. The doorbell again! The doorbell! She hears a kind of tune within it, one long note that races forward then retreats in three, one step forward, three steps back; she imagines a dance, one two, one two three, one two, one two three, two two three, three two three. For a moment she is in a swirl of movement, one arm crooked, the other arm out, the floorboards vibrating, the room spinning. She looks down to the two men standing on the stoop dressed in bulky dark rainproof jackets. They might be proselytising types come to convince her, but she knows who they are and she knows what they want.

She walks downstairs. Opening the door she is unafraid, fatalistic.

There is nothing to safeguard really, there is only surrender. She stands before them in her dressing gown.

– Ms Reid?

It strikes her that everything can be denied.

–Yes.

– We'd like to ask you some questions about Ms Sheila Deane. This is Detective Sergeant Keaney and I'm Chief Investigating Officer Moore.

Such a brusque tone. He presents his credentials as does the smaller one, Keaney.

Everything is predictable but she finds no solace in that.

– We understand that Ms Deane was staying with you shortly before she died.

– Come in.

She brings them in to the living room and invites them to sit on the new three-seater.

–Would you like a cup of tea? she asks.

– No thank you.

She feels unkempt. She wonders if she is slurring. Her heads aches but she feels oddly calm. She predicts their questions pointlessly. Question, response, question, response. That's ok.

The small one, Keaney, flips open a notebook and makes an initial notation.

– When did you hear reports of her death?

– Yesterday evening.

– Why didn't you contact us?

– I think I'm still in shock. I haven't been able to go into work these past few days. I have a doctor's cert if you'd like to see it.

– Perhaps later. But it doesn't really explain why you didn't contact us.

– I feel responsible for what happened. I'm trying to deal with that.

– All the more reason to contact us.

– I wanted to. I just didn't feel able.

– When was the last time you saw her?

– On the twenty-second.

– Two days or so prior to her murder?

– That's right.

– We've spoken to Mr David Shaw, your ex-husband, who mentioned that Ms Deane had been staying with you on account of some phone calls you'd received.

– Sheila was one of my oldest friends; when she heard what I was going through she offered to come and stay.

– What were you going through?

– I was receiving threatening calls.

– Do you still have the recordings?

– No.

– But an officer came to investigate?

– I realise now he was impersonating an officer. He used the same name as the Sergeant here.

– We realise that, which is partly why I've included Sergeant Keaney in the investigation. We'll need to get a detailed description of the impersonator. We already have one from Mr Shaw but we'll need you to corroborate that. Before coming to see you we checked your phone records and there is no evidence of a call placed to our emergency number or to the local police station.

– That's because I didn't call. I was about to do so from the living room here when I saw an officer standing on the opposite side of the street. He came in and behaved exactly as you are now. I had no reason to suspect anything. I know he went to interview David, I'm sure he'll say the same thing.

– Might he have been the person making the calls? Was the voice similar?

– I didn't make a connection at the time but it is possible.

– Is there any chance that this character may have mistaken Ms Deane for you or indeed shifted his focus onto her?

– I don't think he could have mistaken us. We were the same height more or less, but that's as far as it went. Sheila and I had spoken of it as a possibility, but it was just chat.

– Mr Shaw also said that you had joined a dating site and made contact with some other members.

– David appears to have told you everything you need to know?

– He did come forward.

– You keep coming back to that. You don't seem to realise how this has affected me. I can't sleep, I can't eat, I've been drinking too much just to numb the pain. Sheila and I had been friends for over twenty years. And now you're interrogating me. I don't know how much more of this I can take.

– I'd ask you to be patient Ms Reid, believe me there is no quick route through this, the more thorough we are now the more likely we are to be able to close off certain avenues of investigation. We need to limit the elements so to speak.

Mary goes through the louvered doors into the dining room and gets her laptop. She brings up the dating site.

Moore examines the page.

– This is your profile here?

Mary nods.

Long leggy blond. Lust for life. Seeks man with same.

Mary turns away.

Moore hands the laptop to Keaney.

– We'll need to take this to the station with us.

Mary's attention is drawn to the back of Moore's left hand. There's a dense, plum-coloured birthmark, in the shape of a small hand. She wants to touch it, and reaches out only to draw her hand back in. Sergeant Keaney puts the laptop to one side.

– Why did Ms Deane leave when she did?

– She had only planned to stay for a short while. She left somewhat abruptly.

– And why was that?

– I had suspected that Sheila and my ex-husband David had had an affair. When I confronted her she admitted it. We had a row and I asked her to leave.

– So you were angry with her?

– I was disappointed.

– That seems very reasonable of you.

– I felt it as a betrayal, I don't deny that, but it's been over between me and David for a long time. They were both free agents.

– You may or may not know that Mr Shaw's current partner left him some days ago. She's on her way back here now. However, I spoke to her late yesterday and she was highly critical of you. She maintains that you are still obsessed with him and that you pinpointed him as the individual making the calls.

– I was confused. David complicates things emotionally, he keeps you connected in all kinds of ways, he moves on but he doesn't like anyone else to do the same.

– Did you kill Ms Deane?

– No.

– Do you know who did?

– No.

It was that simple. They asked questions, you answered with a kind of truth. Kill? Know? They were big questions really.

– If you could get dressed we'd like to take you down to the station. And if you could get the doctor's certificate, please.

– Why? Am I under arrest?

– No. We just need to get some more details that's all, and have you look at a few photo sheets for identification purposes.

Mary goes upstairs.

Moore turns to Keaney.

– I'll take her down myself. If you could interview some of the neighbours see if they've noticed anything.

– She looks pretty wrecked.

– What time is the autopsy report due?

–Twelve.

–We should be able to get a good identikit photo together of this guy. He may have shifted his target when he couldn't get to Ms Reid. We'll work along those lines for the moment. I'll wait for her, you get started on the neighbours, do the whole street. When you're done with that check in with any of her work colleagues we missed yesterday. I'll see you back at the station.

Mary comes down some minutes later dressed smartly in a pale blue suit, her hair brushed and tied back in a ponytail. She looks almost perfect. Moore goes ahead of her through the front door. Across the road Keaney is interviewing Hilda. When she sees Mary she waves.

–You come dinner tonight Mary, we talk!

Not for the first time she realises her destiny is not fully in her own hands. She climbs into the rear of the unmarked police car. Hilda waves her off. Mary conceives that she will not leave the station, she will not return here, it is over, all that is over. They haven't driven more than a hundred metres when Mary cries,

– Stop!

–What?

– I forgot to let Smith out into the garden.

– Smith?

– My cat!

–You'll be back in good time, don't worry about it.

– But what if I don't come back?

–Why wouldn't you come back?

– Because that's what happens, things get out of control.

52

You think you know what will happen, what people will say, how you will feel, but you don't. You are betrayed by discrepancies. Lies are such fragile things. The lie is made, a small platform with stick and sail and floated on the water, the lie is drifted by happenstance towards obstacles confronted and circumvented, or else capsized by them. The best lies escape their water, disappear and are forgotten as having been lies at all. These are the beautiful lies.

The police station is a theatre of lies, you can see them scattered on the floor, embedded in the furniture, alive in the pale green paint of the walls, you can feel them clogging the air, making themselves available to be drawn down. Mary is seated at a long formica-topped table, a small meshed window opposite, three wooden chairs, a clock, assorted photographic templates of head shapes, eyes, eyebrows, which she goes through in the company of a female officer introduced to her as Duty officer Helen Cloake.

They spend an hour working with a computer model, moving through the variations of haircuts, jawline, nose, until they finalise an image of Maurice with his slicked-down police hair, not the soft bouffant clubby style he would be easily recognised for. It's strange to her, looking at him like this, boyish, refined, soft. It's hard to align the benignity of the image and its corrupt reality. Helen solicits more details about hands, body posture, voice, but it will be hard to source Maurice on foot of this complex portrait. Mary doubts if he is even in the country, his mother will have spirited him to their summer home in Provence. Money is the simplest defence.

Duty Officer Cloake leaves and is replaced by Moore. More questions about Sheila, her routine, the men in her life, the women, back to Mary's anger, back to David. She tries to predict what Hilda will have said, what she saw, what she believes she saw. Hilda is the one who confounds her imagination, she is the one who complicates the pattern of her divulgences. What is Mary protecting after all…her freedom? Blighted freedom of a failed life. Yet she acknowledges the unpredicted urgency to keep that freedom unchanged. The idea of being incarcerated, of being withheld from a freely determined life, is not something she would survive.

At one o'clock Moore is called outside. Mary catches a glimpse of Sergeant Keaney before the door is closed. Faced with the prospect of the inevitable complications to come, she determines then and there on silence. She will stop talking. She has spoken her last words. She will allow them to fabricate their truth aside from her.

Keaney hands Moore the autopsy report.

– Have you had a look at it?

–Yeah.

Moore flips through the standard two-page report.

– Anything?

– Looks like it may have been gang rape. We should get DNA samples from work colleagues, ex lovers, see if anything shows up.

Moore reads the relevant passage.

– Anything from the neighbours?

– Seems to have been a fair amount of activity around the house. Decorators. Otherwise her story stands up. The neighbour across the road saw Sheila Deane going in and out, and had a conversation with her about a week ago. She mentioned something about the house having been lit up one night and then glossed over it, saying that Ms Reid had simply left the lights on, but that she had been worried for her. In fact she seems to be worried for her generally but in a motherly kind of way. Most of the other neighbours are away during the day and what with the fog these last weeks… Aside from Ms Deane's car parked outside they hadn't noticed anything unusual. I have a few call backs but that's pretty much it.

– Has her car been located yet?

– No.

–Try to get a line on the decorators. Do you have a name?

– No.

– She's still inside. I'll check it out with her.

– We need to get photos of this guy to the media. Call a briefing.

– Will do.

– I'll get her home. But let's keep an eye on her. There's always a chance he may come back. Unfinished business and all that. You never know, one kill may lead to another. It wouldn't be the first time.

Moore goes back inside.

Mary, who has been toying with a piece of hard skin in the centre of her palm, stops.

– When did you decide to redecorate the house?

Is this it? Should she clam up now? This is the circumstantial foray, this is how they make inroads.

– A few months ago.

– And the name of the company?

– They were recommended to me by someone I met casually. He came by one day and said he was ready to start. We went through what needed to be done. He made a few suggestions and that was it.

– And you paid him by cheque?

– He asked for cash. He had some Mexican workers on the crew. I figured it was black work. It was a good price. I had no complaints.

– And his name?

– Jack Buckman I think it was.

– And you'd no qualms about potentially disreputable types coming into your home and leaving them unsupervised?

– There's nothing in that house that I value so I've nothing to lose.

– Ok that's it for now. Do you need a lift home?

– No I think I'll walk.

– We'll keep an eye on your place and keep you informed of any developments. If you think of anything in the meantime that might be of importance give me a ring.

He hands her his card.

– Try not to worry.

His tone, which had been hard and clipped up to this, is almost solicitous.

– I'll try, but I think the worst is over, don't you?

53

The fog is merely a memory now, something to be recalled as a bad time.

The terrible fog of such and such,

the gross fog that devoured lives.

All gone.

Clear now.

All given the all clear.

Thank god for that.

Clarity at last.

Normality.

You lose a sense of the rhythm, the white rhythm of absolved movement, you lose it for a while then you get it back and, you re-establish the pattern, and it seems as though you had never lost it. It makes you feel less fallible, more resourceful, to think that you can withstand the worst of everything and come back batting better than ever. In the days following her interrogation by the police something changed for Mary, she knew that she could continue with her life. She felt as she had felt maybe six months previously, in control, work-focused. She had a short conversation with Dr Lavender and cancelled all further appointments including her group therapy sessions. Dr Lavender had asked her to come in and see him for a final time. There would be no charge. She could hear Maurice's admonitions in her head. She declined. He seemed unhappy with her but what could he do.

Each day you make it through builds to a compendium of days you make it through, until it is no longer in question that you will make it through, only how you will make it through, and refining how you make it through becomes the business of the day. She makes it through, day after day, week after week, and makes it home.

– Darling, I'm home!

She brushes the hair off her face and looks in the mirror. She doesn't look that bad for a woman her age. She goes into the living room. Smith follows her. They sit on the sofa together and she checks her messages. Nothing, just one or two saved calls.

She's been back at work a few weeks now. Today has been a good day, a major deal finalised, a bonus in the offing. She thinks about pouring herself a drink then thinks again. Skip that! She goes to the kitchen and fills a tumbler with apple juice and slugs it back. It is early evening. There are still a few hours of daylight left, still a span of hours to fill before sleep. Maybe she should have stayed in the office. There was paperwork on the deal to complete.

She looks out through the back window. The days are definitely getting longer. This spring she will definitely get to grips with the garden. She will spend the summer evenings on the patio drinking chilled Italian whites, maybe even have a party, a barbecue. The sight of the rubbish bin gets to her. No time like the present. She puts on some old clothes, grabs some old newspapers and builds a small fire stack with some twigs and bits of wood.

The fire dies almost immediately so she gets the plastic canister of petrol from the boot of her car and douses it liberally. It flares spectacularly. She throws the first of the plastic rubbish bags onto the blazing fire and stands back. She is enthralled. There's almost no wind. The fumes are acrid. But the black bags burn. Successful days have a kind of momentum. Everything works out. Bag after bag goes on the fire, the plastic singeing, melting, combusting, the cartons, tins and other detritus visible for a moment then invisible. Half way through she throws on another bag, smaller and heavier than the rest. The plastic melts away disclosing a tangled cluster of rags and clothes. They confuse her. She hadn't put any clothes in there. Within minutes the fire dampens and extinguishes. She gets a rake from the garden shed and pulls them free. The clothes are blood clotted, ferrous, rancid. White festering maggots squirm from the opened-out bolus. She recognises Sheila's white bra and the tracksuit top she had worn the first night she arrived. All of the horror of what she has so ably forgotten, returns. She feels the clothes as a sign, evidence of something that cannot be fully cancelled. She feels Sheila's presence as witness, standing behind her watching, not admonishing just watching, not speaking just watching. She turns fretful, stark-eyed, guilty. She grabs the petrol and pours the last of it over the clothes. The match falls from her fingers and traces of petrol glistening on her fingers connect to the finger-surge of flame and in one transformative moment she is on fire, for life, for death, for denial, for untruth, for capably forgetting, for all that she has done and not done irreversibly. She watches her hand burn as though she is looking at a painting by Frida Kahlo: a woman in a white dress in a desert landscape, giant aloe vera plants about her, her arm aflame. She walks calmly into the kitchen and places her singed hand under the flowing faucet. Her whole hand cools into pain. Deep, just, pain. The doorbell rings as the doorbell was always going to ring, at the worst possible time.

She walks to the front door in a daze of irresolution and opens it.

It's Hilda.

When Hilda sees Mary's arm hanging stiffly by her side, the phalanges of her fingers melted and raw, she steps towards her.

– I saw smoke. What happen?

– Just an accident, I'm fine.

Hilda puts her right arm around her shoulder and guides her towards the kitchen. She sits her down.

– You need drink?

– No.

Hilda doesn't listen to her. She gets the liquor from the living room and sets it down on the kitchen table. She pours Mary a couple of fingers of whiskey and hands it to her.

– Thanks.

Mary sips it slowly. Her burnt hand has fallen off her lap

and hangs as a kind of shunned and darkening thing.

– We go to hospital.

– No, it's not necessary.

– I see like this before I know what necessary or not. First we keep cool the hand, okay.

Hilda proceeds to fill a basin with cold water, dumping all of the ice cubes from the freezer section in as well. She lowers Mary's hand in slowly.

– How it happen?

Mary turns towards the still-smouldering pile of bags outside on the patio.

Hilda looks out through the kitchen window above the sink.

– That against the law!

– Is it? Yes, I suppose it is. I wasn't thinking about that.

– I check.

– No!

When Hilda doesn't return after a minute or two Mary goes to stand under the lintel of the door. In the light thrown by the automatic porch lamp Hilda looks at the matted clump of blood stained clothes, making her own sense of them.

She turns to Mary: cold eyes, complicit, commanding.

– You vant I burn everything?

– Would you?

– I burn everything okay?

– Okay.

– You go inside. I do it good. Keep hand in water.

Mary dutifully goes inside and does as she is told. She feels the weight of Hilda's directive as a kind of love. She listens to the sound of the fire outside and feels a lessening in the guilt she felt before, an understanding, a tolerance of who she is and what she has done or not done. The weight of her burden both dissipates and complicates. This kind of solidarity is strangely affecting. Hilda calmly completes what she had begun.

They go to the A&E department of the local hospital and Mary is patched up, her hand smeared with anti-burn ointment followed by wrappings of lint, gauze and binding. She is told to attend her local GP who will change her dressings and she is given six codeine tablets for the pain.

They get a taxi back and Hilda insists on coming in to undress her and get her ready for bed. After four hours Mary finds Hilda's attentions cloying but generous. They have a cup of tea together before going upstairs.

–Why are you being so nice to me Hilda? I hardly deserve it.

–We all make mistakes. No reason you go under.

There's a pause.

– During war my mother and father we live beside camp in Goltzenberg. My father he vork in camp. My father take some gold from Jews, we live good, we do good after war. With brother and me we give some cabbage to women at wire, little thing but no good. But I remember cabbage, remember their faces, so happy for so little. My father good man but do bad things. You good woman do bad thing maybe. Hilda don't know nothing. Hilda know but don't know. Hilda understand.

–Thanks Hilda.

–You okay?

– I'm okay. Sometime it comes back at me. It's like a darkness and it swamps me.

They go upstairs. Hilda helps Mary to undress and puts her to bed.

Standing in the doorway Hilda asks her,

–You pray?

– No.

– Maybe you try, maybe it help.

– I don't think so.

– No?

– No.

– OK. Sleep gut! It all over now, ja?

– Sure. Everything'll be okay now.

54

The weather improves. Clear blue late-winter skies for the first time in weeks. Mary stands at her office window looking down on the plaza below. There's no pain in her hand any more but it exists as a signal wound. She finds it harder to go an hour, two hours without thinking of Sheila in some guise or other. She feels her as a presence, and a weight. She senses her as a vagrant entity about her. Only this morning she had found a bracelet of hers under the rope mat by the kitchen door. She thought of taking down the photographs of her but the gaps they left only emphasized her absence and loss. If anything, she saw the images more deeply once removed, and so she left them accusingly in place.

Guilt as the shatter mirror, guilt as the impossible jigsaw.

Her intercom buzzes.

– Call line one.

– Mary Reid, how can I help you?

– Ms Reid, it's Detective Inspector Moore. I wanted to inform you personally of a development in the case concerning Ms Deane, before you heard it on any upcoming news reports.

Mary immediately thinks of Maurice, his fragility, how he will capitulate, and how inevitably he will incriminate her. She will come clean herself. That is what will be demanded and what she will offer.

– Are you still there?

– Your news Inspector, what is it?

– The DNA tests came back from the lab this morning. Semen from two men was identified. One remains unknown to us at this point but we have a positive ID on the other. You were perhaps right to suspect David Shaw all along.

– Was I?

– He has been charged with rape and murder in the first degree. He is being held pending bail at Christenville Prison.

– David! That can't be right. It must be a misunderstanding of sorts. I'm sure he wanted to protect her, that's all he ever wanted to do. And he never wanted to hurt me.

– I'm not sure I understand you. Are you saying he had no motive?

– Of course he had no motive.

– We don't know what the nature of his relationship with Ms Deane was. On his own admittance they met in Clinton Park two days before the murder. She appears to have been seeing someone else. His own relationship was in crisis. He may have snapped.

– No.

– You sound so convinced. Why are you so convinced?

– I don't want to believe that someone I loved, someone I love, could do such a thing.

– That I understand but the evidence contradicts your faith. He has asked to see you but I would advise against it personally.

– To see me?

– Yes.

– Christenville Prison. Where is that?

– It's upstate, off the North Highway.

– Which exit?

– 51. It's an ugly place. If you're determined to go be prepared for that.

Mary puts down the phone and sinks back in her chair. She tries to remember why she did what she did. Was it like an anointing, grace of the man they had shared, a final sharing out of the man they had both loved, his essence as an emblem of that care? And now Sheila was dead, David ensnared, his relationship with that other woman over. There was only Mary and David left really. It was funny how things worked out in the end.

In the stillness of the office Mary recalls how she had emptied all of the condoms during their last six months together into separate plastic containers and frozen them. She had even bought a special freezer unit online to maintain them. David hadn't wanted them to have a child. It was a way for her to secure that against his wishes. And then after he left she used to put it in herself when she was fertile. David and Mary's baby. That would have been nice. That was just what she wanted. It is what she wants still, and baby glue is ok.

David in prison. She sees the years ahead pass. She will visit regularly, perhaps even daily. Dependency is the natural eventuality of love. She will wait and he will love her. She will go there now. Not a minute to lose. She will set the pattern in motion. For the first time in years she feels a kind of happiness. It is not too strong a word she thinks for what she feels. To feel connected, responsible, wanted. Better than love or merely other words for love. The truth she distils is that there is a fatedness to things. There are things that are simply meant to be, and she and David together is a reality that she has always known was meant to be. Everything they have shared, their long pairing, and now perhaps a future of light, a future in which they will be, and love, and fade.

55

Three days later and the designated visiting time arrives. An hour and a half outside the city Christenville Prison lies on the outskirts of the bleak town of Pachett. She stops at a food store with cellophane-wrapped stems of red carnations stuffed into a plastic bucket by the front door. The shopkeeper, a gross woman with a dyed-chestnut bob stretches out her hand to take the flowers and scan them. Mary wants to put some paper around them so she slips them out of their cellophane wrapper and hands it to the woman to scan.

– Don't you want the crystals?

– No.

–They'll fade.

–That's ok.

– Everybody wants the crystals. Everybody who comes in here at least. Keeps 'em fresh. Are they for a man or a woman?

Mary doesn't answer, then she does.

– Okay I'll take the crystals.

– I can always find a use for 'em if you don't want 'em.

– No I'll take the crystals.

–You'd think crystals were bad or something.

– Just give me the crystals.

– I'm just trying to help.

– Do you have any wrapping paper?

–Wrapping paper!

–Wrapping paper, repeats Mary. Plain is ok.

– Just these ones.

She fans a group of square folded sheets on the counter. They are ugly and inappropriate. Mary selects the least offensive of these, a purple one with the words 'Get Well

Soon' multiply and diagonally written in cheap gold.

– So your friend's in hospital?

– How much is that, please?

– Everybody's got some kind of illness these days. You think you're special then you realise you're sick just like everybody else.

Mary has had enough. In managerial mode she eye-checks the woman's laminated name tag.

– Listen Mildred, just tell me how much it is and let me get out of here.

– Listen Lady, maybe I don't want to sell you these flowers after all.

– You hold that thought Mildred but as you can see I'm holding the flowers and the paper. I'm going to put my money on the counter. If it isn't enough just nod.

Mildred just looks at her.

– There that wasn't so bad. Thank you Mildred.

– You may dress like a lady…

Mildred continues to burble banalities and slurs as Mary exists.

In the car Mary wraps the twelve carnation stems in the purple-and-gold paper. Once out of town the monolithic concrete structure of the prison becomes visible, surrounded as it is by acres of featureless brown-stemmed scrub. Having expected something more catastrophically forbidding she relaxes into the odd atunement she instinctively feels to the emptiness of the landscape, its jagged currents, its flatness, its big oppressive skies. She will not mind making this journey again and again and again. The sky, uniformly grey, merges with the charred perimeter walls of the prison. Some traffic begins to back up behind her. Other visitors she presumes. She will probably get to know them too, in time. She drives on a little more quickly, passing a farmstead with a fire raging in an open field some distance from the barn and ramshackle house. The field of old dreams is burning, she thinks. The field of old dreams and the field of loss is burning. In the cold understanding of what it is in her nature to lament, or to celebrate, she sees the legend of her past unfurl and vanish.

She drives on, her eyes addicted to the chill kingdom of fire in her rear-view mirror; she drives on from elegy, from the scarred past of her extinguished ground; she drives on into her unlikely future.

She is stopped at the outer checkpoint where a guard notes the reason for her visit and the name of the prisoner she is visiting. There is form, decorum, structure. She is not unpleasantly treated. The air is heavy. She is brought through doors and security systems like those in airports. Her nail file and other items are kept to one side for collection on departure.

There is nothing really to divert the eye except the rigour and routine of containment. Mary reacts well to commands: sit in here, wait to be called, present anything you wish to be given to the prisoner for examination, and so on. She waits in a dull room with a high window, painted grey floor, pale green walls, strip lighting, a hatch and a counter. She imagines how hard it will be for David to survive this absence of stimulation, its atonality, its lack of sensuous contours, its delimited colour. He will petrify. She is dressed in blue. She should have dressed in green or red, with a startling faceted broach or necklace, or brought a luminous thing that he could cling to. Does he ever really think of her? He has asked to see her. That is enough. She will offer what she has to offer. Perhaps her love will be returned. This is the substance of her faith.

David is brought to her in the large visiting room. He is brought to her. She asks and he is brought to her. Some things are unparalleled. To think that it would ever have come to this. There is nothing between them. She could touch him. She leaves her hands on the table so that he can touch her. She will touch him if he doesn't touch her, she is sure of that. He looks well, a little drawn but that is only to be expected. His blue prison uniform makes him look a little boyish. Perhaps blue wasn't such a bad colour for her to choose after all; it creates a mirroring, an echoing, an alliance. The red carnations lie between them.

–Why did you bring me flowers?

It feels like an accusation.

– Don't you like them?

– They're useless to me here.

– I wanted to bring something. I didn't know what you needed.

– What I need Mary is for you to help get me out of here.

– How can I do that?

– Sheila was seeing someone. She hinted at as much when I met her. Who was it?

– I don't know.

– She said it was a policeman.

– I never saw her with anyone David. You think I would keep that from you if I knew? Do you really think I would keep that to myself?

– I don't know.

– David!

– I don't know, Mary. I can't make sense of anything anymore.

– Whatever mistakes I've made in the past is one thing but you can't blame me for this.

– I'm not blaming you.

– But you don't believe me.

– I don't know what to believe. I need you to help get me out of here.

– I'm here aren't I?

She can hear his voice almost breaking. She has rarely seen him this emotional before. The whole situation is oddly exciting. It feels in a way like the thrill of capture. She remembers capturing birds as a child. Her mother always said the trick was to trap them without killing them.

– David, I want to be here for you. I'll do whatever I can. You're a very important part of my life, David. These last years all I've wanted was to get back to where we were. When I think of it. You know all that stuff! All my stuff. You know I was never very good at loving, not in the proper way, or what I guess is the proper way…

– Don't, Mary…

– No let me finish, it's important. I've done work on

myself, David. I think you know I've done a lot of work on myself. Things will be better. I'll be better. When I was driving here David I thought of what I wanted to say. And what I want to say David is that I've never really thought it was over between you and me, despite everything, *despite everything*, and I think that says something, don't you? Despite everything we can re-imagine our future.

– But I have no future in here.

– If I thought that you could love me, that we could love each other, then the future would take care of itself, I know that.

– I can't think like that Mary, I'm just so far away from being able to think like that. I don't understand why or how this has happened to me.

When she looks at David he is crying. It's so beautiful to see him crying. He looks so beautiful. She'd never have thought vulnerability would be so becoming, but it is.

– Isn't it something that we can talk like this after all that has happened? says Mary.

She begins to cry.

– Look at us, blubbing like lovers. I wish I could hold you, says Mary.

David just sits there in front of her, slumped over. A long silence weakens the space they share.

– I'd better go. I don't want to exhaust you. I'll come another day if you want. Whenever I'm allowed. I'll bring whatever you want, no flowers, whatever you want. Tell me what you want.

David doesn't answer.

– What do you need, David?

David doesn't answer.

– Don't go quiet on me, David! Don't do that! Don't shut me out David. Talk to me.

– I can't think of anything to say. I'm not going to survive this, Mary.

– It's only the beginning. It will get easier.

– You should go. Thanks for coming. I didn't think you would.

– It just shows how little you really know me.

David signals for the guard. As he stands, Mary reaches for his hand, but misses.

She stands and watches him being led away. The flowers remain on the countertop. She will take them home, put them in a vase, let them symbolise clipped wings, enshrined beauty.

After collecting her bits and pieces from security she asks the information officer about the protocol governing conjugal visits.

He gives her the guidelines concerning long-term prisoners, together with a brochure and a form for her to fill in. Driving through the darkened landscape on her return to the city she feels oddly compounded, more or less elated.

56

The house doesn't feel so empty when she's there now; maybe it's her buoyancy. The days pass more fluidly, with a kind of ease, a kind of joy. The art of being human, she thinks, is the art of survival.

Sitting on the sofa, the evening dusk still vaguely light, she examines in greater detail the brochure and form the prison guard had given her. The brochure itself is of reasonably good quality, glossy, although the photographs of the two types of accommodation available are unprepossessing. The one for families comes with a bedroom, kitchen, playroom and dining area. The one for couples comprises merely a bedroom and shower unit. The photograph shows a very pale blue room with drawn royal blue curtains. Mary wonders what the window looks out upon – yellow brick deeply grouted, or perhaps a tree. In the centre of the room and stemming from the wall is a concrete bed with a cavity form for the mattress, and night tables to either side. It looks cold, impersonal, and she imagines it smells of cheap disinfectant or pine-scented air freshener. And no easy chairs, everything directs you to the bed. Couples are allocated rooms on a morning or evening basis for periods of twelve hours.

Twelve hours! Twelve hours together. You could resolve so much in twelve hours, naked body to naked body. The stunning possibility of loving within such parameters. There is something in this construed narrative she finds compelling, breath taking.

Reading through the form she discovers that she needs a certificate from her doctor stating that she is in good physical health. She makes a mental note to herself to watch her weight and to contact the local Health Clinic for a consultation. In a paragraph under the heading *Eligibility* she finds that prisoners on remand or awaiting trial may be allowed conjugal visits but in the main these are reserved for long-stay inmates. All applications will be reviewed by the Prisons Service, and each form must be signed by both consenting parties before being forwarded for approval. She fills out her part of the form then and there.

Over the next few weeks Mary visits Christenville Prison every Wednesday afternoon. It is without doubt the high point of her week. She could go other days too. Some days she wakes up and thinks to herself, I really must see David again today, but something stops her, some little inner voice tells her to wait, wait until Wednesday, it will be better that way. And so she waits. She has become known to a few of the guards. Sometimes they compliment her on her clothes, her look. They don't search her that thoroughly although they once found a pencil-sharpening blade which they asked her about. That's what she brings mostly, art supplies, eau de cologne, health food supplements. It's amazing to her how having some art materials has secured him, has returned to him a kind of inner balance. In the past she had never understood how that worked, and so she never really respected it, or accepted the time it subtracted from the time he made available to her. She is so indulgent with him really. How she is with him is so removed from how she is with almost everyone else. Desire for him brings her home to another place in herself. She tries to do whatever he asks her to do. She has met, at his request, with Sheila's acquaintances and work colleagues, with her surviving family and relations. She has visited Sheila's apartment, but only briefly, acknowledging to David that being there assailed her memory, and she had to leave. She writes up her conversations with those she has met and offers them to David in the form of reports. He has admitted finding them impressive and useful and has indicated that they will bolster his case.

Mary has tried to determine who else is coming to see him but he seems wary or disinclined to tell her. She doesn't understand why, and has had no success in trying to elicit the information from the guards. Irrespective of how many people he has *on side* he still finds things for her to do. Do this! Do that! Through it all, she does what he asks because she knows what she wants.

She thinks of what she will need to bring to the conjugal room when the time comes. She has already assembled most of it: plain white sheets with an embroidered detail, feather down pillows, massage oils, scented candles, chocolates. She also intends to buy him some fresh pyjamas, not that he'll need them, she jokes to herself, but still they won't go to waste, and a dressing gown – she has seen some fine silk ones in a small oriental store downtown. Other things will come to mind and other things become obvious once she has spent an evening or a morning inside. She vacillates as to which she prefers, the mornings or the afternoons. She freely admits she prefers morning sex, but an evening session would lead more naturally into intimacy. She has raised the topic with David once or twice in a casual manner.

– You know that compound to the right of the entrance gates, any idea what's going on there?

– No.

– Really! I must ask.

Or on another afternoon…

– Is it true conjugal visits are allowed?

– I've no idea.

– As far as I know it's true. Enlightened isn't it?

There comes a Wednesday, a day she feels to be auspiciously ordained. The day, however, is outlandishly bad – teeming rain, violent winds. On another day she might have read this natural inclemency as an omen. She passes through security with her usual assortment of items, the one special thing this week – a bag of pretzels.

When he comes to her he is carrying one of the sketch pads she bought for him. He sets it down on the countertop. His fingertips are covered in charcoal. She takes one of his hands in hers and begins to rub the charcoal off. He withdraws his hand.

– Let me draw you, says David.

This entreaty pulls her back to him immediately.

He begins to sketch her. Throughout the drawing she feels an alliance in their eyes, a truth and solidarity. There is a warmth to some of the things he muses on.

–Your hair's in great shape. Is that why you're not wearing wigs at the moment?

– I guess so.

–You look healthier than I've seen you for years.

–Thanks!

– Almost finished.

She imagines for a moment that he will pin it to a wall in his cell. But when he turns the drawing towards her to inspect he says,

– Here, it's yours! Something to remember me by.

– I need more than this.

–What do you mean?

She takes out the form she has carried in her purse for weeks and hands it over to him. He glances at the brochure and notes that she has filled up one section of the form.

–This is an opportunity David. We can reclaim something.

David tries to suppress a smile.

– Don't make fun of me! says Mary.

– It's just I don't think …This is ridiculous Mary!

–You should see the rooms, David. We could make it really nice, and just talk. I know it says conjugal but we could take it easy in the beginning at least. It's an opportunity. Isn't it the future?

– I'm sorry Mary. It's not going to happen.

–Why don't you at least consider it?

– It's not going to happen Mary because that past, our past, can't be retrieved.

– You're so definitive. You're so unthinking David sometimes, and so cold. Maybe if I just leave it with you so you can think about it; so much depends on it David.

–What depends on it?

– I depend on it.

–There's no point Mary. I'd be lying to you if I said there was.

– These last weeks, well…it was important for me to be some kind of help to you.

– And?

– I just thought…

– Let's be clear here Mary. I value your support, I depend on it, in part, but I never entered into a pact that equates your act of friendship with getting back together. Aside from everything else I don't have the strength. I feel kind of dead.

Mary feels suddenly cold.

– Others find me attractive.

– I'm not surprised.

– You've got a very high opinion of yourself David; not too many other people share it. You're not getting out of here. In most people's eyes you killed Sheila.

– They're wrong. You know that. I loved Sheila. I would never have hurt her, never.

– You hurt me.

There's a pause.

– Did you love Sheila more than you loved me?

– It's not like that. I loved you both, says David.

– Loved!

– Love, says David, correcting himself.

– You're a liar.

It isn't what she meant to say. She feels a remote anger swell.

– You were always good at meeting your own needs, says Mary.

He looks at her coldly.

– This isn't about us. This is about you, says David.

– It will always be about us until I understand why you left me.

– Ok. You want to have that conversation, let's have that conversation. You make it sound like you wanted it to continue but you didn't. You couldn't stand how I related or didn't relate to you. Anyway this is a useless conversation Mary because I don't love you.

There's a kind of pity in his voice, an anger and condescension. She hates it.

– You never saw me as anything other than flawed. With you I was always going to feel diminished. I feel that way now.

– So let it go, if it was that bad, if I'm that bad let it go, let your hopes go and settle for something plainer. We still have something to offer each other.

– I thought so too. Why do you think I've been making the efforts I've been making these last weeks? When you look at the people who have remained loyal to you there aren't too many left standing David, and all you can say to me is that you don't love me! Well, that's good to know. I hope it makes you feel better to be able to articulate the fact that there is yet one more person you definitively don't love.

– It's not like that Mary. That's not what I said, that's not what I meant.

– But it is what I heard, it's probably what I've been hearing from you for years but just not accepting.

Her tone has gone hard.

– I just hope you feel liberated by your rejection, says Mary.

– I'm not rejecting you.

– Oh but you are. Maybe using me like you have is your idea of revenge but I won't set myself up like this again.

She stands to go.

– What do you want from me? asks David.

– I was hoping you cared enough David to lie, at least until we got to the point where we could explore things again, but the only truth you have is an ugly one so you can go to hell.

– I'm there already in case you haven't noticed. You say you want me Mary but it's not true, you're too fascinating to yourself, you're the most complex thing you know.

– You were always hard David, in your heart you were always hard, now you're a killer. Some day soon you'll know how it feels to be despised. I was going to come again, I may even have remembered something, but not now.

She begins to walk away from him.

– You think this will cripple me, says David, but you're wrong. It will cripple you. I'll be out of here in no time, with or without your help.

By the time Mary reaches the door she knows she will not come again. She wants to look back one last time but doesn't.

On the drive back into the city the skies darken and rain

torrents down. She watches as streams of it gather and sluice down street grilles. She feels adrenalated, angry, passing back and forth over the details of their conversation. What kind of a life does she have? She needs so little really, just a point of absorption, a focus to deflect her sense of alienation, a sense of normality to structure her emptiness. It is only when she feels her blouse dampen that she realises she is crying and realising it she cries more deeply, unstoppably.

By the river she pulls the car into a vacant parking space, her eyes still watering, and watches in the darkening light as a pair of birds gather rushes for their nest, pure activity, equal beings, tender dedication. She is entranced by their... she searches for the word and comes up with affection, but this she knows is merely transference, and she is angered even by the birds and what she transposes to them. She thinks of stoning them, of ruffling their equanimity and concordance. She gets out, locks the car and walks along the cindered path by the side of the river, the tubular orange streetlights glowing in the degenerating light. She sees a young man urinating against the red brick wall opposite and an image of her rape is appallingly promoted. A night such as this, rain such as this, and those remorseless moments. She thinks about holding this young man's cock, of squeezing it until it bulbs and bursts. There is a payment due, she thinks, for all the pain.

She continues along the riverfront and across a narrow transept bridge to the other side. The plane trees are larger here, the darkness deeper.

She is wet through. She stops and leans against the moss-and-ivy-covered trunk of one of the trees. She squeezes her wrist until it aches. She takes out her phone and looks at it. Who is there to call now? Sheila is gone, David is gone, Maurice is gone. She punches in her own number. In the strangeness of this night, in its blackness and rain, in its soundless lonesome music, she retreats to the cover of her own darkness.

– 'Mary', she speaks into the phone, her voice deeper, guttural, male. I know you're there Mary. It's time you weren't. You sad little fucking bitch. Every unlived life has its haunting aftermath. Your eternity is mine. Be prepared to suffer. Come on Mary I know you're there. Pick up Mary. You should always pick up for Daddy. Daddy's little bitch. Some things are inescapable. Some identities are inescapable. Some lives never rise except in flame. Be prepared to burn, Mary. Be prepared to burn.

Mary drops the phone suddenly and begins to retch. The curdle of grey vomit splashes her shoes. She falls back and slides down to the concrete pavement. She closes her eyes against one reality and sees a darker one. She was foolish to believe there would ever be freedom. Freedom was for the birds.

57

It is seven o clock when Mary finally makes it home. Cleansed though the house is after the redecoration she feels it to be a prison, the house a tomb, a weight of capsizing memories and walls. When she thinks of a place that offers her relief, she rekindles memories of a summer house they had taken regularly in the years before her mother's death. The winding lane that led from the rented shingle-roofed farmstead, the marram-banked beach, the dark house they passed daily, set back from the lane amongst a grove of beech trees, the emaciated horses that grazed the thin grass in the adjoining field. That big grey house was an inevitable presence, a necessary counter-colour to the Venetian blue skies, the buoyant water. They were the years before her mother's death, before Sally's death, before the whole irreplaceable construct shattered. For a moment she thinks that she would go there now, but she knows in her heart that all of that past is an illusion. To go and see it would be to seed the past with the pathetic fallacy of the present.

She sits, vacant, without invention, momentarily. From one moment to the next she is full only of the images in the room, the painting above the fireplace, the pink lamp, the white sofa, the acred city of lights beyond, the namelessness of what is critical. Inevitably there is a thought, inevitably there is an act, inevitably there is invention, a need to locate an otherness, to dislocate this...

She pulls the telephone towards her, retrieves a number from her contact index and calls.

– Hello!

– Germain, it's Mary.

She tries to impel her voice, to perk its tone, to imbue a languorous, relaxed liveliness, carelessly opportune, inviting.

– Mary?

As though there might be a thousand Marys in his life.

– Am I that forgettable?

– No you're not. But you surprise me. I didn't think I'd hear from you again. In fact I'm not sure I wanted to.

– I find it's always hard to name what you really want. Wants are obscure, don't you think?

– But you wanted to call me. Why?

– You never got your pound of flesh. I've been feeling guilty about that.

– Believe it or not I don't mind you feeling guilty, you probably deserve it, and as for my pound of flesh maybe you should wrap it up and give it to someone else.

– Don't be cruel, says Mary, I'm making an effort here.

– That's just it. I'm not sure why you're making an effort.

– I made a mistake. I'd like to see you again.

– Some people are emotional masturbators. You're not one of those, are you Mary?

– I'll behave better this time, I promise.

– What does that mean?

– It means you have to decide whether to take a risk with me or not.

– You can understand my *apprehension*.

– It's been a difficult time Germain. There are few enough people I can talk to. Please!

– I can connect with anyone who is open and honest with me. Are you prepared to do that?

– I think so.

– Okay. So what now?

– I was wondering if you'd like to come over.

– When, now?

– I could cook something simple.

– I've already eaten.

– Drinks then?

– Now?

– Why not?

– What time?

– Say an hour.

There's a long pause.

– Okay. I hope I'm not going to regret this.

– You won't.

Mary replaces the phone. She gets up. She feels as though she is surfacing from deep water, so much water below her, so much water above her. She stands breathlessly for a moment, then breathes.

Upstairs she changes into a red dress. She takes her wig of flowing red hair and combs it out. She fixes it to her scalp then brushes it again. She plumps out her eyelashes with mascara; feather-brushes some bronze eye shadow onto her eyelids, refines the line of her eyebrows with soft pencil, and applies gentle swathes of liquid red lipstick.

Standing on a low stool she retrieves a box from the upper shelf of her mahogany wardrobe and empties it onto the bed. She checks the various items: leather straps, handcuffs, corded rope, whip, ball gags. She takes the whip in her hand and fingers the tasselled tip. She gives it a gentle lash, her blood seized by the sound. She does it again, a little fiercer this time.

58

Germain, lightly supported by his crutches, walks rhythmically along by the railinged brownstones, stopping in front of the quartet of dimpled slabbed steps ascending to Mary's door. He looks up. The house is aglow with light from the top floor down. He walks up. The door is ajar. He enters.

Standing in the hallway he looks at himself in the long mirror just inside the door. Mary watches him. He is as she imagined he would be, mutable, as are we all. He brushes some hair off his forehead and removes a speck of shaving foam from below his ear. He rests his arm on the curl of polished wood at the base of the banister rail and calls out Mary's name.

– Mary!

There is no reply.

He calls her name again.

– Mary!

On hearing footsteps from behind, he turns.

– I see you let yourself in, says Mary.

Mary walks through into the hallway from the living room.

– Wow! You look…red! You look amazing.

– I felt like dressing up. It's been one of those weeks or months, I hardly know anymore. Everything has felt interminable this last while. I guess you can imagine.

– I was thinking about our conversation. I let my anger get the better of me. I should have been more sympathetic. As you said it's been a difficult time.

– Yeah. I don't really want to talk about it, or I'm exhausted talking about it. I just need to unwind. You can kiss me if you wish.

Mary turns her cheek to him and he kisses one and then the other.

– Let me take your crutches. You don't need them inside, do you?

Germain takes a bottle of wine out of the carryall draped over his shoulder and hands it to Mary.

– Don't take them too far away. After I've had a few glasses of this the world begins to veer. Anything can happen.

– I suppose you're right.

– So were you at work today?

They walk into the living room.

– No, I went to visit David. He thought I could help him. I couldn't.

– Will you go again?

– No. There is no reason for me to go again, which is something.

– How was he?

– Defiant.

– I still find it hard to believe he was involved.

– All artists are corrupt, says Mary. It's what makes you attractive. David wasn't really painting, he hadn't for a while. Maybe something snapped. David! David! David! Enough of David, what would you like to drink?

– Whiskey if you have it.

– Water?

– On the side, please.

– I'll be back in a minute.

Germain leans on the sideboard.

– Don't lean on that! says Mary.

– Sorry?

– It was my mother's. I don't want it marked.

– Sorry.

Mary takes the bottle of whiskey into the kitchen and pours double measures into two tumblers. She opens the cupboard above her head and takes down a sachet of Ketamine. She pours the powder into one of the tumblers and stirs until the grains dissolve. There is a little sediment in the glass but nothing very noticeable. She returns to the living room.

Germain has seated himself on the sofa. She places the tray of drinks down on the glass table and hands him his. He raises his glass to her.

– To us!

– Cheers.

– Don't put your glass down on the table like that. Use one of the coasters.

– Sorry.

– Here I am giving you orders, why don't you give me one.

– How do you mean?

– You know tell me to do something for you.

– Like what?

– I don't know, anything.

Germain looks at her.

– Get me some ice, please! says Germain.

– No please. Say it again, harder.

Germain smiles.

– Get me some ice!

– Harder.

– Get me some fucking ice!

Mary goes and gets some ice.

– There that wasn't so bad was it? Now drink that down and I'll get you another.

Germain drains his glass. Mary refills it.

– At this rate I won't be able to move. I'll have to stay over.

– Would that be so bad?

– Not at all.

– Good. I'm just going to put a snack together. I haven't eaten. You can follow me in.

Germain remains seated on the sofa. He can hear the remote clatter of pans coming from the kitchen.

He rises and calls to her from the hallway.

– Do you mind if I put on some music?

– Go ahead.

– He puts on Dylan's *Time Out Of Mind,* then limps awkwardly into the kitchen.

Mary turns the omelette on the pan with a steel spatula.

– You can touch me if you like while I'm cooking.

Germain moves over to her, a little nervous, tentative. He touches her bottom.

–Your ass...it's beautiful!

Mary lashes back with her arm, the side of the spatula catching Germain in the face. He falls backwards onto the floor.

– I'm sorry. You tickled me. It was just a nervous reaction. Come on, get up. There's a good girl.

Mary helps Germain up and sits him down on a chair on the opposite side of the kitchen.

– How is my face?

– It'll be fine, no scars, although women find them attractive you know.

– I like my face just fine. They'll have to find something else. Can I have a mirror?

Mary brings him a hand mirror.

–That was quite a belt!

– I didn't mean it.

– I know.

– I had a boyfriend once who liked me to slap him. Sometimes he really freaked me out. Men are strange.

– Some men are. Me, I'm pathologically normal.

–That's what I like about you. It was what I liked about David.

– Don't compare me to David, not after what he did.

– No.

– He's unattainable now. Does that make him more attractive?

– Don't be glib, and don't make assumptions.

– I'm not sure I like all these orders, says Germain.

–You'll get used to them.

– So what happens if I disobey?

– Go on, disobey me.

Germain pushes his almost empty glass of whiskey to one side.

– I don't want anymore of this fucking whiskey. Get me some wine!

Mary demurely takes the whiskey away, opens the bottle of red wine and brings him a brimming glass.

– If I'd known command structures work as well as this on women I'd have started a long time ago.

– Women like to obey. I learned that a long time ago.

Mary transfers the finished omelette to a plate and brings it over to the table.

– Sure you won't have some?

– No thanks. In fact I feel a bit queasy.

–You're not going to get sick are you?

– Maybe if I had some water?

– Get it yourself.

– No *you* get it.

Mary grabs the knife from the table and points it towards him.

Germain chuckles quietly.

– Okay, okay!

He gets to his feet and wobbles slightly.

–That's weird! My legs feel kind of numb.

Germain moves forward. Mary lifts her foot slightly and he trips. He bangs his shoulder on the radiator as he comes down. He lies sprawled face-down on the floor. Mary laughs quietly.

–You tripped over my foot.

– I think I'm okay. Just help me up.

– I have to turn down that music first. I can't hear myself think.

Germain struggles to his knees. There's a sharp pain in his left shoulder as though the bone might be bruised. Using his right arm he levers himself onto the chair and waits for Mary. The blood has drained out of his face. He looks ashen and drawn. When Mary returns she is carrying a pair of pyjamas.

–You need to lie down, Germain. I have a pair of David's old pyjamas here, if you can bring yourself to wear them, and the top room is all ready for you. Come on, we can take a rest together and who knows, you may perk up later.

– I feel completely fucking zonked, like I'm tripping.

–You can lean on me.

They shuffle out along the corridor and into the hallway. As they climb the stairs Germain's legs become increasingly slack. It is fast becoming a struggle for both of them to ascend the stairs.

–Where did your friend Sheila sleep?

– In the spare room on the first floor. I haven't been in there since it happened. I won't go in there again, ever.

They struggle forward step by step in silence.

–You know what my daddy used to say when he took me up to bed?

Germain is hardly listening to her, focused as he is on trying to maintain his balance and get up the rest of the stairs.

Once more Mary's voice takes on a male tone.

Think of all the bad things you did today Mary.

Think of all the bad things and for every step you take you tell me one.

In a child's voice she answers,

Step one – I wiped my bum with the face towel.

Step two – I said I hated you to my friend Jane.

Step three – I spat on Marjorie's anorak.

– It went on like that every night. I'd have to stay on the same step until I thought of something. Sometimes he'd go ahead and wait at the top on the landing. In the end the hardest thing of all was to think of so many bad things. So I'd say the same ones over and over.

Step forty-one – I said I wanted to run away.

Step forty-two – I wished I was dead.

Step forty-four – I wished you were dead.

They move up towards the second floor landing. Germain slumps.

– Stand up! Stand up, you lump. What kind of pleasure am I going to get from you tonight? You deserve to be beaten. You deserve it.

They make it to the second floor landing and begin the ascent to the top floor. She drags him up by his arms. She gets frustrated with him,

You're a bad fucking little girl. You're a scheming fucking cunt. I know you're well able to stand up. I'll beat you. I swear I'll fucking beat you.

She drags Germain into the room and onto the bed.

The room itself is red. Mary merges with it, becomes part of it. Photographs of her father clutter the wall space. Old fire extinguishers lie stacked in one corner. Mary begins to undress Germain who is now almost comatose. When he is naked she pushes him back onto the bed, takes the handcuffs and manacles his hands and feet to the four bedposts. She takes a comb and combs his hair forward over his face so that his eyes and nose are covered. The long leather straps she throws over his chest and legs, then crawls under the bed to buckle them securely. When everything is finished she sits down and lights a cigarette. She continues to sit there looking at him trussed up, immobile. The cigarette burns down quickly. She thinks of stubbing the cigarette out on her own skin but grinds it into Germain's leg instead. When he winces, she thinks, there's life in the old dog yet.

59

Hours later, Mary is still sitting in the same position. The room might be empty, or silent, or dark. She imagines herself in a place where these are essential acts, necessary acts. She imagines herself in a place where none of this is happening, where Germain is merely a figment, a figurative thing she imagined, a strange figure in a gross reality. She thinks herself to a place where nothing she believes has passed, has passed, and nothing she knows will come, will come. A place of outstanding realities, of rooms leading to lives created and extinguished at will.

The light overhead appears to dimly illuminate the strategy of bodies, guardian and prisoner, child and father, lovers. She looks at Germain's body and wonders if it isn't indeed hers. Is that Germain's body stippled with burn marks, or is it hers? Time passes. The darkness outside begins to lighten. Germain stirs. His eyelids open and close and open. He appraises the room. He sees her. He *sees* her. He shakes the hair from his eyes. He feels his pain. He struggles against the manacles. He screams.

– Don't scream! You'll wake the neighbours. You'll have to exercise a bit of control if you're going to enjoy this.

He begins to shiver.

–There's no point in being afraid, there's nothing you can do.

– Mary, I want you to let me go. I want you to let me fucking go NOW.

He raises his head as far as it will go and looks at his body.

– O for Christsake! What have you done? What have you fucking done to me?

HELP ME SOMEBODY!

HELP ME!

Mary grabs one of the ball gags and stuffs it in his mouth and despite his struggles buckles it around the back of his head. She slaps him a couple of times with the stick-end of the whip. He struggles, but inevitably his struggles subside. He makes a kind of humming noise, a kind of abstract enunciation. It is obvious what he wants.

Time passes slowly in the room. At five a.m., Mary takes a pair of scissors from the side table. He writhes in anticipation of the pain to come and hums his screams. When Mary brings the scissors over his groin there appear to be only three grotesque options: to sever his penis, or his balls, or both. But her act is gentler, almost a ministration. She clips his thick pubic hair, letting it fall about him, and then she drifts to his chest. She lathers his body as she had seen Maurice do and for a moment this man beneath her seems to contain a trinity of men, Daddy, David, Maurice. She shaves him clean and covers his groin with a piece of tape.

– David I have a fantasy. You're lying naked in a kind of coliseum. Busts of all the women you've fucked are in a semicircle looking down on you. I am the priestess officiating. You want to die but cannot. You await a lover to kill you. I am the one chosen because I am the one you have loved the most. I feel incredibly calm. I feel like rain falling on your body. When I bring the tiny knife down again and again, your body becomes a sieve. I collect a goblet full of your blood and offer it to each of the women in turn. But they cannot drink your blood. Only I can stomach it. Isn't that what it's about, knowing finally the blood you can stomach.

Early-morning light squares the window on the opposite wall. Mary goes to the far corner of the room and takes a chime box in her hand. She opens it and a little plastic ballerina pops up and turns exquisitely to the tune of *Für Elise*. She replaces the box as it plays. Taking the whip she flays Germain's pale body. Her voice is high-pitched, squealing.

I love you daddy, please don't hurt me anymore!

I love you; I really, really love you.

Germain groans.

The chime-ballerina stops.

60

Mary dresses for work in a finely tailored tweed suit, her hair swept up and coiled in a bun. Although she has not had any sleep she looks refreshed. Her briefcase is on the table. She swallows some black coffee and bites on a piece of buttered toast. She glances at the clock, sets the unfinished piece of toast to one side, and looks out the window. The rain, which had continued throughout the night, is now merely an intermittent drizzle. She grabs her overcoat, picks up her briefcase and takes a final glance around the kitchen. At the hall door she stops, looks upwards through the well of the stairs and calls out,

– Darling, I'm off! See you later.

61

When Mary is away from him she never stops thinking about him. She sees him lying on the bed, burns and whip-marks over his body. He struggles, but there is no give either in the manacles or in the straps that bind him. He looks towards the window, to the drawn red curtains and to the light flowing through them. It is difficult to breathe with the gag in his mouth, and his throat feels constricted and dry. She knows that he is beginning to concede that he may die here and perversely he calms in acknowledgement of that reality. He looks at the various photographs of the man pinned or framed on the walls. The man is tall, athletic, blond. In almost all of the photographs he appears to be in his late thirties, dressed in loose chinos and shirts. In some he is pictured with two small girls, in others with a little girl in a print dress. Mary knows that he will recognise her child self, he will sympathetically note that she was a beautiful child.

As his discomfort grows he will find himself angered by his incomprehension as to the why of his incarceration. What did he miss? Was there a prelude to this? The way she had left him on the side of the road, the death of her friend, her relationship to David.

When he is honest with himself he will recognise the curious tension that existed between them, her attractiveness, her oddness, her skewed intriguing nature. He has rarely made good choices with women in the past, and he will view this as his absolute nadir.

Alarmingly, he begins to cry. In the midst of it he wants to stop but cannot, crying tears almost for their own sake, tears that make his pain, and the expectation of his death all the harder to endure.

62

Days pass.

In the evenings Mary sits with him. She cleans him as she would a baby. It is good to have a baby, or something like a baby. It is good to have real company again after so long. She tells him about her day, its small trials, the people in the office, the deals she has structured, the frustrations she has had to contend with. She tells him she has never felt as resolved as she feels now. Just when she thought everything was over, her life had begun again. Sometimes she reads to him from the newspaper. She does not call him Daddy, or David, or Maurice, or Germain, simply you.

–You'll like this...

– Here's something for you to think about...

She hardly notices his weakness any more. She has taken to putting dark glasses over his eyes, since they have developed a language of their own which she dislikes. As he diminishes he grows more like a child. It is a kind of saintly reduction, a kind of cleansing or purification. He has stopped struggling. Sometimes she drizzles water over his face. She doesn't have any plants in the house but she waters him as she would a plant. The water is the one thing that stimulates a response in him now; he twitches, trying to get little drops of it in the side of his mouth. In the last few days she has also brought containers of diesel into the room. She is unsure what she will do with these but she will probably burn him eventually. Sometimes she climbs onto the bed beside him and falls asleep. He seems to like her warmth, which is heartening.

63

When the weekend finally arrives she has all day to spend with him. On impulse she retrieves some of the dresses she had worn as a teenager. She has grown thin, thinner than she ever remembers having been. She irons the crinkles out of them and puts one on – a pale cream crinoline dress with a pink satin bow around the waist. It fits her perfectly. It's such a joy. She prances around the house, dusting, sweeping, vacuuming. When the telephone rings she answers it.

– Hello 374935!

Even her voice sounds adolescent.

– Hello Mary. This is Dr Lavender.

– I'm sorry, I think you have the wrong number.

– Mary is that you?

– Yes, this is Mary.

– Are you all right?

– I'm all right.

– You don't sound all right.

– No?

– Do you know who I am?

– No.

– I'm your therapist. Do you know who I am now?

– I suppose so.

– Who am I?

– You're the rapist.

– I don't know what you're talking about. You sound confused Mary. You sound unwell. Are you unwell?

– No.

– All right then. I wanted to tell you that I had a call from your ex-husband David, and he wishes to talk to me. I have agreed to do so and I wanted to let you know that. Of course there will be no breach of our confidentiality. Do you understand?

– I have to go now. I have things to do.

– Mary, why don't you think of returning to therapy? I think it would be good for you and if not with me then I can suggest someone else.

– No.

– I know your story Mary. If you want to talk at any time just pick up the phone.

– I don't have a story.

She puts the phone down and walks away from it. Then she returns to it, picks up the unit, pulls it from the wall, goes outside into the yard and puts it in the bottom of the bin.

She stops dusting after that and sits in the living room with the blinds drawn. Someone knocks on the front door but she does not answer. The house grows alive with sounds and with voices. She moves from one room to another but they follow her. She feels hands tug at her dress and fingers move over her body. She believes the man in the room is orchestrating these effects. She walks upstairs; the door to her bedroom is open. She closes it. She walks up to the second floor landing and closes the doors there too. She walks finally to the top floor. He hasn't moved. She prods him and he reacts slightly. She takes the dark glasses off and he turns his head to face her and then turns away. She opens the canisters of diesel. She inhales the fumes. She douses the floor and bed and furniture.

When the floor is slick with it she stops.

She looks out the small window at the outline of the spired city. There must be moisture in the air or some other atmospheric condition that makes the city appear so close. She remembers standing in the same place as a child, this was her place, the small room at the top of the house. She sees some neighbours across the way lighting cinders for a barbecue. She tears off a strip of newspaper and twists it into a stiff wand. She lights the match and glances over at the man. She touches the burning match to the paper and hears the echo of words from another room.

Save yourself Mary! Save yourself!

There are tears in her eyes. She sees an image from the past of her daddy asleep or comatose on the bed, and of herself as a little girl standing beside him with a flaming piece of paper in her hand. She feels tired suddenly. What she wouldn't give just to lie down. She goes over to the bed and releases the straps around the man's body, followed by the manacles. He continues to lie there, unaware of what has happened, uncaring. She draws his arms down by his side and takes off the gag. When he doesn't stir she lies down beside him. The stick falls from her hand and the place ignites. He tries to raise his exhausted body and finally does so. He turns and whispers in his dry voice,

– No one has to die. No one has to die Mary.

She looks at him for a moment and sees her father, David, Germain, Maurice, then shifts her gaze to the photographs on the ceiling. He tries to pull her, and it is not that she resists but that he is unable. He tests his legs, stands feebly, and struggles through the slick oil and flames. The door appears and he opens it. When he looks back at her, her dress is already engulfed, but she does not cry out. Her eyes remain focused on her father. He stumbles down the steps to the second floor and on his bottom down to the first floor and to the hallway. She imagines him taking her overcoat from the hallstand and wrapping it about himself. In the hallway Smith comes towards him, he looks back up the stairwell at the fulminating smoke beginning to spiral down. He takes Smith in his arms and for a moment appears reluctant to leave, or is waiting for something, a terminal cry or scream to end it, but there is nothing. He wanders out onto the street, leaving the heavy hall door half-open. Someone will call emergency services, he thinks, but it won't be him.

A flame of orange gold light fills the rectangle of space at the end of the road. For a moment he is blinded. He hears a woman's cry from behind him, he looks back to the house instinctively, only to see the windows explode outwards and flames spume haphazardly, colonisingly upwards. The woman, stout, with a red apron about her waist, gesticulates wildly, screaming for help. Within moments there are other neighbours clustering about her on the street. He walks close to the railings using every second one for support, Smith mutely secured inside his coat. He comes to the arcade, and to the sex shop window now blacked out, though the blue-and-pink neon sign above it continues to flash on and off. He reaches the inevitable river, sunset-streaked and slack. He stops and leans on the bridge, and looks down into the water, into its muscled currents, slowed by a pier before its passage onwards. He listens to the river, and to the river-sound of feet flow on.

THE END